COLD WAR ON THIN ICE

Daniel Fludgate

Published in 2021 by FeedARead.com Publishing

Copyright ©Daniel Fludgate

Cover image by wk1003mike, through Shutterstock

Cover font of 'Russian' by Manfred Klein, through dafont.com

A CIP catalogue record for this title is available from the British Library.

"A man who wants to lead the orchestra must turn his back on the crowd."

Max Lucando

PROLOGUE

NO ONE EVER leaves the KGB.

She'd understood these words from her handler to be both a justification for what she was about to do, and a warning about what would happen should she not succeed.

Mistaking her shivering for cold rather than fear, the Austrian deputy ambassador offered his dinner jacket.

"Thank you, Herr Koller," she said. The small of her back was damp with sweat. "But I'm already warming up now that we are inside the theatre."

"Very well, my dear," he replied with a small bow. "It would seem a shame to cover up that beautiful gown. The audience will be watching you rather than the opera."

His attention wasn't on her dress. Her handler had been right to make her remove the bra.

In the private box reserved exclusively for the deputy ambassador and his guest she was quick to take the seat on the left, a detail she remembered from her briefing as being important for the success of her task. But this was just one of many potential obstacles, and she would have to endure her nerves through all four acts of Mussorgsky's *Boris Godunov*.

Liquid affair was a peculiar euphemism for murder, she thought, smiling at the patrons in the neighbouring box. Traitor to the Soviet Union was a more unambiguous expression, and the file she'd read proved Herr Koller's guilt.

Reminding herself of what she knew about him helped to ease her anxiety about what she had to do, but not enough.

Her hands were shaking.

She was no murderess. The KGB expected too much of her.

At what the other girls colloquially called the swallow's nest, she'd willingly slept with the men her handler instructed her to seduce, and she'd been good at that. Over the last few months she'd also demonstrated a skill for finding the vulnerabilities of these men and gaining their trust, the deputy Austrian ambassador included. She'd betrayed their confidences with neither hesitation nor guilt. But state-sanctioned prostitution in a honey-trap was something quite different from the assassination of a middle-aged foreign diplomat at the Bolshoi Theatre during a live performance.

The assignment had seemed exciting when she was given Herr Koller's file to read; the girls were never usually trusted with such details about the men they were seducing.

At the weapons centre in Kuchino, having the effect of venom from the marine cone snail explained to her, the mission had suggested adventure and excitement. The choice of a knife as the preferred method had been a surprise, but a welcome one; the encounter with such things was thrilling. The weekend outside Moscow spent with a handsome KGB officer practising finding the blade's entry point on a mannequin had been yet another intriguing aspect of this stimulating new experience.

She wanted to serve the country and the cause to which she'd sworn a faithful allegiance.

When she reported Koller's meeting with the British agent at the GUM department store to her superiors, she'd felt a surge of pride at having been chosen, at having her assignment changed to something more decisive. Koller was using his position in Moscow to feed at both the Soviet and British troughs. He had become unreliable, and no one ever leaves the KGB.

The trepidation had arisen only when the actual weapon had been given to her earlier that evening, along with the dress she was to wear.

She was no assassin. But failure or refusal would call her own loyalty to the state security apparatus into question. It had become a choice between Koller's life or hers.

The thought of his death, a man she'd had inside her, and who'd treated her well, troubled her conscience almost as much as being the one responsible for that murder. The anxiety was made worse by the fear of making a mistake.

The state security apparatus was both sword and shield to the USSR; she'd been willing in her role as shield at the swallow's nest, but never expected to be the one to wield the sword.

She tried to clear her mind, as she'd been advised to do. Thinking about it made the anxiety worse, *they* had told her.

She noted how comfortable the plush chair was. The red curtains and gold tassels were luxurious. The theatre was exquisite. The orchestra tuned-up their instruments, and the expectant buzz from the chattering audience hinted at the start of something impressive.

Herr Koller's palm was warm against her leg. One of their neighbours glanced across disapprovingly over the low partition that separated the seating areas. The murder would easily be seen, perhaps even stopped before she could succeed. The mission couldn't work, she thought.

A bell was heard alerting those still at the bar to the imminent start of the performance.

This was madness. She couldn't kill anyone.

Koller shuffled his seat farther back. His strong hand gripped the underside of her chair and drew it towards him. He was unknowingly making his own assassination easier for her.

Another obstacle had been removed. She realized she might actually have to do this; to kill someone in cold blood.

His hands explored her body, taking full advantage of the additional privacy the curtained area of the private box offered. Seduction was what she had been trained for, and her body responded, lying to the diplomat, reassuring him that she was eager for his touch.

Love, she could fake. But sexual enticement as a prelude to murder was the coldest of deceptions.

Killing someone was real.

The lights of the auditorium dimmed to candle illumination as the conductor entered the orchestra pit to enthusiastic applause.

LIKE THE chorus on stage, she was at the theatre to do a job. She was in a costume and playing a role, but hers was one for which she felt there had been insufficient rehearsal.

The actors shouted 'Catch him' as the character of Grigori, discovered to be plotting the overthrow of the Tsar, fled out of a window at the end of the first act. Watching this, she reflected to herself that Koller, himself guilty of deception, had already been caught, even if he didn't yet know it.

He deserved to be punished. But could she really be his executioner?

Her apprehension intensified during two more acts of the opera; the greater punishment seemed to be hers rather than his.

"Shall we join the others for refreshments?" he asked.

She quickly dried her damp palms on the seat fabric. She fumbled getting up from her chair. She hadn't been concentrating on the opera and the intermission surprised her.

"Begone, begone child! I am not thy murderer." His tone was heavy with menace. His hand rested on the door handle, blocking her way out.

Her heartbeat quickened. Her hearing became muffled. Her vision lost focus.

"The opera," he said, noticing her panicked expression. "Weren't you listening? Boris, choking with guilt and remorse." He clasped one of her hands around his own throat and pretended to be suffocating.

Perhaps he was hinting that he knew of her plan. Was this his way of warning her? She couldn't interpret what was happening with any clarity.

"Refreshments?" She snapped her hand away. "That sounds delightful, Johannes." She had neither an appetite nor a thirst. The lies were accumulating.

He held her gaze for a second longer than was comfortable. His expression hinted at suspicion. In not recognising the quote from the last scene had she already betrayed herself? If he asked her anything else about the third act of the opera, she would be unable to answer, and his suspicion would surely ripen to mistrust.

She stepped closer to him and kissed his unshaven cheek.

"I'm thirsty," she said in a tone that implied a sexual meaning; this was a more familiar weapon to her than the blade in her evening bag. She uncurled his fingers from the handle and opened the door.

"Please excuse me for a moment," he said once they'd left the darkness of the box. "I shall join you presently." He walked off towards the toilets, leaving her in the horseshoe-shaped corridor that connected the auditorium to the bar. Others pushed past her, eager to be first to the buffet of meat, fish and fruit. She was reluctant to move.

Was he about to make a hasty dash to the diplomatic protection of the embassy on Starokonyushenny Pereulok? Should she alert someone? But what if he really was just going to the toilet? A trained assassin would know what to do, she thought.

In the bar she stood apart from the other patrons. Despite telling herself not to look, she instinctively glanced at every person who stepped through the doorway. By the time the interval bell rang, the deputy ambassador had not been one of them.

She would not have to murder anyone, and the disappointment surprised her.

Something about her character had made the state security services put their trust in her for this, a high-profile assassination in the centre of Moscow. She valued the Soviet Union and wanted to protect it. That was why she'd willingly gone to the swallow's nest with those men, and that was what had brought her to the Bolshoi Theatre this night. Others had, perhaps, seen in her a propensity for murder that she hadn't noticed herself.

But she'd failed and, in doing so, she had jeopardised herself.

Her hand, holding a full glass of champagne, stopped shaking. She was the only patron still in the bar.

9

"You must *leave* now," barked the usher, his hand grasping at the glass. The unsympathetic face was one she recognised; he was not really a theatre usher.

The mission had failed. She would be punished for her mistake, and *they* were already watching her.

"No one ever leaves the KGB," whispered the state security handler dressed as an usher.

She pushed his hand away and emptied the glass in one long defiant gulp.

The muffled sound of the orchestra could be heard as the prelude to the fourth and final act of the opera commenced.

She surrendered the empty glass.

Pinching the fabric of the gown just below the waist to raise the hem off the floor, she stepped slowly towards the door. For her, the evening's performance was already over.

"There you are, my dear," said Herr Koller. "I was waylaid by a colleague and became worried when you didn't return to your seat."

"I thought you'd left, Johannes," she replied, trying to damp down her relief. She glanced behind at the usher, who hurriedly stepped away to collect other glasses from the tables.

"That would be an unforgivable crime," joked Johannes as they hurried back along the corridor to their box. "Although a four-act opera is perhaps a little too heavy." He took hold of her arm and turned her towards him.

His kiss was forceful and unexpected. He pushed his body against hers. She masked her surprise and softened her lips in response to his impulsive passion.

"Shall we leave?" he suggested breathlessly. She could feel his erection pressing against her thigh.

"No!" Her reply was too quick, too vigorous, and ill-judged.

The diplomat's brow creased in confusion at being told something that contradicted what her kiss had indicated.

"I mean, people will notice our absence," she said.

"As if I care!" he exclaimed.

"But Johannes, *people* will be watching outside the theatre."

This was a risky admission. Letting him know she was aware of the state security agents who monitored foreign diplomats might raise Herr Koller's suspicions about her. It might also make him nervous about the risks he'd been taking lately with the British spies.

He looked at her quizzically.

To mask her momentary panic, she kissed him on the cheek, a promise of what would come later. It was a reassurance that her interest in him was unchanged.

"I can wait a little longer," she purred, running a finger down the fabric of his shirt from his chest to his waist. "Can you?"

The squeaking of the usher's rubber soles on the hard floor signalled his approach along the corridor.

Johannes gave her another questioning look. She pushed her fingers beneath the waistband of his tuxedo trousers.

The squeaks grew louder and faster.

Johannes glanced at the exit stairwell door, and then back at her.

He removed her hand from his underwear.

"It would be rude to the performers not to stay for the whole opera," he mused.

"Perhaps there will be a surprise ending," she said.

He kissed her again and opened the door to the box as the usher's shadow spread across the opposite wall of the corridor.

SHE HAD sacrificed much to defend the Soviet Union. This was her opportunity to demonstrate the measure of her loyalty to the communist ideology. And Koller was a traitor.

Her brow was damp. She hoped he wouldn't reach across for her hand, which was shaking and sweaty.

She rehearsed in her mind the steps practised during her weekend outside Moscow at the weapons facility. The instructor had assured her that muscle memory would compensate for her nerves, but she needed to be sure.

The opera reached its final scene.

The fabric of her gown stuck to her clammy skin; she pulled it away from her body.

The bass vocals of the leading man were heralding the end of the opera. Sitting in the near-darkness next to the ambassador, she knew the moment had come for her own leading role. There wouldn't be a second chance, and there was no opportunity for doubt.

She hesitated.

Would Herr Koller protect her if she confessed the real finale of tonight's opera? She dismissed the thought. It had been the bitter taste of treachery that pushed her towards the Soviet state security apparatus. The consequences of failure were preferable to the shame of treason.

The actor playing Tsar Boris sang 'Punish treason without mercy,' after which the funeral bell began to toll. It was also Herr Koller's death knell. The libretto was prescient.

She took the plastic tortoiseshell comb from her evening bag but her trembling hand dropped it.

Herr Koller, seeing his companion reaching down for something, shuffled his chair back a few inches.

"Allow me," he whispered.

He handed the comb to her.

"Thank you," she mouthed. She flicked it through her hair and glanced towards the stage. His eyes remained on her.

He turned back to face the stage, and she dislodged the handle of the comb to reveal a long sharp blade. Finding the entry point on the back of his neck would be easy. The courage to drive the blade in with the force required was more difficult.

Her hand steadied clutching the instrument of death, as her handler had told her it would. Her conscience was not yet satisfied that Herr Koller must die. But if he turned around, he would see the blade and she would have failed.

It was too late to back out.

She trusted her training, and the orders she'd been given. It was not for her to contemplate the morality of those instructions. She was merely the sword, not the commander.

The tip of the blade was millimetres away from the indent at the base of Koller's neck.

Tempestuous music accompanied the entry of the chorus on stage following the Tsar's death. It was her insurance policy in case she missed and Koller cried out.

She didn't need it.

With a firm thrust forwards at a forty-five-degree upwards angle the sharp metal blade pierced the medulla oblongata. It shut down Koller's motor senses as quickly as flicking off a light switch.

She stood behind him and cupped her hands around his ears. Turning her shoulders slightly, she jerked his head. The brain stem snapped.

The long final note from the wind section ended, bringing momentary silence to the theatre.

Hurrying along the corridor, she heard a rapture of applause break, accompanied by shouts of 'Bravo.' The adrenalin release made her tingle with euphoria. Pretending the plaudits from the audience on the other side of the corridor wall were for her, she stopped and performed a curtsey. This wasn't how she'd expected to feel.

Reaching the foyer, patrons from the stalls were already spilling out through the auditorium doors. She scanned the lobby for the agent dressed as an usher.

She handed him her programme, the sign confirming the Austrian diplomat's death. This would prompt the state security apparatus to initiate the misinformation campaign, nudging any suspicion about the assassination towards the British.

In the middle of the foyer she smiled at the departing patrons. It was an unashamedly self-satisfied smile. She had conducted her own tragic opera on behalf of Mother Russia, and it was a job well done. Her nerves had been for nothing. She *was* a killer.

She would have to leave Moscow for a while, but she was reassured by the thought that no one ever leaves the KGB.

1972

Moscow

Friday 1st September

THE SMELL of boiled cabbage intruded into his room. The aroma stirred Alexei from yet another fretful sleep. He woke quickly: one of many enduring habits from his time in a dormitory and, before that, the barracks. He now had his own room in a communal apartment but was unhappy to be alone.

Alexei wanted the first scent of his day to be Vassily's distinctive smell from the leather collar of his jacket that rubbed against his neck. He wanted his lover's face to be the first thing he saw, and his unshaven cheek the first thing he touched. For that, even just once, five years in the gulag branded as an enemy of the state might be a price worth paying.

In Moscow, personal space did not mean privacy. He'd forgotten to lay a towel across the base of the door the night before, so the trace of Veera Sergeevna's stewed vegetables had been able to encroach into the nine square metres of living space allotted to him: considerably less than the fourteen each citizen was promised.

He didn't mind the trespass of the vapours, nor the smallness of the room. He was pleased not to have accepted the special treatment offered either by his job, or by his mother's connections.

The elderly *upravdom* for the building had been apologetic when showing Alexei, a man from the KGB, such a modest room. It was the smallest in the apartment, but had the best sunlight, the old man had said. He'd reassured Alexei that nothing much could be heard through the plywood walls. He'd enthusiastically promised that the apartment's elected steward would ensure Alexei moved to a larger room when it became available. The unsmiling mouth and deep frown of that steward, Maria, a woman with a hairstyle even more severe than her expression, did not indicate that the *upravdom's* promise would be honoured for the newest resident.

Living in the male dormitory for the previous three years, Alexei had patiently watched his name creep up the waiting list with other Muscovite bachelors. The room was enough for Alexei, perhaps even too much.

The front doorbell rang. It was early for visitors.

Alexei stopped counting after the third ring, the code for his room number; it was a visitor for one of the other families who shared the apartment's kitchen, bathroom and toilet.

The iron-framed single bed rattled as he turned over onto his back.

Hurried footsteps ran to the front door. He listened to a whispered conversation in the hallway about a returned bicycle, and his eyes followed the pattern of the crumbling cornice moulding on the ceiling of his room. The decorative plasterwork depicting vine leaves crept from two corners to connect with the rose feature which once held a chandelier. There was now a naked bulb hanging from a frayed cable.

He sat on the edge of the bed. His bare feet felt the roughness of the pre-revolutionary parquet floor in need of polishing. Alexei decided to ask Maria for it to be covered with the same linoleum that ran through the communal areas, which was much easier to keep clean.

Should he ever be elected steward, he thought, there was much that needed changing about the building. It was a cemetery of splendour, with cracked marbled wall panels in the once-grand stairwell, and a creaking wrought-iron lift with most of its mirrored tiles missing. Alexei was glad to see the grandeur crumbling and fading into its rightful place in Russian history, but it couldn't depart fast enough for him.

He moved the plastic table aside to get to the large window. It was still plugged up with rags where the frame had fallen away with decay. He'd forgotten to replace the mouldy cloths as his immediate environment was not a priority for him. The musty smell didn't bother him.

"Good morning Alexei Ivanovich," said Veera. She didn't even knock as she entered his room. Wearing just his underwear, Alexei covered himself with his overcoat. Veera chuckled at his modesty.

"Always keep your head cool and your body warm," she advised. She passed him a pair of pyjamas from the top of the washing pile she was carrying.

"Thank you, Veera Sergeevna," he replied. "It is cold for the start of September."

"It's summer in a winter dress," she said.

"And you really didn't need to ..." He emptied the pockets of the trousers he'd been wearing the day before to find some money, but she waved away his gratitude and walked off, shuffling in her slippers across the rough floor.

He'd bought the threadbare nightwear from an old man in the street the day before but hadn't noticed them missing from his room. Buying them had been charity. There had never been any intention of wearing them, but now they'd been washed by his kindly neighbour he put them on. Both the sleeves and the legs were far too short for him. He'd bought a pair of battered shoes also, even though they weren't his size, but it was all the old man had to sell. Alexei left these in the stairwell, knowing they would be taken by someone whom they did fit.

Saving some of the black bread from his evening meal to feed the birds that perched on his windowsill each morning had already become a routine. He watched as the city birds cautiously landed and pecked at the crumbs as he spread them across the flaking balconette.

The first three matches broke but the fourth ignited to light his cigarette. Good quality matches had become hard to find.

A small tree sparrow hopped uncomfortably. The other birds easily kept it away from the breadcrumbs. Alexei balanced the cigarette in the corner of his mouth and used his towel to capture the injured animal. Holding the bird upside down clamped between his legs, he untangled the wire which had wrapped itself around the creature's foot. Once back on the windowsill the sparrow tentatively tested the now-mobile limb, then pushed its way towards the food with enough confidence to take the biggest crumbs closest to the window where Alexei was sitting.

He collected his own toilet seat from beside the wardrobe along with several strips of newspaper and stepped out into the corridor. It was still early, and the apartment was quiet, so he hoped to be undisturbed.

The toilet was blocked, and he remembered it was his week on duty as the apartment cleaner. A thin metal tube that was once a chair leg was hanging on the back of the door to deal with this frequent occurrence. He scooped the urine-soaked paper out of the toilet and into the bin. Using a broken piece of plasterwork he wrote on the wall in large letters: *Comrades! Don't flush big pieces of paper!*

There was an impatient knock on the door before Alexei had even sat down.

"Put up with it!" barked Alexei. He then muttered to himself, "Every medal has its reverse." It was an acknowledgment that his outburst had been out of character. He considered himself to be a Soviet 'new' man, happy to live in a collective existence. Mostly he was pleased to be part of such a community and relinquish his privacy. But his sexuality was a private thing; those thoughts and emotions had to kept inside. He knew it was un-Soviet. It was the only aspect of his life which was. Having to keep the secret occasionally made him angry and defensive.

In the apartment everyone knew intimate details of the other's lives, but they were all still strangers. Alexei reminded himself these people were his neighbours, not his friends nor his family. He'd kept his feelings secret during his time with the Baltic Guards, and the three years living in the dormitory since returning to Moscow. He was KGB, so keeping secrets was his job.

"Good morning, Stepan," he said to the large Georgian man who was shaving at the kitchen sink. There was nowhere else for Alexei to wash his hands.

Stepan acknowledged Alexei with a lift of his eyebrows and nod of his bald head. Stepan never spoke, neither to Alexei nor any other resident. He seemed to enjoy the interest this mysterious solitude generated, and was unconcerned by the risks it held for him. Maria referred to his individualistic behaviour disapprovingly, describing it as *chastnyi*. It made Alexei feel as though he had more in common with Stepan than with any other neighbour in the *kommunalka*. Stepan's residency permit identified him as a schoolteacher, but none of the residents believed that.

Alexei swept the floor of the kitchen then pushed the broken brush through the dysfunctional labyrinthine corridors that constituted the shared space in the apartment. The layout was not the design of the original architect's, but a result of hastily erected partitions constantly being moved to reconfigure the floorplan based on the whim of the building superintendent, or to accommodate the newly decreed square metre allowance.

Alexei was pleased that an apartment which once contained only one family now housed nine. He was sure it could accommodate even more than that.

The light from his own corridor bulb was insufficient for the task of taking readings from each of the families' electricity meters. The old ladder he was using to reach each box felt more unreliable with every jerk of his body as he struck more matches that wouldn't ignite.

The kitchen was bustling when he returned there. The radio blared with announcements listing productivity figures by region. Alexei knew these numbers to be ludicrously inflated. He was disappointed that his country had to import grain from America to feed themselves, but glad the radio broadcasts kept this detail a secret. It would have been different but for the drought, he thought, as he wrote the electricity meter readings on the chart.

Six-year-old Nadya crushed a bug on his recently swept floor, but he bit his tongue. This was just one of many insects that shared the communal space with the human residents. The death of one had little effect on the infestation but made a huge difference to Alexei's clean floor.

Veera Sergeevna, perched on the stool in her section of the kitchen, gave Alexei a toothless smile when she saw his restrained reaction to the dirtying of the cracked linoleum. She paused from pushing a meat cutlet through the hand-cranked grinder and beckoned Alexei closer. She tugged at the sleeve of his pyjama top. Her expression betrayed no confusion at Alexei wearing such ill-fitting clothes. The seventy-year-old always had the countenance of someone who had seen everything she needed to and couldn't be surprised by anything. Alexei had liked her immediately when they'd first met.

"You need a wife," she said.

"I think I'm too young for you, Veera Sergeevna," joked Alexei.

"I prefer them a *little* older." She leaned away from him, squinting through the only eye that worked. "But I can always make an exception, Alexei Ivanovich."

"This floor is dirty," snarled Olga, Veera's sister. Having found no mathematical errors on the electricity chart to reprimand the newest apartment resident over, she commented on the crushed bug as she left the kitchen.

"She *does* need a man," joked Veera, returning to her meat preparation.

"Has Olga Sergeevna ever been married?" asked Alexei.

"In love," said Veera, "but not married. She has always lived here with me."

The sisters were the daughters of the apartment's original aristocratic owners. Every decade since the Revolution they had seen their living space reduced by several square metres. Veera was always dressed in several layers of clothing as if she feared sudden eviction.

"She was in love with a dancer from Leningrad during the war. His disappearance has never been explained to her," said Veera. Alexei sharpened the pencil stub he'd used for the electricity readings, shaving the lead with a kitchen knife. "The medals she wears are a happy memory of the war, of the time she fell in love."

Alexei unclamped the heavy meat grinder from the side of the table and carried it over to the sink that Stepan had vacated. He washed it thoroughly, wondering how Veera would have managed such a task if she and Olga still lived in this apartment on their own. One day, when he was older, there would be a young resident in the apartment to help him.

He turned the volume up on the radio as he left the kitchen. The benefits of communism needed to be heard, even the untruths.

"Just take any," said Yuri, noticing Alexei staring at the washing line of black socks. Yuri had quickly become a friend, despite being married to Maria, the unyielding apartment steward. He was a doctor who worked long hours.

"What if they're not mine?" replied Alexei.

"As long as they're clean, who cares?" said Yuri, taking his place in the queue for the toilet behind Boris, a janitor at the local bathhouse. Alexei was pleased to see two men from such different backgrounds taking an equal place in the line for the toilet. He often noticed small details like this, fragments of life that proved Lenin's philosophy that different social groups could unite happily under the Soviet Union banner.

Alexei pulled down two random socks, unsure whether they were his, or even if they belonged together.

"Oh Yuri, I have something for you," said Alexei. He collected something from his room, then dashed back down the corridor. "Here are the tickets I promised."

"Marusya, look," Yuri called across to his wife, who'd poked her head out of their room to investigate the noise of someone running in the corridor. "Alyosha's got us tickets to the hockey match. Isn't that generous?" Maria grunted her acknowledgement of the kind gesture and returned inside her room.

"They're for the final match of the series on the twenty-eighth," said Alexei, leaning carefully against the thin walls to put the socks on. "Hopefully we'll have already beaten the Canadians by then."

"I tried to get tickets, but it seems only Party members are allowed, and Maria refused to use her influence for something she calls a distraction from the revolutionary struggle against the West."

"I'm sure she'll still go to the match, though," whispered Alexei. Yuri slapped his friend on the back, winking conspiratorially.

Alexei propped the back of a chair against the door handle to prevent any intrusions while he got dressed. Positioning himself in front of the section of mirror with the fewest cracks in it, he smoothed down his dark hair. He already looked older than his twenty-seven years, he thought. He pulled at the skin covering his angular face to check for early signs of sagging.

Keeping secrets was ageing him.

GORKY STREET bustled with eight busy lanes of traffic. A trolleybus missed Alexei by inches as he weaved his way through the vehicles at a sprint. All seven million of Moscow's residents seemed to be conspiring to make him even later for work than he already was.

His duties as apartment cleaner had taken longer than expected, and he was angry with himself. Lateness implied arrogance.

He'd been working from a different building for three months now, long enough to learn the short cuts via the backstreets of different architectural styles. For him, the last fifty years of Moscow's development outshone the previous eight hundred. Pre-revolutionary stucco-fronted pretentiousness gave way to Stalinist examples from the thirties, and now that slice of history was being replaced by the modern glass-and-concrete monoliths that Alexei admired most. To him, this demonstrated the success achieved by following the path set by Lenin.

He was out of breath as he entered the side entrance of the Intourist Office on Revolution Square, the information centre for foreigners. His surveillance team occupied one of the upper floors of the building, a location that was perfect for the work of the KGB's Seventh Directorate.

The decorative façade of the building contrasted starkly with the industrial-green painted interior. The furniture was sparse and utilitarian. The layout was based on functionality rather than comfort. The exterior was unique to Moscow, but inside it could have been any KGB office in the vast Soviet Union.

Alexei disliked the dated environment, most especially the foetid smell. It seemed as if freshness itself had been forbidden. It was reminiscent of old KGB; of something no longer fit for purpose; a stench that was, at last, dispersing.

"Honour the work, comrade," mumbled the middle-aged female security officer standing by the door to the main office. She'd become so used to repeating the phrase that her tone suggested it had lost all meaning to her. Alexei considered whether a reprimand was needed, but his lateness risked an accusation of hypocrisy.

"Morning, comrade," replied Alexei. He waited patiently for her to check his identification, over which she took her time.

In the Directorate everything moved at the pace of the slowest functionary. In the Guards the political influence of the Party had provided the soldiers living in difficult conditions with a morale boost. In self-important Moscow, Alexei had noted how politics made bureaucracy sluggish. The city's petty, pallid-faced officials sought to maintain rigid compartmentalisation to protect their own positions.

Even though he saw the same guard every morning, she checked his name against the authorised list with unfaltering and frustrating diligence.

After gaining admittance, he checked the large taskings board, as was his routine.

Under his supervision were several part-time civilian spies as well as entry-level KGB officers. He scanned the list of parks, museums, theatres, barbershops, hotels and transport hubs where he had people embedded.

The drivers of a fleet of public taxis used by foreigners had reported good intelligence results the previous day. A maid at one of the larger hotels had installed covert surveillance equipment in the room of someone from the United Nations who the KGB was particularly keen to listen to. A concierge at the same hotel had reported top-quality overheard information that would be passed on to another department to follow up.

Alexei was pleased with the results.

Steadfast vigilance was the standard he set for those fighting with him against the foreign capitalists and those Soviet nationals sympathetic to that dishonourable cause.

Moscow was a battleground to him, no different from the border territories he'd patrolled as a soldier.

Alexei's personal ambitions had always been modest, which was why he'd turned down the offer of a place at the esteemed Institute for International Studies when he left school. It was not the route he'd wanted to take, most especially because admittance had been secured for him by his influential mother who wanted to see her son fast-tracked into the elite of Soviet foreign intelligence.

He'd chosen the Border Guards instead, a rebellious decision vindicated by the happy years he'd spent there. In the Guards, Alexei found he wasn't just a soldier, but a defender of Soviet ideology. He volunteered to lead the six hours of weekly political education for his platoon, a demonstration of enthusiasm that led to him being made editor of *Pogranichnik*, the monthly communist journal of the regiment.

Alexei's political skills and enthusiasm were noticed. To the mind of the Chief of the Guards Directorate who posted Alexei to a civilian job in Moscow, the dedication shown had been rewarded. But the honour of a posting in Moscow had seemed more of a punishment to Alexei, rather like a man of God having his conversion of the masses acknowledged with a posting somewhere inhospitable where greater numbers of non-believers would be found.

He'd left his detachment in the Baltic region, and with it the green uniform of which he was so proud. The transfer taught him that pride had its price, in this case the non-descript brown suit that he now wore.

The stain of favouritism was also obvious to Alexei. Zyryanov, the Border Guards chief, was a friend of Raisa, Alexei's mother, a woman determined to get for her son what he seemed so reluctant to seek out for himself. But he could not refuse his commander's offer.

That he was being groomed for a higher office in being sent to Moscow, Alexei was aware. But every step taken further up that ladder increased the risk of his sexual preferences being found out. He would soon have to choose between the Communist Party and his own secret desires.

The ideology of Leninism had satisfied him in the Guards. He would have made any personal sacrifice, even his life, for his platoon and his country. But since coming to Moscow, he'd met Vassily, and the choice was no longer an easy one.

"Good morning, Alexei Ivanovich," said Pavel, one of Alexei's team.

"Good morning, Pavel Fedorovich," replied Alexei. He straightened his frayed tie and sat down at his desk.

The colleagues sat opposite each other, sharing adjoining scuffed and scratched steel-grey metallic desks. The furniture had been in situ since the fifties and was bolted to the uncarpeted floor. This measure was ostensibly to avoid the risk of theft, but also prevented the furniture being moved to suit the current occupant's personal choice or comfort.

"The squirrel is here today," warned Pavel in a hushed tone.

Fedor Borisovich Yukalov, their head of department, was a man who shared little operational intelligence with his workers, believing that knowledge was power. Vassily had once commented that their boss was like a squirrel keeping his nuts in store just in case there was a bad winter, and the sobriquet had stuck ever since. He only came into this office when there was trouble. Alexei worried the squirrel had come for him.

"Why?" asked Alexei. He'd been scanning the room looking for Vassily, but quickly stopped.

"No one tells me anything," replied Pavel with a shrug.

For a KGB agent, Alexei had often been surprised at his middle-aged co-worker's lack of curiosity. Pavel's attitude of unquestioning obedience had apparently remained as unchanged for the last twenty years as his hair style. But such conformity had kept him safe during a perilous period.

Pavel was ill-suited to espionage. He trusted people too easily and seemed tormented by the broken pledges and ruthlessness of his daily work. But Pavel's naivety benefitted Alexei; such an unquestioning optimist would be the last person to suspect Alexei and Vassily were anything other than colleagues who got along well together. Pavel unknowingly helped to protect Alexei's secret.

Alexei flicked through a copy of an Australian magazine confiscated at the airport from a visiting student. He was supposed to review it for intelligence material but was distracted by its content. He lingered on the pictures of shirtless young men with long hair and bare feet dancing with topless young women in floral skirts at something called the Sunbury Festival. He wondered what the music of *The La De Das* or *Billy Thorpe and The Aztecs* sounded like.

The debauchery of the magazine both offended and intrigued him. The photographs suggested a dangerous kind of freedom. The young men, some even holding hands, were about Alexei's age, but living an entirely different experience.

He tore the magazine in two, threw it in the bin, and picked up surveillance reports that had been left for him to review.

"Will you be listening later?" asked Pavel.

"Listening?" Alexei wondered what surveillance job Pavel was talking about.

"Doesn't look good for Spassky."

"I predicted Fischer had the victory days ago," replied Alexei, realising Pavel meant the international chess championship. He allowed himself another quick check to see if Vassily was in the office.

"Don't let the squirrel hear you say that," whispered Pavel. "You'll be shuffled off into exile for circulating falsehoods derogatory to the Soviet state and social system."

"But it's true," said Alexei.

"We haven't lost such a chess tournament since the war," rebuked Pavel.

"We'll lose in Reykjavik. Then comes the hockey series against Canada. Things will get unpleasant around here if we lose that too," joked Alexei. "Three thousand Canadians are due here this month for it. How are we supposed to keep watch on all of them?"

"Shhh, do you want us all to get denounced," warned Pavel, only half in jest. "Anyway, remember what Orwell said about sport?"

"Serious sport has nothing to do with fair play. It is bound up with hatred, jealousy, boastfulness, disregard of all rules, and sadistic pleasure in witnessing violence: in other words, it is war minus the shooting." Alexei was still looking for Vassily as he quoted the passage perfectly.

"Exactly. *We* won't let our side lose," replied Pavel. "Vassily already left," he added.

"Oh," said Alexei, worried that he'd made himself too obvious.

"The full works has been ordered for a guest at the Yaroslavskaya," added Pavel. "Remote controlled cameras in the concrete, pin-holes, and telephone transmitters."

"Rather him than me," replied Alexei. "Let's hope the mark doesn't ask to change rooms when he arrives."

"Hotel's full I'm afraid sir," said Pavel, imitating a female hotel receptionist. "Industrial conference in the city this week."

They were both laughing when Pavel stopped abruptly and looked down at his work.

"Good morning, Comrade Dimichenko."

Alexei recognised the snake-like hiss of Yukalov behind him. Their boss had perfected a way of walking almost soundlessly, so there had been little warning of his approach apart from Pavel's reaction.

"Good morning, Comrade Colonel." Alexei straightened his suit as he stood and turned around. "I trust everything is in order?"

"Come with me," replied Yukalov. He held Alexei by the elbow and led him to one of the private meeting rooms.

The main office fell unnaturally silent. Nobody dared to look up from their desk, yet Alexei felt their attention directed at him.

Yukalov must know about Vassily, he thought. A spread of panic-sweat from his armpits dampened Alexei's shirt. It was now clear that Vassily was not fixing surveillance material at a hotel, and Alexei would soon be joining his lover in an adjacent cell at the Lubyanka. Siberia would then follow for them both, but not together.

He would never see Vassily again.

Once in the privacy of the office Yukalov attempted to smile. It was something so unnatural to him that it seemed sinister. Alexei became more unsettled.

"I …" Alexei started to speak, not knowing what to say once he'd begun.

Yukalov raised his hand, gesturing for the junior officer to be quiet.

"Things have not gone unnoticed," said Yukalov.

Alexei looked back out into the office, expecting to see uniformed police searching his vacated desk. There were none.

"Comrade…" Alexei began to speak again, hoping the right words to explain himself would flow.

"I cannot tolerate lateness," barked Yukalov. "It sets a bad example of laziness; of arrogance!"

"I'm …I apologise, Comrade Colonel." Alexei was confused.

"But that is not why you're here. Please, sit down." Yukalov gestured Alexei into a chair.

Was this a trap, thought Alexei? The tactics of the KGB had changed under the chairmanship of Andropov. It had been recognised that agents could achieve more by cunning than brutality. The amiable, courteous, civilised approach was now the accepted method of interrogation. Calm firmness had been proved to secure greater compliance. It produced a different form of fear; a more effective one.

Alexei had practised it as the interrogator, now he was experiencing it as the accused. It was working. He was alarmed.

"To be a great nation, you need great enemies, comrade." Yukalov sounded as if he were about to recite a Politburo speech. Alexei gave a shallow hesitant nod of agreement. "And we have great enemies!" exclaimed Yukalov.

"Yes, Comrade Colonel," stuttered Alexei, waiting to be told his relationship with Vassily made them such an enemy.

"I fought with the Western imperialists during the Great Patriotic War, but they betrayed us. They are war mongers and our greatest enemy."

"We are with you in solidarity, Vietnam!" said Alexei, repeating the slogan found on the current propaganda poster affixed to every metro station doorway; it seemed the right thing to repeat now.

"It is not just America," said Yukalov.

Alexei held his breath, waiting to be accused of treason.

"Britain expelled our diplomats and accused us of subversion. It is they who subvert us, comrade!" Yukalov wasn't shouting, but his voice was being projected across the small office as if he were addressing a Red Square military parade.

Alexei nodded in agreement with everything.

"Détente!" The word exploded from his mouth. "They are fools to believe it. We should not accept a weakening of the ideological struggle. On the contrary, we should be prepared for an intensification."

"We should follow the true path," said Alexei, hesitantly starting to calm down.

"Exactly," replied Yukalov, "and I have noticed you, comrade." He leaned down until his face was uncomfortably close to Alexei's. There was a hint of threat in his expression.

Alexei's eyes widened with rapidly returning fear.

"We shall defeat the Evil Empire, together!" Yukalov smiled so broadly that his yellow, coffee-stained teeth were fully exposed. He looked to the ceiling in a moment of reflection as if expecting a greater power to immediately acknowledge him and require his presence because of the speech.

When no ascension came Yukalov regained his composure. His voice returned to the slithery conspiratorial tone that came naturally to him.

"I have an important job for you, Alexei Ivanovich."

"Yes, Comrade Colonel?" asked Alexei. His breathing returned to normal. He might see Vassily again.

"What do you know about something called ORCHESTRA?"

3

THE TACTIC to be used was one which Alexei had designed himself. He'd perfected it over the last three years as a surveillance technique so simple in its design that its record of success seemed almost unmerited.

"Remember," he told his small team at the briefing, "make yourselves so obvious to the mark that he has to notice you and realise you're KGB following him."

One of the newest agents, a young woman being deployed as a taxi driver, looked confused.

"I want him focussing on you," clarified Alexei, noticing the woman's puzzled expression. "Even if he really is just a businessman, his company will have made sure he received some basic training in surveillance evasion techniques. Let him use them; make sure he loses you."

"But comrade, are you sure the comrade colonel wants the mark to know we're following him?" The young woman was bold enough to query the instructions. Alexei liked that. Pavel had never asked why.

"This is my operation," replied Alexei. "When I say so, you drop back, and I might keep one of you on his tail. The mark will assume his evasion has worked or he'll focus entirely on the one he knows is following him, and he'll relax."

"So that he won't notice you?" asked another agent.

"Exactly," said Alexei. "He'll be enjoying the feeling of beating the KGB on their own turf at their own game so much that his pride won't allow him to see any other shadows."

"Sounds risky," said the female agent.

"I've seen it work on some of the most experienced foreign agents, and even KGB defectors," replied Alexei. "Being part of this is a privilege, comrade."

"Yes, comrade." She lowered her head in acknowledgement of Alexei's reprimand. When she glanced back up, her expression had changed to one of admiration, and something more. Alexei recognised that her half-opened eyes were now inviting him to seduce her. Perhaps she wasn't all that perceptive, he thought.

PAVEL STARTED following the American as soon as he left the Mir Hotel. Crossing over the newly built part of Kalinin Prospekt, the American noticed his shadow.

Alexei had dressed Pavel in a ridiculous bright red cardigan confiscated from one of the female secretaries in the office. It worked as expected, capturing the American's attention to the exclusion of all else.

The American entered the Melodiya music store.

Alexei waited in the section dedicated to vinyl albums of Russian folk music. There was no need for him to follow the American, as he and Pavel were wearing transmission units.

The neck-loop antenna was worn under their shirts. A discreet microphone was clipped inside their clothes and couldn't be seen. The transmission receiving unit was concealed in a smoker's pipe; when the pipe stem was bitten down on, it conducted the transmission through the teeth. Earpieces could be seen easily, so the pipe was Alexei's preferred tool: one which he'd asked the technicians to make for him. He'd nicknamed it the tooth-fairy.

The surveillance team were tuned to the primary KGB surveillance frequency for that day: 103.25Mhz.

As the American walked towards the exit of the music store, Pavel dropped back.

"*Dvahd-tsaht awdeen*," muttered Alexei into his microphone, confirming he had the American in view.

The female agent pulled her borrowed taxi up and sat outside the music store, just in case the American decided to make a quick exit. Several people tried to solicit her services, but she refused their fares.

The taxi wasn't required.

As the American walked out of the music store, he glanced back several times. He was looking for the man in the red cardigan and didn't pay any attention to the young man in the brown suit who emerged with a record tucked under his arm.

The mark's stride increased in speed and length as his confidence grew. In the shadow of the great high-rise buildings of the New Arbat district he approached the Moskva river.

Stopping briefly outside The Lilac perfumery, the mark pretended to be looking at the perfumes while checking the reflection in the shop window for any signs of the man in the red cardigan. Alexei's instinct was to stop also, but he discarded the record he was carrying in a dustbin, took off his jacket, and walked past the American. He then slowed his pace to ensure he would be overtaken.

They passed the disc-shaped conference hall of the Council for Mutual Economic Assistance. Crossing the Kalinin Bridge, Alexei closed the distance between them even more, testing the tolerance of his surveillance technique. The bogus taxi had driven ahead and was waiting at the end of the bridge, just in case.

The American stopped abruptly and turned once again. He smiled with an apology at Alexei, then looked past him. The smile was dangerous. Alexei had been noticed.

"He's turned down Taras Shevchenko embankment," advised the female agent from the taxi. Alexei had been forced to continue in front of the American and had gambled that the man's destination would be straight ahead. He'd been wrong.

Of course the American would have followed the embankment, Alexei thought. There were fewer people there, and a clearer view behind him. He was annoyed at the stupid mistake.

"Follow him," said Alexei to the agent driving the taxi. He quickly reconsidered. "No," he said, "drive along the embankment and pick up a real fare at the end but take your time before moving off." He couldn't risk the taxi also having been recognised at three different points along the route.

Alexei made a fast run along Kutuzov Prospekt. He turned left past the Artistic Fund Building and had regrouped on Bolshaya when he saw the American up ahead crossing over to Kiev Railway Station. The mark continued to glance behind, unaware that his shadow was now in front of him.

The American checked his watch against the clock on the grandiose façade of the pre-revolutionary train station.

Was this a signal to someone? Alexei scanned the crowd of midday travellers heaving luggage across the forecourt of the station. Experience had trained him to notice any peculiarities in behaviour. Fortunately, people were pack animals. Alexei saw nothing suspicious.

He followed the American into the ticket hall through the entrance topped with a majolica mural of St. George which was obscured and dulled by grime and vegetation.

The glass-canopied ornamental platform hall was busy with people travelling to and from the south of the country. The American presented a ticket to the gate inspector and merged with the bustle of other passengers. Alexei made another mistake. He watched the crowd instead of the train.

Not seeing the American, Alexei was about to board the train at the first carriage when he noticed his mark disembark further down. The departure whistle had already been blown. Had Alexei boarded, he would have been trapped. Luck also played a part in espionage, thought Alexei. The American was proving better than expected; it added weight to the KGB's theory that he wasn't a businessman after all.

The American strode past Alexei. The fabric of their sleeves touched but the American didn't show any signs of recognising the Russian in the brown suit.

In the high-ceilinged restaurant of the railway station Alexei checked the direction of the sun and asked to be seated at a specific table. His back was turned to the stained-glass window, so his vision wouldn't be obscured, and he was opposite the American, who was sitting several tables away.

A fat-faced woman with peroxide bouffant hair reluctantly took Alexei's order. Her dark blue button-front dress was almost bursting open with the flesh she'd tried to restrain inside it.

Alexei lit one of his Prima cigarettes. It made him cough. He checked the splutter hadn't drawn the American's attention.

Another drag confirmed that the cigarettes had recently started to be cut with paper and wood flakes now that production of tobacco had slowed due to the drought.

He took out the thin paperback novel which was always kept in his pocket. It was a book he'd read many times before, but it was the perfect size for the jacket, which meant that he always had something with him to pretend to read if he needed to look distracted. In his other pocket was a dog lead ready to be lassoed around a stray dog's neck if required. No one expected a dog walker to be a KGB spy.

Such everyday items had proved to be far more useful to Alexei over the last three years than any of the sophisticated gadgets or disguises suggested to him by the artistic types in the Eleventh Department. It generally took several months, and countless forms completed in triplicate, to procure such elaborate items anyway.

A dog lead and a well-thumbed paperback required no bureaucratic tenacity to acquire and served his purpose much better. Alexei disliked the pretensions of his colleagues and their elaborate equipment designed to compete with the CIA. He still considered himself to be just a Border Guard on secondment rather than a full-blown KGB spy.

He lit another cigarette and continued to monitor his subject.

The American looked at his watch intermittently and checked the restaurant clock. He was waiting for something to happen, or for someone to arrive. Whichever it was, Alexei realised by the American's agitation that it was late.

In the field of espionage lateness meant danger.

Alexei felt the pressure of an added worry. If something was about to happen, he needed to be ready to act fast, even if he was in danger himself.

The American drained his coffee mug, placed the napkin on the table and was about to stand up when he saw the person arrive that he'd been expecting.

A young man sat down at the American's table with his back to Alexei.

Even from behind, Alexei knew it was Vassily.

The double-crown at the back of his head - two opposing swirls of messy dark-blond hair - and the broad shoulders of the young man brought up in the countryside were unmistakable. Alexei even recognised the shoes Vassily was wearing.

The burly waitress slammed down another cup of coffee in front of Alexei with an indifference bordering on contempt. His continued presence at one of her tables was unwelcome. Alexei ignored her surliness, but the noise of the clanking cup jolted him out of momentary shock at seeing Vassily here.

Pavel had said Vassily was installing surveillance equipment at a hotel on the other side of the city. Surely Yukalov would have told Alexei if he'd assigned others to this operation?

Applying logic and calmness to unexpected circumstances was something he'd been trained for. And he was very good at his job.

A mistake must have been made at the Centre. Two teams had accidentally been assigned to follow the same mark. This was not unheard of, thought Alexei as he began to relax. They would find it amusing later, and someone, somewhere would be posted to the Personnel Directorate for a period of punishment.

Vassily had made contact with the American so he was taking the lead. Alexei would provide back-up with his own small team if required.

Alexei took a large gulp of his coffee.

He scanned the faces of the staff and patrons of the restaurant again, checking to see whether he recognised anyone else who might be part of Vassily's surveillance team. He saw no one he knew.

The waitress dropped a tray of glasses next to Alexei's table, drawing everyone's attention to him. She walked off with a shrug of her rounded shoulders to fetch a broom, but not in any hurry.

Vassily turned towards the noise and saw Alexei.

They held each other's stare for longer than two strangers would. This was noticed by the American. He'd stood up before Vassily had even turned round again, and walked away quickly.

It was Vassily's expression that had told Alexei everything. It was not surprise at seeing another agent on the same operation; it was the same look as a young boy caught doing something he shouldn't by his parents. Fear and panic.

Because of their relationship, the expression had been unguarded and honest. Because of love, the truth had been disclosed.

In that brief connection between them, Vassily had revealed that he was not meeting the American on official KGB business. Had that been so, he would have signalled for Alexei to help him follow and catch the American.

Vassily's shoulders slumped forward and he looked up to the ceiling in a gesture of defeat and resignation.

Alexei knew he should be following the American or alerting his team outside to re-instigate their surveillance measures. Instead he stared at the back of Vassily's head, and at the broad shoulders he'd spent many an evening massaging.

Neither man wanted to move.

Vassily stood up. He drained his coffee mug, smoothed down his shirt, and turned back towards Alexei. He walked slowly towards Alexei's table, biting his top lip.

Alexei hoped Vassily would sit down with him and offer some reasonable explanation. He wanted to hear a lie that he could fool himself with. But Vassily never lied to him, and he wouldn't do so now.

Vassily stopped next to the table. Alexei's hand was clutching a fold of the tablecloth as Vassily's fingertips brushed his. It was as if a charge of electricity had passed between them. Vassily took a large step over the debris of glass then quickened his pace towards the exit.

The surly waitress whacked Alexei's shoe with the broom, forcing him into motion. He stood up but didn't chase after Vassily.

The moment had come, the one he'd feared. Alexei now had to make a choice.

It was the KGB or Vassily.

4

COOPER BAIN was in danger.

His KGB contact recognised the man sitting at the other end of the railway station restaurant. That was not supposed to happen.

Cooper stood up and walked away from the table quickly, before his KGB contact had even turned back around. In espionage, hesitation increased risk.

The veteran CIA agent knew how to escape.

Outside the entrance to Kiev Railway Station he dashed down the steps of the Metro entrance. It seemed satisfyingly perverse to use Stalin's underground rail network to help him evade the KGB.

On the platform for the Circular Line there was one other passenger who didn't board the train that Cooper let arrive and depart without him. Cooper recognised this man as the one who'd followed him into the music store earlier, although he'd now taken off the red cardigan.

Cooper calmly walked up the steps towards the exit.

A taxi pulled up in front of him, braking harshly. The female driver looked directly at Cooper, then behind him, as if she were waiting for someone else. She appeared confused, perhaps even nervous.

Cooper crossed the street, ignoring the honking of car horns as he weaved dangerously amongst the vehicles. There was more tooting for the man following him.

He walked down the steps of another entrance to the same Metro station. Hearing a train arrive on the platform for the Arbatsko Line, he ran across and leapt on board as it was about to leave.

He wedged his foot against the door in case he needed to get off.

The male KGB agent burst into a sprint. Cooper knew then that his pursuer wouldn't make it. He moved his foot and let the doors close.

The carriage accelerated.

Cooper turned his back to the KGB agent as he passed by, separated by the glass pane of the carriage window.

Changing trains at Arbatskaya, Cooper later emerged from the exit of Kirovskaya Station.

Before leaving Washington, Cooper's handler from the president's re-election campaign had advised him never to contact the US Embassy or any of the active CIA agents in Moscow for help. In an emergency, Cooper was told to get a haircut. He knew what that meant; this was not his first mission to Moscow.

"Welcome comrade," croaked the elderly barber as he fastened a nylon cape around Cooper Bain's neck. He'd recognised the American when the bell above the door tinkled and Cooper walked in to join the others waiting for a haircut.

He struggled to tie a knot. His hands were shaking.

"Hello Arkadi Leonidovich," said Cooper. He spoke Russian with a Moscow accent. "I always ensure I have a trim for the celebration of my name day."

"We shouldn't bow and scrape to religion, comrade," replied Arkadi as he began to cut Cooper's hair.

"Tell that to my wife!" joked Cooper.

The barber was reluctant to ask the question he knew he must.

"Today is the feast day of Nikolai of Pskov isn't it?" asked Arkadi. His hands were still trembling as he gave the first part of the coded phrase. He'd waited for years to see Cooper again, knowing when he did it meant he'd been activated. Arkadi had hoped that day would never come.

"No, Arkadi Leonidovich. Have you forgotten, my name is Vassily?" Cooper laughed. "Today is the feast in honour of Vassily the Blessed. The celebration starts in an hour."

Arkadi knew Vassily the Blessed was more commonly called Saint Basil. In his reply, Cooper had secretly given the barber both the location and time for a later meeting: St. Basil's Cathedral in one hour.

Arkadi continued the haircut without speaking. His hands eventually steadied.

The gruff, bearded West Texan flicked through that day's copy of Izvestiya but without reading any of the propaganda published by the Soviet government. As his hair got trimmed and his Rasputin-like beard re-shaped to disguise his appearance, Cooper Bain's mind was planning his next moves.

The KGB contact at the railway station had either been followed or had himself betrayed Cooper. Either way, ORCHESTRA was compromised.

The White House counsel had been insistent with Cooper that another screw-up like the Fielding burglary in Los Angeles wouldn't be tolerated. Worries over the Watergate break-in had made Washington as volatile as a powder keg. If the State Department found out about ORCHESTRA, and the cooperation with a faction in the KGB, that keg would surely explode.

Cooper did not panic. In Beirut in the late forties he'd learnt his tradecraft from Archie Roosevelt, the best there had been in the Agency. Of even more value, daring Archie had proved that a set-back didn't always mean disaster.

In over twenty-five years of spying since, Cooper had been kidnapped, tortured, and double-crossed, but more missions had succeeded than had failed. The White House had sent him to Moscow without any CIA or Embassy cover because of that pedigree.

ORCHESTRA might not yet be a failure.

Cooper noticed Arkadi flinch each time he caught his own reflection in the mirror. The barber seemed concerned by the only other customer waiting in the barbershop. They both knew that man could be CIA or KGB, but Cooper hoped it was just someone who wanted a haircut.

Cooper's age put him on the cusp of becoming an old man, but the thrill of uncertainty and danger still affected him as it had done when he'd been a young man recruiting agents to blow up railway lines in the Levant with Archie Roosevelt. He was still a man of action and glad when the haircut was finished, and he could leave. A moving target was harder to hit.

"THIS IS too dangerous," whispered Arkadi leaning close to Cooper. The American was admiring the huge iconostasis of the light-flooded central chapel under the twisting onion-shaped domes of St. Basil's Cathedral in Red Square.

"Don't whisper," replied Cooper, "it makes your whole body act like you have a secret." He walked slowly out into the decoratively tiled gallery that connected the eight small chapels.

"Are you still in contact with our friend?" asked Cooper.

"No." replied Arkadi. Cooper didn't believe him.

A young couple approached.

"That is where a bomb caused damage during the Revolution," said Cooper, pointing up at an irregular part of wall masonry. The young couple also glanced up at the high part of the wall. They returned Cooper's smile.

Arkadi fidgeted.

"When this building was finished Ivan the Terrible asked the architects if they could ever build anything finer," said Cooper, loud enough for the couple to hear. They stayed in the small chapel, obviously interested in what he was saying. If they were KGB, Cooper reasoned, they would have walked away, worried that staying would make them too obvious.

Arkadi wiped dampness from his forehead.

"'Yes' the builders told Ivan, 'we can build something even more beautiful'," continued Cooper. "So Ivan had them both blinded," he laughed.

The couple walked to the next chapel, also smiling.

"I don't understand," said Arkadi.

"Be careful how you answer questions," warned Cooper. He stepped out of the building onto the platform at the top of a covered staircase. He closed the wooden door behind Arkadi. The two were alone.

"Why have you come back?" asked Arkadi. "After all these years."

"I need you to contact our friend," said Cooper.

"I can't."

"Telephone our friend and suggest a haircut is due." Cooper ignored Arkadi's protestations. "Ask if ORCHESTRA is still safe."

"I won't," implored Arkadi. He was almost in tears. His whole body was shaking.

The broad-shouldered Texan stepped close to the Russian, using his body to emphasise this was not a request but an order.

"You will," demanded Cooper. "Our friend will know how to contact me."

Without waiting for Arkadi to reply, Cooper walked down the steps, through the grilled fence, and paced casually across Red Square without looking back.

Arkadi would relay the message. Then Cooper would know if ORCHESTRA was still active. Until then, he had to hide in plain sight in his enemy's own territory.

Leaving Red Square, Cooper crossed Marx Prospekt. He walked up Gorky Street as far as Soviet Square, then doubled-back down Pushkin Street. Taking Neglinnaya Street, he turned right and arrived at the hotel.

"Chesney Hoyt," he said to the receptionist.

"Of course, Mister Hoyt," she replied in unconfident English. The room key was handed over. Cooper returned her smile but was unsure whether to be nervous. Where the KGB one step ahead or behind him?

He unlocked the door to his first-floor room. He never stayed in a room higher than was possible to escape from.

His muscles stiffened, preparing for whatever might be waiting inside.

He moved in quickly and closed the door behind himself. There would be no point in running. He would have to fight if the KGB had found him.

The room was empty and undisturbed.

He knew by now the KGB would have raided the room of Mr. Jeffrey Johnson at the Hotel Mir, but they would find the personal effects of a ghost.

Mr. Chesney Hoyt, registered at the Berlin Hotel by Cooper the day before, seemed to be safe. He had a third alias at the Moskva Hotel if needed.

Cooper carried out a series of activities that had become routine.

From Beirut in the forties to Tehran in the fifties, and many cities since, Cooper had built a career on half-truths, evasions and disappearing bodies. The taste for adventure and trickery kept him alert so that even routine tasks were still carried out with thoroughness.

He methodically searched the room to identify where the listening devices were. He only found the quantity and type that would be expected to monitor any regular foreign businessman. With a damp cloth he wiped the pair of shoes he'd left in the room, removing the traces of nitrophenyl pentadienal the hotel maids sprayed on their guest's shoes to make tracking them easier.

Cooper slid the window up just enough to guide his arm under. In his hand was a small rock he'd collected earlier. He flicked this at the window, which smashed easily and sent the shards of glass into the room. He eased the window frame back down and locked it in place.

"Yes, Mister Hoyt?" asked the receptionist on the phone.

"Someone has thrown a rock at my window and there's glass everywhere," said Cooper.

"I don't understand," replied the receptionist, "rocket?"

"No, a rock," repeated Cooper. "I'll need to change rooms."

"The hotel's full I'm afraid, sir." The receptionist's reply sounded rehearsed. "Industrial conference in the city this week."

"Even so, I need another room," insisted Cooper.

There was a pause and a clicking sound on the line.

"A porter will come and show you to a new room, sir." There was a tone of defeat in the receptionist's voice.

"Thank you."

Cooper sat in an armchair to wait for the porter. His suitcase was already packed.

He checked his watch. Seeing that the time was three-thirty, he switched on the travel-sized transistor radio to tune into the commentary from the chess tournament in Reykjavik.

5

THE CLOCK in Alexei's car read three-thirty.

The radio relayed commentary from the chess tournament in Reykjavik but he wasn't paying attention to it.

This was a route he'd driven many times, but never in such circumstances. Vassily would be waiting for him, but this time Alexei would arrive as a KGB agent, not his lover. Alexei needed to hear a reasonable explanation for Vassily meeting the American without permission from the KGB. He feared what his lover would say.

A black Volga appeared in the rear-view mirror. It was a KGB car like Alexei's own.

He put both hands on the steering wheel and pushed his foot against the pedal. The weighty car responded sluggishly. There was a reason why the sedan he'd borrowed was nicknamed the 'barge' by his colleagues. It was heavy to drive.

He easily overtook a school bus that proudly waved the Soviet flag from one of its rear windows. He swung in front just as the second lane was blocked by another vehicle, cutting off the other Volga. Cars moved aside for him, recognising his vehicle as an official one, but so too did the traffic behind him for the other Volga.

The highway passed beyond the ring-road heading to the western reaches of the city.

Alexei weaved in and out of the three lanes of traffic paying little attention either to his speed or to other road users. At times he accelerated, keen to get to Vassily's flat, then he'd slow down as doubt over his course of action made him hesitate. Seeing the other Volga in the mirror as they entered Vassily's suburb of Molodezhnaya made him quicken the pace.

Alexei had the advantage of knowing the area well. He turned off the main road into one of the complexes of prefabricated character-less concrete rectangles. He lost the other car easily. They would give up and return to the main road. That gave Alexei precious minutes.

Vassily's boxy little economy car was parked in the usual place. Alexei slowed down as he drove past. That Vassily had not fled didn't ease Alexei's mind.

Something was not right with Vassily's car.

The wheels had been turned as far to the left as they could, away from the road. There was a bunch of flowers on the rear parcel rack. Vassily never bought flowers.

It was a signal.

Alexei had intercepted enough CIA communications to know that Vassily was using the car to ask the Americans for help. Had Vassily been exfiltrated? Was he already in the sealed compartment of a truck with just a piss-pack and some water to sustain him as the vehicle crossed to the West?

Almost any outcome seemed preferable than Vassily living in Kansas, renamed as Chuck, and working at a gas station.

This wasn't the first time Alexei had loved and hated someone at the same time. Vassily had betrayed everything. He was a traitor, just like Alexei's father.

The brakes of his car screeched as he parked up next to the block of flats where Vassily lived. He flung the car door open, but his legs wouldn't move.

He could hardly breathe.

Rage coursed through his body, which shook with adrenalin.

His senses were alert to everything. He could smell the honey-like scent of the lime trees. He noticed the green leaves had started to turn yellow as autumn approached. He could hear the flapping of a cloth that a young woman in the flat next to Vassily's was shaking out through the window.

The other black Volga pulled up a short distance away.

49

Alexei could tell them Vassily had left and order the agents back to Moscow. There was time to save Vassily if he was still in the flat.

On the car radio Alexei listened as the commentator announced from Reykjavik that Boris Spassky had resigned the latest chess game, making Bobby Fischer the new world champion for the Americans. The hatred of America had been something the two young men believed in, or so Alexei had thought. Had everything been a lie?

"Comrade, you drive like a maniac," joked one of the burly KGB agents who'd walked over to Alexei's car.

"What are you waiting for?" barked Alexei. "I gave you my orders before we left."

He switched off the radio and waved his hand at the other vehicle, signalling for the planned arrest to take place.

"Yes, Comrade Captain." The agent rushed towards Vassily's building.

Alexei stepped out of the car to have a cigarette. He also wanted to make sure Vassily saw him when brought out; he owed his lover the respect of eye contact.

Vassily held Alexei's gaze. He was led to the Volga and forced into the back seat. An unnecessary kidney-punch was delivered by one of the agents to encourage continued compliance.

Alexei looked for an expression of forgiveness, but there was no such absolution. But neither was there anger. Alexei couldn't hide the painful expression of a lover who'd betrayed Vassily for the Party.

"Wait here," said Alexei to one of the agents.

"But -"

"I said wait," interrupted Alexei.

Already Vassily's flat seemed unfamiliar to Alexei. It had been tidied up, something Vassily never did. The rubbish had been bagged-up and left outside the door. Even the cold space carved into the exterior wall of the kitchen had been emptied of its perishable food. He'd clearly expected that either Alexei would betray him, or the Americans would rescue him. Either way, Vassily had not intended to live in this flat any longer.

The mini Orljonok transistor radio on the kitchen table had been left on. The commentary from Reykjavik was being relayed. He and Vassily had been listening to the same broadcast. Was that the last thing they would share?

Alexei picked up a picture of Vassily as a teenager. He slid it out of the frame to study it.

They were opposites in many respects, both physically and in character. Alexei was an elite city-raised Soviet with access to comfort; an extravagance he had grown up despising. He had the fastidious neatness of most military men. His features were distinguished, angular, even noble. His physique slender and toned.

Vassily shared none of these things. It was only because of his intelligence that he'd escaped from the kolkhoz farming community depicted in the photograph. Party officials had seen in the young Vassily a propaganda opportunity and he'd hungrily followed the path that Alexei had shunned in accepting a place at the elite Institute in Moscow.

Alexei proudly lined up to buy food and clothes from the poorly stocked stores, happily queuing for hours with his fellow comrades. Vassily was like a stray dog finding a door to a restaurant left open. He was a peasant with a talent that he was determined to exploit to access an apartment of his own, western style clothes bought at the KGB-only store, and the new furniture that Alexei now surveyed from the doorway to the main room. The new bed where he'd lain next to Vassily's stocky muscularity and kissed his rough weather-worn face had only been delivered two weeks before.

But what they had in common had seemed much stronger than what set them apart. They shared a purity of belief in the Communist Party, a commitment to an ideology which held sway over them with the power of religious devotion.

They'd met when spending time helping with the harvest during the late summer months two years before; something all city dwellers were supposed to do but which most managed to find an excuse not to. Only the true believers made such sacrifices.

For Alexei, espionage was a way to protect the ideology from the enemy. For Vassily, joining the KGB had been a rebellion against those in his village that lacked the same faith as him.

But Vassily's belief had not been strong enough, thought Alexei. Whilst his own had been too strong, strong enough to betray his lover.

"Alexei Ivanovich, we must go," wheezed one of the agents, out of breath from running up the three flights of stairs. "The Centre has radioed."

Alexei nodded an acknowledgement. He took one last look around the room, walked along the corridor, and closed the front door.

On the second from top concrete step Alexei noticed the toy action figure of a Soviet soldier he'd bought Vassily as a joke. Vassily had said it looked so much like Alexei in his green Border Guards uniform that he would always keep a small Alexei with him.

The arm had broken off.

Had it been dropped by Vassily as he was pushed down the stairs, or had he left it out with the other rubbish by the door and an agent had knocked it?

Alexei picked up the figure and the broken arm and put them in his jacket pocket with the photo of Vassily he'd taken from the flat.

AS THEY approached the city centre, the lead vehicle with Vassily in turned right after crossing the Moskva river instead of continuing. The Lubyanka was straight ahead.

Alexei had stipulated they were to go to the Lubyanka. He'd arranged for someone he trusted to be there for the interrogation.

Turning right could mean only one thing. The orders had been changed. They were taking Vassily to the Serbsky Institute.

Alexei's hands gripped the steering wheel as a sense of horror and regret overcame him.

6

THE BLOOD in Alexei's veins chilled.

Vassily was en route to become the newest patient of the Serbsky's special diagnostics department for political nonconformity, a euphemism for the application of psychiatric terror.

Serbsky was more feared than the Lubyanka, and for good reason.

Earlier that day Alexei had asked Yukalov, the department head, why Vassily was at the railway station. He knew there would be two possible outcomes. But his commitment to the Party, to what he, and what he thought Vassily, believed in, meant that he had to ask the question.

Yukalov did not seek to blame someone for their mistake in not coordinating the surveillance teams. Nor did Yukalov dismiss the question as unimportant. Instead, he made several phone calls, debriefed Alexei, and summoned an arrest team which he insisted Alexei lead.

A period of detention at the Lubyanka, followed either by enlistment as a double-agent with America or exile to Siberia had seemed like Vassily's fate. Even for the man he loved, Alexei could accept that consequence, as he had years before when his father was executed.

He had loved both men, and both were traitors. The state had chosen to protect his father's memory. But that same government apparatus was going to destroy his lover. What

Alexei had never considered, otherwise he may not have asked Yukalov the question, was Serbsky.

Only a few months before, Alexei and Vassily had been in the rear seat of another Volga en route to Serbsky. Squashed between them had been the principle male dancer for the Kirov ballet in Leningrad. The Jewish dancer had made the mistake of requesting permission to emigrate to Israel with the other refuseniks.

When he'd disembarked from the train in Moscow, expecting to get his export documents from the Foreign Ministry, a police officer sent by the KGB falsely accused the dancer of spitting in the street. He was arrested for hooliganism and spent fifteen days in prison with inmates who were all amputees and cripples.

Confinement with limb-damaged prisoners hadn't been enough of a warning to the dancer. His demand to leave for Israel only became more insistent. So Vassily and Alexei had been asked to escort him to Serbsky and the promise of a hellish, almost mediaeval, captivity.

The dancer had been released from Serbsky weeks later. Bursts of voltage had shaken his brain into a state of permanent idiocy. His body shook with terror. His mind had become that of a child's and his legs those of an old man. He would never dance again. His export permit for Israel was granted. Alexei had felt sickened by what the state security service he worked for had done. They were now going to do it again, because of him.

Vassily turned around in the car. His eyes found Alexei's with an expression of hopeless terror. A guard punched Vassily in the stomach.

Denouncement by the lover who felt betrayed, Vassily would have understood. But not torture. This was a consequence of the events initiated after the Kiev railway station sighting that Alexei could not allow.

Alexei pressed the accelerator pedal. He swung the Volga out to get adjacent to the lead vehicle. Banging his palm on the horn and gesticulating wildly for the driver of the other car to stop, Alexei was ignored.

He increased his speed and cut in front of Vassily's vehicle, then slowed to force a stop.

The other driver turned sharply down a side street.

Alexei took the next street but emerged behind the other car. There was no room to overtake.

He revved the engine and thrust the heavy vehicle forward, ramming into the lead car. The bumpers crunched against each other.

As worried pedestrians pinned themselves against buildings, the lead Volga sped off.

They were nearing Serbsky.

The Makarov pistol from the glove box gave Alexei hope. The weapon was in his hand and the anger coursing through his body, but the street was busy with people. Even firing a warning shot would result in his own arrest.

He couldn't help Vassily that way.

He had to remain calm and clever.

Vassily's car turned into Kropotkinskiy Pereulok.

Entry to Serbsky was via a huge metal security-controlled gate attached to a non-descript building in a residential street. The unremarkable exterior increased its power to those who knew what took place inside.

Any erratic behaviour from Alexei would raise suspicion. Even with a KGB pass, the sentry at Serbsky could deny him entry.

He approached with his car at a crawl. He smiled at the guard and showed his pass, hoping the guard would not notice his shaking hand.

The steel gate slid open slowly. He was waved through.

The vehicle that had been carrying Vassily was already empty, but the driver was inspecting the damaged bumper.

"Your orders were to take the prisoner to the Centre!" roared Alexei, hurling himself towards the driver.

The driver raised his hands in surrender.

"Other orders comrade," he said

"From whom?" demanded Alexei. The driver shrugged. "Get the car ready, we're going to Dzerzhinsky Square. I already have an interrogation team waiting there." Alexei pushed past the driver on his way into the ominous building.

"Who's in charge here?" demanded Alexei, knowing the only chance he had of getting Vassily over to the Centre was by intimidating people at Serbsky. If they believed a mistake had been made, the staff would release Vassily to another KGB officer rather than risk a charge of incompetence or insubordination. In Russia, a show of strength sometimes meant more than the truth.

Alexei hoped a mistake might really have been made. Vassily could still be saved from torture.

A guard checked some paperwork.

"Get out of my way!" exploded Alexei. "The prisoner just admitted is in the wrong place." The guard's confused expression hinted that he was convinced by Alexei's explanation.

"There's been a mistake," insisted Alexei. "You'll be culpable if you don't stand aside right now."

"There's been no mistake comrade." The silky voice came from behind Alexei.

As Alexei swung round to berate whoever had emerged from the office, the sight of three stars on the shoulder boards of the uniform, and the menacing expression on the man's face immediately deflated Alexei's bluster.

"Comrade Colonel I ordered the prisoner taken to the Lubyanka," said Alexei calmly. "I have interrogators there waiting for us."

"We have better interrogators here," said the KGB colonel.

"I ordered the men to take him to the Centre," said Alexei, hoping he could appeal to the colonel's military respect for chain of command.

"And I ordered him brought here," replied the colonel. His reply did not encourage any further challenge. "I'm Vladimir Mikhailovich Roskov," he said, extending a hand in greeting. Alexei shook the colonel's hand. He looked too young, perhaps only forty, to be wearing the insignia of a colonel. That could only mean he was favoured and connected. This made him very dangerous.

"But comrade colonel, I…"Alexei felt he had to say something to try and save Vassily from his brutal fate, but there was no argument to be made to a KGB colonel who'd taken charge.

"Please, Alexei Ivanovich," interrupted Vladimir, "let's go through to the hospital."

The sentry stood aside. The two men stepped through the door into the prison.

Alexei knew Vassily was no longer his to protect.

THERE WERE no howls or screams from people being tortured.

The halls were silent, made more so by the thick carpet that even muffled their own footsteps.

Serbsky was quiet, calm, orderly. This made the place more sinister. Alexei shivered with an instinctive fear.

As they passed the locked rooms Alexei scanned the faces of those whom he could see through the windows in the ward doors. He dreaded seeing Vassily's face amongst those pressing themselves against the glass.

Everything was white. The walls, doors, and linen were white. Even the metal-framed beds and door handles had been painted white. The only hint of colour came from the dark grey tracksuits the patients were wearing. These uniforms removed their individuality whilst setting them apart from the clinical whiteness elsewhere. The patients themselves disrupted the consistency of their surroundings. They were otherness. They were disorder.

"He's not here," said Vladimir. "These are the observation wards for those already receiving treatment."

"Wh…Where is Vassily?" asked Alexei tentatively. Self-preservation made him hesitate, lest he be considered an accomplice. "The prisoner?"

Vladimir didn't reply.

Had Alexei already betrayed himself? Had his behaviour in the car already been reported? Was he about to be issued with a grey tracksuit?

Alexei cursed his stupidity. In the reception area he should have apologised to the colonel, returned to his car, and hurried away. Instead, he stepped willingly into this prison with a man who's blunt, Slavic, reptilian features warned of the very

57

sadism and brutality the Lubyanka plan had been put in place by Alexei to avoid.

Two faces with lifeless eyes peered out from one of the windows. They were jostling to see out into the corridor. The noticeboard above the door showed that all fourteen beds on that ward were full. Alexei imagined that behind these two patients twelve others were surging forwards, pushing against them. The vacant eyes followed Alexei as he walked past. One of the men gave a knowing smile; the expression suggested this patient knew Alexei would soon be one of them.

Two rows of chairs faced a large window in the small room Vladimir led Alexei into. Once both were seated the lights behind the glass were switched on to reveal a clinical room with a metal-framed bed, an unusual bathtub and medical equipment that Alexei didn't want to consider what the use of might be. The light in their observation room was switched off. They were in semi-darkness.

"What you did today was heroic, Alexei Ivanovich," said Vladimir. Alexei could no longer see the coarse features of Vladimir's face. The deep-set eyes, like black caves, were obscured. The cruel face might be hidden, but the excited voice, almost girlish in its tone and tempo, revealed Vladimir's enjoyment in whatever was about to happen.

"Heroic, colonel?" asked Alexei. He felt anything but.

"Please call me Vladimir Mikhailovich. In me you have made a friend today. And yes, it was heroic." He clasped a meaty hand of stubby fingers on Alexei's knee. "We know you and Vassily Petrovich had become…" he paused for effect, "very close."

They knew.

This whole thing had been an excuse to capture them both, thought Alexei.

From the moment Yukalov had asked him to carry out an unplanned surveillance operation that morning, the KGB had set a trap for him and his lover.

Betrayed by his lover, Vassily might already be in another room telling the KGB everything about their relationship.

Alexei recollected a passage about homosexuality from the 1964 Soviet sex manual. It had stayed with him since being taught it: 'Such people should be immediately reported to the administrative organs so that they can be removed from society.'

Serbsky ensured removal.

Alexei loosened the knot of his tie and undid the collar button of his shirt. He couldn't remove his jacket because his shirt was damp with sweat that would incriminate him, betraying his sense of panic.

"It shows true loyalty to the Party to denounce a close friend." Vladimir removed his hand from Alexei's knee and folded his arms across his bemedaled chest. "As Comrade Lenin said: 'No revolution is worth anything unless it can defend itself'. You defended it today, comrade."

"Thank you, Comrade Colonel," replied Alexei hesitantly. He was still unsure whether this was a trap. More flies are caught with honey than vinegar.

"He is a traitor," said Vladimir. "He betrayed you. He betrayed us. And he was in league with the Americans. We shall soon see how deep that treachery is, comrade." Vladimir banged on the door, which could only be opened from the outside. As he left, a uniformed guard entered and stood blocking Alexei's exit.

Alexei couldn't leave. He was being monitored.

7

TWO MALE orderlies led Vassily into the examination room.

Alexei knew the principles of interrogation well.

Stage one from the manual of tactics was captivity. The gates of Serbsky closing behind Vassily's car had removed the last of hope of rescue.

Stage two taught interrogators to strip the prisoner of his individuality. To make him vulnerable.

Vassily was naked. His head had been roughly shaved with electric clippers. Uneven patches of dark blond hair were deliberately left to dehumanise him further.

"Let the criminal see himself in the mirror," suggested one of the orderlies. Laughing, they turned Vassily to face the reflecting glass, on the other side of which Alexei felt sick.

Alexei walked towards the door. He couldn't watch the humiliation of the man he still loved.

The guard stepped forward one pace and moved his hand to the holstered pistol. Alexei sat back down. He was expected to watch. Both he and Vassily were being investigated, albeit by different methods.

Perhaps Vladimir had designed it so that Alexei's loyalty to the Soviet Union would be further tested by witnessing the interrogation and torture of the man he had accused of treachery.

A doctor entered the examination room. From behind thick, black-rimmed glasses his eyes scrutinised the new patient. Vassily turned his head to follow the doctor.

"Face forwards!" barked the doctor. When Vassily refused, a nod from the doctor to one of the orderlies prompted a hard slap across Vassily's face.

The doctor took his time inspecting Vassily's body. He scribbled notes in a file as he did so. He prodded Vassily's muscles. He grabbed Vassily's genitals and smiled when his patient flinched.

"Open your mouth," said the doctor. Vassily ignored the order. Without needing a signal, the two orderlies wrestled with Vassily's head, holding it in place so the doctor could prise open his jaw.

Another nod from the doctor signalled for the two orderlies to release Vassily and see whether he still fought. The doctor was testing Vassily's compliance.

"What is ORCHESTRA?" asked the doctor in a low non-threatening tone, as if he was asking someone their plans for the weekend. He didn't expect a confession this early on.

"I don't know," replied Vassily. He stood with his bare feet shoulder-width apart and his arms rigidly by his side. He stared straight ahead at the mirrored glass.

Alexei could tell he was lying.

He imagined how scared Vassily must be. He wanted to bang on the glass and plead for Vassily to confess. They both knew what treatments were administered by the clinic-prison to those who did not comply. Once the aminazin, sulfazin and reserpine combination drug treatment was administered, Vassily would give up the information the doctor wanted anyway, but by then his mind and body would be irreparably broken.

The peasant boy from the kolkhoz who had defied all expectations to become a KGB officer was tough. Alexei knew that, if Vassily still believed in whatever ORCHESTRA was, he would make the vivisectionist work hard to break him.

Alexei looked at the face, every blemish and crease of which he knew better than Vassily himself. In bringing Vassily to Serbsky, the KGB had tricked Alexei, another betrayal. He wanted to fight back.

Vassily was the only person he'd ever loved. He couldn't endure watching the lobotomization of that person, even if Vassily was a traitor.

"Comrade, I need to see the colonel," said Alexei.

The guard didn't respond.

Alexei reached forwards to knock on the door. The sentry stepped across to block Alexei's arm. Alexei couldn't help Vassily. He couldn't stop what was going to happen; what he'd started.

Perhaps it was a fitting punishment to witness the brutality. The pain would be the last thing he and Vassily would share, and it would be a suffering that would stay with them both. Everything else from their relationship would be ruined. Perhaps that was Vassily's intention in refusing to cooperate. He must have known Alexei was on the other side of the glass.

Alexei sat back down.

Vassily was strong. He had rescued Alexei from a future of shameful and illicit alley-way sex with the feminine male prostitutes who loitered around outside the Bolshoi. He had shown Alexei that being in love with a man, a masculine man, was not just possible, but natural. That was the man standing in front of the mirror now. That was the man Alexei loved. The person who'd sat down for coffee with an American spy earlier that day seemed like an illusion.

What was ORCHESTRA? And why did Vassily betray everything for it?

"You wanted to see me?" asked Vladimir, stepping into the darkened room.

"What is ORCHESTRA?" asked Alexei.

"We shall soon find out, comrade." Vladimir sat down next to Alexei. Their arms were touching. This was Vladimir's performance to direct. Alexei didn't move his arm.

The doctor checked various items of medical equipment. The two orderlies watched their prisoner.

Vassily stared at the mirror, at Alexei.

Minutes ticked by.

"Why doesn't he ask him again?" said Alexei. He was worried his voice betrayed more than it was safe to, but the waiting was intolerable.

"He won't ask again, not yet," said Vladimir. "The doctor knows if stages one and two of interrogation haven't loosened the tongue, there is no point in repeating the question which still won't be answered. That only emboldens the prisoner into thinking he has some control. It boosts his self-esteem with a show of feeble, pointless defiance." Vladimir leant forward, closer to the glass, he was enjoying this. "And the prisoner will be expecting the question. It's more effective to do the unexpected."

The doctor nodded to the chief orderly. They'd played out this sequence so many times before that nothing more than a gesture was needed to understand each other.

Vassily resisted.

A third man, one in military uniform, ran in to help. The orderlies pulled Vassily by the arms whilst the soldier lifted Vassily by the ankles. His limbs were tied to the four corners of the metal bedframe, but he continued to struggle.

"Get me off this bed!" bellowed Vassily.

"This isn't a bed," replied the doctor. He rolled up the sleeves of his white coat. "The South American's call it a *parrilla*." He smiled at the writhing patient. "In case you don't know Spanish, that means barbecue, or grill."

Alexei felt faint. His breathing was quick and shallow. He couldn't swallow.

"This is peppermint oil," said the doctor as he massaged the ointment onto Vassily's genitals, "in case you're wondering." He sniffed the bottle as if testing a perfume.

"It increases the sensitivity," added one of the orderlies, smiling sadistically at Vassily.

The doctor inserted a thin metal rod into the urethra of Vassily's penis. It was a rape of sorts and designed to be as such. He placed a wire mesh bag over Vassily's genitals.

"That forms the fixed electrode portion of the *parrilla*," explained Vladimir. Alexei didn't want a commentary. He wanted to be sick. He suppressed repeated surges of nausea.

The doctor washed and dried his hands slowly. He whistled a jolly tune as he did so. He plugged a device into a wall socket and handed this to one of the orderlies with a gesture of magnanimous generosity. The orderly took the other end of the device, which was a moveable electrode.

The doctor forced a rubber cylinder between Vassily's teeth.

With a further nod, and still without repeating the question about ORCHESTRA, the doctor indicated for the orderly to commence.

"This is stage three of interrogation," said Vladimir. He rubbed his podgy hands together in excitement. "Pain."

The contact of the electrode with Vassily's left foot made his body contract violently. He growled in agony. His jaw clamped down on the bit in his mouth.

The doctor looked puzzled that his patient was not divulging information freely. Usually one shock was enough.

"Oh, how forgetful of me!" exclaimed the doctor, as if genuinely annoyed with himself. "The Peronistas in Buenos Aires would be so disappointed. 'Dumb Commie' they'd say." He chuckled to himself. From his coat pocket he produced a blindfold and tied this around Vassily's eyes. The orderlies held the head steady.

"Sensory deprivation increases the sensation," said Vladimir. He stood up to be as close to the glass as possible. This allowed Alexei a moment to turn away, to cough properly, and to take a deep breath. He mopped the dampness from his forehead and hair with his hand.

Vassily writhed against the restraints, not knowing when and where the next shock would come. He was unable to tense and prepare himself.

The orderly touched the device to Vassily's neck. The scream of agony was a visceral wailing. Alexei had heard the sound only once before. When helping with the harvest in the countryside a kitten had slept next to the engine of his car. Without realising the animal was there, Alexei turned the ignition and heard the death squeal of the trapped cat. It haunted his dreams with nightmares, as Vassily's scream now would.

Tell them, thought Alexei. Make this stop.

"Ask him again!" implored Alexei.

"Remarkable," said Vladimir, ignoring Alexei. "The application of the oil to their scrotum is usually enough to make them tell us everything."

Vladimir was overcome with enjoyment. He banged on the door and left.

When the doctor saw that Vassily had untensed his muscles he nodded his permission to proceed. The orderly touched the electrode to Vassily's testicles.

The convulsions of agony were so violent that Vassily's right wrist snapped against the leather restraint. The broken bone ripped through the skin. Vassily spat the bit out, with it came a mouthful of blood and broken teeth.

The doctor waited.

The blindfold was removed.

Vassily sobbed uncontrollably.

The doctor waited a few more seconds.

"What is ORCHESTRA?" he asked.

Vassily didn't answer.

The doctor looked worried. He bent over Vassily to check his eye reflexes. He was too close. The mouthful of bloody spit showered the doctor's flabby face. A hard slap from the doctor sent another stream of blood squirting out of Vassily's mouth.

Alexei knew what Vassily was doing. Humiliating the doctor might make him lose control. Uncontrolled violence could result in a quicker death.

The doctor didn't even replace the blindfold. He grabbed the electrode from the orderly's hand and thrust it down to Vassily's genitals. He jabbed it to the wire mesh but Vassily smiled at him with a bloodied mouth of missing teeth and swollen, torn gums.

The doctor lifted the electrode and rammed it down again. Still nothing happened.

"That's enough, Comrade Doctor!" bellowed Vladimir in an almost falsetto voice. He'd disconnected the device from the wall socket.

Alexei recovered from having vomited. Breath was at last returning to his lungs.

8

THE GUARD escorted Alexei back to the observation room. A cup of strong black coffee had stopped his body shaking.

A patient was cleaning up Alexei's vomit. The middle-aged man made eye contact just once, briefly, with Alexei. Despite the glassy deadness of his eyes and the hollowness of his cheeks, Alexei recognised the former Naval commander who'd given the commencement address for his Border Guards graduating class several years before. The former Soviet hero kept his head bowed in deference to Alexei as he left the observation room.

Vassily's wrist had been bandaged. He was clothed in a grey tracksuit and sitting uncomfortably on the bed which now had a mattress.

Vladimir sat on a chair next to the bed. He was smoking a cigarette.

"It is unacceptable, comrade, unacceptable," said Vladimir. "The doctor does not honour the work with such an outdated approach. Even the KGB still has its relics."

"I preferred the Stalinist approach," replied Vassily. His voice was weak, croaky. His trembling hand slowly guided a cigarette to his damaged mouth.

"Stalinist?" asked Vladimir.

"Show trial and firing squad," said Vassily. He coughed on the cigarette smoke. This aggravated his other injuries and he winced in pain.

Alexei stood with his back to the guard blocking the door. He closed his eyes.

"The KGB has always been its most brutal against the Soviet people," said Vladimir, ignoring Vassily's tears of pain. "I suppose it's because of Russia's size. People must be compelled to accept things. Don't you agree?"

Vladimir's comments criticising the KGB were enough to get him sent to Siberia. Alexei had met this type of official before. Non-believers. Time-servers who'd joined the KGB because it paid more. Vladimir assumed Vassily was the same, someone who'd been turned off from the ideology and sought a new religion elsewhere, to the West.

Alexei now suspected Vladimir's assessment was wrong.

He knew Vassily better than anyone else.

Whatever ORCHESTRA was, for Vassily to not divulge anything under this level of brutality, it must be the most important thing to him. Only Communism had ever held that pre-eminence. The political belief was strong enough to make Alexei betray his lover. Perhaps, thought Alexei, something to do with that same ideology was preventing Vassily from yielding to torture.

"The truth is that ideas are more powerful than guns," stuttered Vassily, as if he'd heard Alexei's thoughts. He discarded the cigarette on the floor. Vladimir shrugged his shoulders and crushed the cigarette out.

"The truth is whatever enhances the state's interest at that moment. In the Soviet Union, there is no such thing as a lie, comrade." Vladimir studied Vassily as if he were something never seen before.

"I'm here to help you," said Vladimir. It was a phrase Alexei had been expecting to hear. Help was the favourite word from the lexicon of the new breed of interrogators. "Tell me about ORCHESTRA and I'll make sure you're released today. You could redeem yourself, comrade, and help us."

"I was helping *us*," replied Vassily. He looked directly at the mirror, at Alexei.

For nearly an hour Vladimir tried every possible civilised approach with his questioning. At one time he invoked pro Soviet sentiments, then he criticised the system. He pretended to know about ORCHESTRA, insisting Vassily just needed to confirm the details to secure his forgiveness and release. America had abandoned him, he told Vassily. The Soviets still valued him. Rapid questions were followed by long silences.

Vassily said nothing.

"You leave me no choice, Vassily Petrovich." Vladimir had been pacing the room, but he now stood next to the bed and glared down at Vassily. "If you won't prove your loyalty by talking to me, then we must use another method."

One of the orderlies fully opened the taps on the large bath. The water gushed into tub.

"This is something I'm very proud of," said Vladimir. "The grotesque human barbecue or drug treatments of the comrade-doctor's are old fashioned." He tested the water with his hand then adjusted the taps. "This is a test, not torture. Come over here."

Vassily remained on the bed.

Vladimir rolled his eyes and gave a 'tut' of annoyance. He waved for the orderlies to drag Vassily over to the bath.

"At the bottom are two large straps, one for your arms and chest, the other goes across your legs. We submerge you with a breathing tube in your mouth. When you're secured, I remove the tube and start the clock." He took a stopwatch out of his tunic pocket. "I've calculated the lung capacity of a man your size and condition so I know how long you can hold your breath for, even after the horrors the doctor inflicted upon you."

He splashed the water again and turned both taps off.

"When the time's up we'll pull that lever. The bottom of the tub falls away and the water drains completely in two seconds. Simple and clever isn't it?" He looked at Vassily for a reaction, perhaps even admiration. There was no response.

"It's a test because the submerged person has no idea how long they need to hold their breath for, or even if we'll pull the lever when the time's up." Vladimir settled for the smiles of appreciation from the orderlies. "Only the truly faithful, those who still believe in the KGB, hold their breath long enough not to drown. They trust me."

Vladimir glanced at the mirror, then back at Vassily.

"Do you trust me, Vassily Petrovich?" he asked.

Alexei stood with his face to the glass so he could see inside the bath. He wanted Vassily to pass the test, to prove his loyalty, to redeem himself from the accusation of treachery that Alexei had shamefully made against his lover.

"Don't struggle," advised Vladimir as the orderlies fought against Vassily, trying to undress him. "My advice is to try and relax. Take slow, deep, even breaths. Let your body slacken. You need the oxygen going to your brain not your muscles."

He nodded for the orderlies to submerge Vassily in the bath. He stepped out of the way of the splashing water. One of the orderlies gripped the broken wrist and Vassily weakened with a scream of agony.

"I'm trying to help you, Vassily Petrovich," said Vladimir, smiling. "I *want* you to prove your loyalty."

The orderlies pushed on Vassily's shoulders. Vladimir forced the tube into his mouth. The straps were fastened, and the splashing ceased.

Alexei looked at Vassily. His face was distorted by the settling water. His eyes were closed.

Vladimir waited.

"He'll open his eyes," he said to the orderlies.

He continued to wait, but Vassily kept his eyes closed.

Vladimir shrugged.

"This is my favourite part," said Vladimir. He smiled at the mirror, at Alexei, who noticed that Vladimir had the bulge of an erection.

Vladimir wiggled the end of the breathing tube, warning of its imminent removal. He was grinning at the power he had over a man like Vassily.

He pulled the tube out of Vassily's mouth and started the stopwatch.

Alexei held his breath also.

After only a few seconds Vassily opened his eyes. He stared at Vladimir through the water. He didn't look scared. His expression was saying 'fuck you'.

Vladimir guessed what the submerged prisoner was communicating to him. He knew what Vassily would do next.

Vassily opened his mouth and gulped at the water to drown himself.

"Pull!" exclaimed Vladimir.

In one mighty torrent, the bath drained through the grill in the floor beneath. Vladimir was already unbuckling the straps before the water had emptied. He couldn't allow anyone to cheat his plan.

Vassily coughed up water.

Alexei took a deep breath.

Vassily was alive but he hadn't proved his loyalty.

Alexei still had no answers. What, or who, was ORCHESTRA?

London

BIL WAITED across the road from the Playboy Club in Mayfair.

The long suicide of William 'Wild Bill' Yaxley was how his remaining friends referred to the last few years, but they had no idea. It wasn't suicide. It was slow murder. The inevitability of it had followed Bill like a shadow for nearly two decades. A slow, planned death.

Suicide was the romantic notion of a noble gesture against a cruel world. But Bill was just as cruel as the world he inhabited. His self-destruction was murder; justifiable, necessary, pre-meditated self-murder.

He'd built his own gallows and tied his own noose.

The autumn evening was warm and wet.

"That him?" he asked.

"Yeah," replied Valerie. She took a drag on her cigarette and watched the Dutchman walk into the club opposite.

"Sure?" asked Bill.

"For Gawd's sake, don't start on me. I said so didn't I?"

"Get yerself back to Dalston, girl," said Bill.

"Me bruvva's gonna pick me up. He's up west tonight."

"Here." Bill handed a roll of pound notes to Valerie.

"Blimey, there must be twenty nicker 'ere!"

"Get yerself some decent clobber then," replied Bill, frowning at the mini skirt Valerie was wearing.

"Charmin'," she said.

"And maybe a nice job in an office," he added, keeping an eye on the door of the club.

"What? Fifteen pound a week and all worry. Nah, I don't fink that life'll suit me," she said, treading carefully on the cigarette butt she'd discarded.

Bill continued to watch the club entrance.

"You stoppin' 'ere then?" she asked.

Bill didn't reply.

"Night then," said Valerie. She adjusted the heel strap of her shoe. She stepped past Bill and hurried off down the road, avoiding the puddles.

Bill felt as out-of-place in Mayfair as the girl.

The lustre from his war years spent earning a commission in the Special Operations Executive had long since faded. The sharp edges of a fighter from his teenage years on the streets of gangland East London had never dulled.

That persistent serration of his character enabled Bill to successfully spend twenty years engaged in the kind of ungentlemanly warfare Whitehall forbade those who'd stayed in British intelligence after the war from engaging in.

Bill still did them the odd favour. Like tonight.

No one had followed the Dutchman into the Playboy Club.

Bill put the last cigarette from the packet in his mouth. He crushed the empty packet in his hand and threw it into the swirling gutter. He ripped the filter tip off and pulled out a few strands of stray tobacco.

The first few matches wouldn't strike. He missed not having the Zippo gifted to him in the War by an American G.I.

The smoke caught in the back of his throat. His fees for an assassination were such that he could easily afford the expensive Balkan cigarettes that were his one usual indulgence. But he was a professional. He never carried his own brand on a job. Nothing could be allowed to identify him.

He held the cigarette between thumb and forefinger, shielding the rest of it and the orange glow of the flame in his cupped hand. The habit had developed over many years of smoking in doorways and staying undetected.

The doorway shielded him from the rain.

A bus drove past obscuring his view for a moment. The dirty water splashing from the gutter just missed Bill's shoes. He didn't care. They were only cheap, bought for tonight, and would be disposed of later with everything else he was wearing or carrying.

A young drunk man with long hair approached.

"Got a spare fag, guv'nor?" he asked.

Bill noticed the green shirt, opened to the navel, and the beads around the boy's neck. He detested these dropouts, but any insult might make him memorable. Bill shook his head to dismiss the hippie.

Bill had a precision of timing to rival a stand-up comedian.

The young hippie, now shouting to no one in particular about the virtues of peace instead of war drew the attention of those passing in the street. Bill flipped up the collar of his dark blue rain mac and crossed the street unnoticed.

The doorman briefly glimpsed Bill, but he was more interested in laughing at the hippie urinating on the steps of a Park Lane mansion whilst shouting about Vietnam.

Even if asked, no one outside the club would be able to recall Bill.

The bunny-girl at the reception desk checked his membership card, made out in someone else's name.

He found Peter van Klaas easily.

The Dutch womaniser, who'd been using some of London's children as mules for his father's imported drugs, was sitting alone at the bar scanning the face of every bunny-girl that walked past. He was looking for the one he'd come specifically to see, but Bill's preparatory work had already ensured Valerie wouldn't be at work that night.

The soft spot van Klaas had for Valerie had established a pattern to his behaviour, and such patterns were vulnerabilities. Bill had discovered that whenever van Klaas was in London, he would make enquiries to check the shift rota for Valerie. In every other respect of his London visits, van Klaas was a man who avoided routine and repetition.

Van Klaas was always in the company of bodyguards providing a level of protection that would normally have made Bill's task much more difficult. But when van Klaas came to the Playboy Club to see Valerie, Bill had discovered he always came alone.

Bill sat at a table rather than take a seat at the bar. He selected the table himself, making sure he could keep van Klaas in his sightline.

The bunny-girl, dressed in a high-cut powder-blue one-piece with matching coloured bunny ears and high-heeled shoes, brought him the whisky sour he'd ordered. To ask for a pale ale, his usual drink of choice, in a place such as the Playboy Club would have made him note-worthy. She turned her back to show off the fluffy white pom-pom tail, looked over her shoulder and, with a practised grace and poise, performed the famous bunny-dip to place the napkin and drink carefully on the table in front of Bill. He gave a tip which was neither too small nor too large, so the girl wouldn't remember him.

The Dutchman moved into the casino area of the club. Bill knew van Klaas did not gamble. Taking his drink with him, he followed van Klaas at a safe distance and watched as the young man sought out the bunny-mother to enquire about Valerie's non-attendance.

Bill stood with a group of other middle-aged men at one of the roulette tables. They were all wearing either wide-lapelled business suits like Bill's, or they'd chosen a jacket and slacks combination with an open-necked shirt unbuttoned far too low for their age. Bill was entirely unremarkable as one of the group.

He watched as van Klaas was told the news that Valerie had not turned up for work that evening. The Dutchman hurried across the dancefloor, pushing his way through the crowd of young people. Petula Clarke was on the stage singing. Bill recognised her for the Sanderson wallpaper adverts in the Sunday Times colour supplement rather than her music career.

Van Klaas went into the gent's toilet. Bill followed him after a couple of seconds, prepared to take a piss and leave if there was either an attendant, or other men, in the bathroom.

The toilet was empty, apart from van Klaas standing at a urinal. Each cubicle had its door open and was unoccupied.

Bill reacted quickly.

He placed the 'closed for cleaning' sign on the outside handle and slipped the lock on the door as he closed it.

Time had creased Wild Bill's face into a grizzled veneer of one whose life experience had left its physical mark, as well as thinning and whitening his hair. But those same decades had not dimmed either Bill's talent for spilling blood, nor his character as a hardened man not interested in excuses, apologies, or bribes. He was ageless, with a single-minded intensity to his approach that left no doubt he was a lion who could still roar.

His dark eyebrows shielded two piercing ice-like grey-blue eyes that gave those reflected in them no hope of leniency. Bill's brooding silence and small gestures could change-up several gears into rapid down-market cockney verbal attacks of unrestrained fury. He had a physical presence that could dominate a room but return to laconic calm just as quickly. Bill had learnt that sometimes a whisper after a storm can hold the most power.

Bill was an assassin. And he was excellent at his job.

"Peter van Klaas?" asked Bill rhetorically. He stood at an adjacent urinal to the Dutchman.

"Do I know you?" replied van Klaas uncomfortably.

"Nah." Bill turned his head and fixed a stare on van Klaas that made the Dutchman's bladder seize up with fright.

Bill dropped a polaroid photo into van Klaas's urinal, showing the body of one of the children who'd died carrying the Dutch drugs into London from the port in Hull.

The hard drug scene centred around Piccadilly Circus had grown rapidly since van Klaas's product had entered the market. The Met police hadn't been able to link this to the Dutchman evidentially. The other London gangs weren't yet in a strong enough position to start a continental drug war on the capital's streets. Van Klaas's use of young children was an unconscionable step too far for even the most brutal of London's mobsters.

Only a mercenary had the freedom to get to van Klaas, so Bill had been asked for a favour. He found Valerie, and that had given him this opportunity.

"But...I..." stuttered the Dutchman. His shaking hand swept the recently permed hair away from his sweating forehead. He ran a finger around the inside of the turtleneck sweater, which now seemed too tight.

Every word spoken echoed around the pristine bathroom that smelt of lavender and honey.

"There ain't nuffink you can say that's gonna change what's about to happen, so shut it," interrupted Bill, turning towards his target.

Van Klaas started to back away. Bill stepped towards him. The Dutchman's bladder suddenly reversed its shock response and the urine started to soak across the front of his flared trousers.

"Fuck sake, Petey, have a word with yerself, son!" exclaimed Bill with a burst of ferocity.

"S...s...somevone vill find you." Van Klaas's Dutch accent strengthened the more nervous he became. He was now backed fully into the corner of the room. "Kill me, and your own children vill end up like that bastard in ze photo." Peter was trying to regain some courage.

"I'm a professional, son, no one'll know it's murder." Bill's voice was now almost soothing in its softness. He patted the young man's shoulder. "But they will find these on ya." Bill gave van Klaas a bundle of more Polaroids, all showed an obscured slim white adult male engaging in some of the most graphic sexual acts with children that Bill could get from a contact in the evidence store at Scotland Yard.

"That's not me...I...." stuttered the Dutchman.

"You and I know that, lad," replied Bill. "But your daddy back in tulip-land won't when the newspapers report finding these on your dead body, will he?"

Van Klaas opened his mouth to reply. Before he could speak, Bill used a noiseless atomiser mist gun to explode a vapour shot of prussic acid in the Dutchman's face. Bill had taken an anti-dote pill with the last gulp of his whisky moments before following his target into the bathroom.

The Dutchman's mouth remained open, but no words came out as his blood vessels contracted. His face contorted as the intense pain gripped him. A quick death released his body, which collapsed to the floor.

Bill swung open a window to disperse the remaining gas. He slipped the obscene Polaroids into the Dutchman's jacket pocket. He then unlocked the bathroom door, and climbed out through the open window, dropping down into the alleyway behind the club. A twinge of pain in his left knee caused him to flinch.

By the time Bill had reached the main road he knew van Klaas's blood vessels would already have returned to normal. The pathologist would assume a heart-attack had killed him. There would be no repercussions against London from the young man's drug-baron father, who would be ashamed of his son's alleged perversions. There would be no one against whom to seek revenge, due to the lack of suspicious circumstances associated with his son's death.

Bill was pleased that he had, with one simple gesture, avoided a drug war on the streets of his home city, but had removed one of the most invidious aspects of the capital's drug scene. The Dutch cartel would be completely discredited by the stain of van Klaas's apparent paedophilia.

There was a stylish creativity to his violence that Bill was both proud of and ashamed of all at once. Each plan was carefully worked out, and there was no element too gruesome or sophisticated not to be considered; it was that lack of restraint which, most times, reminded Bill of the cruelty in himself which he so despised.

Sometimes a message needed to be sent with the assassination. The brutal hammer attack, disembowelling, and hanging from a prominent bridge of a politician who was a target simply because he was in another's way could serve the purpose best in one case, whereas an undetectable gas attack against an unscrupulous drug dealer would meet the requirements better in another, as was the case that night at the Playboy Club.

Bill walked casually to the bus stop.

Menacing to his long list of enemies, loyal to his short list of friends, Bill usually gave off the impression of a man who was unhappily passing time by the only means he knew how.

Whatever regret he felt for the decision to move away from those who'd trained him during the war, had been disguised by an appetite for perfecting effective means of violence and death. The line of morality between Bill's teenage years as an East London villain, and his wartime exploits as a courageous fighter for other's freedoms, had blurred beyond any hope of re-identification over the last twenty years. Savagery was now Bill's way of life, regardless of the motivation.

However, if anyone had cared to ask, Bill would not have claimed to embrace and enjoy his lifestyle; he was just occupying himself and earning a living.

Only his wife might have asked, but Margaret had stopped doing so years before.

He disembarked from the bus and found his car.

In the early days he'd confided everything to Margaret, but now his wife never asked about his work. Bill wouldn't now have answered even if she had. He'd learnt to perfect the separation between his two lives as husband and killer. It was a necessary duplicity.

The melancholy was more difficult to separate. Bill knew that leaving his career in the security service had been selfish. So too was his continuing with the private 'wet' work that had become his employment since.

Margaret had seemed to fluctuate between blaming and then forgiving him almost every week of their earlier marriage. She'd often gone to stay with her sister in France and stopped contact for periods of time. But these long episodes of separation had ceased ten years ago; a sign they were both accepting their lives together. Now Margaret only visited her sister in France for short periods.

BIL YANKED the handbrake of the brown Rover P6 up forcefully and flipped the ignition key to turn off the engine. He sat in silence for a few moments, switching his thoughts from one life being lived to another, as if moving a train carriage onto a different, but parallel track. He ran his hand over the dashboard, sweeping up the accumulated dust, and wondered whether he should trade the car in for the new Ford Granada he'd seen and admired.

A football from the neighbour's young son had found its way into the Yaxley's front garden again, so Bill hoofed it back over the fence with a well-placed kick on his way up the path. He raised his hands and pretended it had been a cup winning goal. The bitter disappointment of remembering Arsenal had lost that year's cup final to Leeds United made him lower his arms and look for his door key; his mind was now getting back to where it needed to be.

He let himself noiselessly into the home he shared with Margaret on the outskirts of the London overspill area of Buckinghamshire. His precision with the key was not out of consideration for his wife, but simply because that had become his habit in life. Covert and cautious was his unconscious nature, it was the only way to guarantee the skills wouldn't be forgotten when in the field and under pressure.

Margaret was asleep in the armchair. An aria from a favourite opera was playing too loudly on the record player. Bill walked over to the sideboard and lifted the needle from the vinyl. The scratching noise and sudden silence jerked his wife out of her light sleep.

"Hello love," said Margaret, slowly adjusting to being awake. She fiddled with her damp red hair. She'd been colouring it in secret for years to hide the grey. Bill leant down and kissed her on the cheek.

"Tea?" she asked.

"Only if you're making one," replied Bill. He was flicking through the post received that day, most of which were bills and circulars.

"Would you like a slice of cake too?"

"Cake, bloody cake?" asked Bill jokingly, distracted by a bill for some new furniture that he was sure must be in error, having not ordered any such items. "At this time of night?"

"I'm keen to see what you think," replied Margaret calling from the kitchen. She poked her head round the door. "I bought one of those electric mixers at the market. Rose has got one, and you won't believe how easy it makes life."

"How is your sister?" asked Bill, not really interested in the answer. Margaret had just got back from yet another last-minute visit to France to see her sister, someone who always seemed to have a crisis that needed Margaret to fix.

"She's…well…she's Rose," replied Margaret.

"A smack in the bleedin' ear'ole is what she needs," added Bill.

"Don't be grumpy," said Margaret. She stood next to her husband in the hallway. She adjusted her still-damp hair in the mirror.

"These suburban ponces don't even know what a market is. 'All alive and every one's got a bright eye and silver belly', my old dad used to shout on his eel stall. Billingsgate, now that was a market."

"Am I going to have to listen to the 'we were poor, proud and happy' stories again?" joked Margaret.

"You may laugh, but my old mum'd get back from charring, Aunt Vi or Aunt Lil would pop round to gossip, and a full spread for tea was still ready when I got home from school each day. The kettle was always on duty from dawn to bedtime. And there was cake. No fancy food mixers for our family." Bill stood behind his wife and glanced at himself in the mirror. The sight of the creased old man's face that he barely recognised offended him. He turned away quickly.

"So, do you want cake or not?" asked Margaret.

"Go on, then, if there's a slice going beggin'." Bill stepped into his slippers and went back through to the sitting room to find the paper he'd been reading earlier that day.

"Fancy a bit of music, love?" asked Margaret.

"As long as it's not some old tart warbling again," replied Bill.

"That *warbling* is opera. We can't listen to Pearl Carr and Teddy Johnson bashing their way through 'Knees Up Mother Brown' every night you know." Margaret put the tea and cake down next to her husband, pleased now that she'd gone to the effort of making a cake earlier for Bill for when he got home.

Theirs was a marriage that now involved effort. Margaret was trying to love a lonely man who felt he no longer deserved that love and wouldn't listen to arguments to the contrary.

With music on the record player, the windows cracked open for the late evening summer breeze now the rain had stopped, and the tea things already laid out in the kitchen hours before Bill came home, it was as if Margaret was a supporting character in a play which had been paused waiting for the main character's entrance.

Bill knew many of his friend's wives suspected their husbands of leading secret lives because of sexual affairs. The difference in his relationship was that Margaret knew hers was a marriage of secrets. The secrets of the Yaxley marriage were relative, but not of themselves a destructive or invidious force; it was the effect those secrets had which caused the barriers to their love.

No sooner had the record player been brought back into life with a Nat King Cole song, than a knock at the front door caused the Yaxleys to stir sharply from their relaxation.

"Take yerself to the kitchen," whispered Bill, shifting himself back onto the mental rail track that was his other life.

The late hour was cause for caution on its own, but the context of the day's events in London raised Bill's concern, not for himself but for his wife. He picked up whatever object nearest to him could be improvised as a weapon, in this case a handful of long fondue forks from the set his wife had bought but never used, and which had become a dust-collecting ornament.

"I DO apologise for this late hour." Sir Hilary Redfern was suitably apologetic about the timing of his visit and lack of a phone call.

Margaret emerged from the kitchen pretending she'd been in there for some time. Bill put the fondue forks down next to the phone.

"Bit late for a social call, Hil, I assume things have gone for a Burton at the Sanity Board." There was hostility behind Bill's attempt to be jovial as he helped Hilary out of his coat and hat.

"Hilary, can I get you some tea?" asked Margaret, trying to mitigate the subtle antagonism from her husband. "The pot is fresh."

"There's cake too," interjected Bill sarcastically, immediately regretting what he'd said. Margaret would be upset by the joke at her expense. He stood to one side, indicating for Hilary to go through to the sitting room.

"Tea would be lovely, Margaret," said Hilary, "but no cake for me, thanks all the same."

"Was I right about the Sanity Board then?" asked Bill. Both men sat down in floral patterned armchairs that Margaret had recently had re-upholstered in a fabric design she'd seen in Woman's Weekly.

"The Committee of Sanctions is functioning just fine, thanks Bill. 'C' has everything in hand." Hilary was a man of perfect English manners, easy charm and immaculate dress sense.

"I doubt that. Rennie was born a ha'penny short of a shillin'. I'm sure he'll remember me from Warsaw though," replied Bill. He disliked the pretentious use of codenames.

"You're a difficult man to forget, Bill, but I'll be sure to pass on your good wishes," said Hilary with indifference to Bill's irascibility.

Margaret brought her guest his tea.

"I'll be off to bed then gentlemen," she said. "Oh, do you need me to make a bed up for you Hilary; you're welcome to stay the night?"

"Thank you, Margaret, for the tea and offer of lodgings, but I have a car waiting and must get back to London post-haste." He stood up and kissed Margaret. "Always a pleasure."

"Goodnight then," replied Margaret. She kissed Bill on the forehead. She closed the sitting room door behind herself to indicate to the men that they could now speak more freely. She climbed the stairs slowly with a head full of worry, knowing that for Sir Hilary to pay a late-night visit, the matter to discuss was not inconsequential. She stopped half-way up the stairs to listen to the conversation.

"How are you, Bill?" asked Hilary, once enough time had passed for Margaret to get out of earshot.

"Bit of jip with my knees, but that's to be expected I suppose. Shall we cut the crap, though? I'm tired."

"I'm sure you are, Bill. I'm assured that your handy-work at the club has already been deemed non-suspicious by the police." Hilary finished his tea and placed the cup and saucer down on the lacquered coffee table. "That should be a comfort to you."

"I know how sacrosanct the weekend is to you chaps, so I'm assuming this is about another quick job which your guys won't deal with before Monday morning. Although Maclean's defection in fifty-one should've shown up the error of fair play at weekends. I've always wondered with Philby's escape whether the English Establishment felt it was sporting to let him have a crack at running for it, or whether letting him go was the punishment, making him accept the unpleasant realities of a life in Moscow."

"I really can't say, Bill," replied Hilary, polite but uncommitted. Bill hadn't expected an answer, he was just giving vent to the excoriating thoughts about the Service that Margaret usually had to listen to with patience and feigned interest.

Hilary had expected a testy reception, but he remained affable and unprovoked.

"Brandy?" asked Bill, to show that his dislike was for those whom Hilary represented, not a personal criticism. For both men, there was a certain respect each had for the other, even if what they each had come to represent since the war was mutually disliked and misunderstood.

"Thank you, yes," replied Hilary. "I am here on a sensitive matter." He quickly moved onto the subject which he'd come up from Whitehall to discuss, denying Bill the opportunity to continue with his denunciation of the Secret Intelligence Service.

"Aren't they all?" Bill handed the brandy to Hilary. Both men were now standing. Bill leant against the mantle-piece, as Hilary pulled back the net curtains to close the window.

"Does ORCHESTRA mean anything to you, Bill?" Hilary came to join Bill by the unlit fireplace.

"Not immediately," replied Bill, adopting a more serious tone. He sniffed at the swirling brandy, knowing that Hilary would have to fill the silence. He knew of a slight connection with a word such as that mentioned, but it was tenuous at best, and from a time quite distant. He didn't like dredging up the past.

"Our chaps picked up some traffic out of Moscow to Washington concerning it. Early stages, nothing much beyond the name."

"Not ringing any bells with me. Is it a person or operation?" asked Bill, taking a swig of the liquor. Hilary did the same.

"Can't say."

"Or won't," replied Bill.

"You know how these things are, Bill."

"It's not my first circus, that's for sure. Another?" Bill gestured to Hilary's empty glass.

"I won't on this occasion, must be getting back. Thanks anyway."

"Seems a long drive just to ask me one question." Bill took Hilary's empty glass.

"Yes, I suppose it does," replied Hilary with a knowing smile; he was not going to give away anything more.

The interaction for both men was more about their body language and behaviour than what was being said. Bill knew Hilary had more to say, or ask, should the ageing assassin-for-hire have shown a flicker of recognition at the mention of the code name. Bill's plausible denial, believable both in answer and physical reaction, meant that Hilary had no need to make further enquiries.

Bill helped Hilary back into his raincoat that had been left hanging in the hallway. It was only once the door was open and Hilary out on the front step that Bill's curiosity got the better of him.

"I don't expect an answer, and I'll accept a sharp kick up the jacksie if I'm over-stepping, but why ask me?"

"Well, you know I shouldn't really, Bill," replied Hilary, replacing the bowler hat on is head, and tilting it to a jaunty angle. "But…there seemed to be a connection to some dormant leads you were involved with ten years ago or more. I'm sure it's just an error on the analyst's part. Anyway, I'll say good night, Bill."

"Goodnight," replied Bill, hoping that neither his facial expression nor body language had changed discernibly.

As he closed the door, the overdue furniture bill he'd opened with the other mail earlier suddenly made perfect sense. It was an old method of contact from a Soviet source that only he had access to back in the late fifties.

Bill realised that CONDUCTOR had woken up after many years of silence.

Washington D.C.

10

THE LOCATION chosen for the meeting was certainly unusual thought Alan Rawlings. He left his office in the West Wing and used the tunnel under West Executive Avenue across to the Old Executive Office Building.

Rawlings was a military man, and his bearing showed it. Although he was Pearl Harbour rather than Saigon.

He ran a hand over slicked down thinning grey hair as his identification was checked at the gate. He was not well known around the eighteen-acre White House complex, and he liked it that way.

Chuck Colson was Nixon's public hatchet-man. His was the face people feared when he stalked the halls. Only Chuck could have convinced Alan to come out of retirement to help Nixon get re-elected.

Nixon would win in November and win big. But Alan had the experience of knowing there was never a sure thing in Washington politics. He'd designed the Moscow plot, codenamed ORCHESTRA, as an insurance policy to bolster Nixon's foreign policy platform if needed. If it went wrong, Alan knew he would be the scapegoat.

Room 37 was half-way along the basement corridor.

He heard a hard-plastic ball smashing into the wooden pins in the bowling alley Truman had constructed twenty years before.

Alan had to stoop. At over six feet tall he was worried about the low ceiling and exposed pipework. The basement was unrecognisable from the elaborate French Second Empire style of the upper floors.

"Fancy a game?" asked the young man from the CIA. His shirt sleeves were rolled up to his elbows and his tie had been discarded on the floor next to his sports jacket.

"I'm more of a tennis man," replied Alan. He didn't disguise the tone of disapproval at the young man's casual manner of dress and longish hair. He looked like a college drop-out.

"Of course you are," replied the CIA agent with a tone of equal disapproval for the old man in a wide-lapelled three-piece grey flannel suit and sombre-coloured tie.

Alan glanced at the geometric wallpaper. He sat in one of the Eames-designed red plastic swivel chairs. He was uncomfortable.

The agent finished totalling his score on a card and slurped from a bottle of coke through a straw.

"Is anyone else joining us?" asked Alan.

The CIA agent pulled off the tri-coloured bowling shoes and walked over to the chairs in his sports socks.

"Didn't think you guys wanted an audience when it comes to ORCHESTRA."

"Quite so," replied Alan. He scanned the seating area for anything that looked like a recording device.

"We won't be overheard here," said the agent, noticing Alan's caution. "We're just two Washington colleagues getting in a few games over lunch. I'd suggest you loosen your tie and take your jacket off. You look a bit too square for bowling."

"Any news from Moscow?" asked Alan. He ignored the advice from a kid who chose to wear flared cords to work.

"VIOLIN's reported in …"

"Please," interrupted Alan, "can we dispense with the codenames. If we're not being listened to then there's no need for the James Bond stuff."

The agent shrugged. He walked back to the edge of the bowling lane and threw a ball down the aisle to maintain the sound of a game for anyone in the corridor.

"The KGB dupe was arrested. But Cooper Bain's been in touch through the barber. And another KGB sucker has been found."

"Any ripples from across the water?" asked Alan.

"Our agents in Moscow picked up a mention of ORCHESTRA on the traffic but nothing to suggest the plan's in jeopardy."

"Good. Anything from State?" asked Alan.

"They're preoccupied with Ottawa. We've planted enough intel strands to make the State Department think it plausible the Canadians are considering whether to join the other non-aligned countries and take command of the neutral ground. That gives the cover story in Moscow the necessary credibility."

"The hockey series couldn't have come at a better time really," said Alan. He wondered what else he needed to know ahead of his briefing with the president.

"I don't think the Canadians can be beaten," said the agent. He saw the expression of horror on Alan's face. "In the hockey I mean." He was amused that the man from the White House could be so easily provoked.

"We haven't forgiven Trudeau over China or the Vietnam betrayal," said Alan.

"Ottawa is trying to position itself as the international honest broker," suggested the agent.

"We can't let middle powers set the tone of world affairs. That's why we've found ears sympathetic to ORCHESTRA on both sides of the Berlin Wall. A re-freeze, shutting down détente, will push Canada out."

"Winning at hockey will be a big boost to Canadian morale."

"Then I'll be hoping the Soviets rout them on the ice." Alan corrected the knot of his tie, straightening it under the stiff collar of his starched shirt.

"If this works, ORCHESTRA I mean, d'ya think the American public's ready for a renewed Cold War?" asked the agent. He twisted the cap off another bottle of coke and offered it to Alan. The older man waved it away.

"The American people are easily led. Assuming their president is a man strong enough in character to lead them."

"And that's Nixon?" The agent sounded doubtful. He enjoyed needling the stuffed shirts who thought of themselves as all-powerful just because of the zip code on their office address on Pennsylvania Avenue.

"*Anybody But McGovern*, don't they say?" joked Alan. "Just look at the Eagleton fiasco."

"I was at the Lincoln Monument when Nixon suddenly arrived just before dawn with his White House butler. When he told the protesters he was no kook, I wasn't convinced." He haphazardly tossed another ball down the lane, sliding along the floor in his socks.

"Peace with honour, not peace at any price," said Alan.

"There's a spiritual hunger growing and a resistance to the concept of traditional allies and enemies, especially amongst my generation."

"All people are happy to accept control by authority," replied Alan. "Freedom and dignity are both illusions." He was getting animated. He even took a swig from the agent's half-drunk coke bottle. "Everyone's happiest under a benevolent autocrat. Surely the Agency knows this? Isn't it your job to help us condition the populace?"

"We leave it to the Bureau to do our dirty work here at home."

"If we reward people with a better standard of living, they surrender their freedom."

"Pavlov's dog?" asked the agent.

"The government turns right and wrong into legal and illegal. To these we attach rewards and punishments to condition people's behaviour."

"All a bit abstract for me." The agent opened a new coke bottle for himself.

"Communism only has the means to punish. Democracy can reward as well." Rawlings was beginning to lecture. "That's all that sets us apart from the Kremlin. But it's enough of a difference for me to do anything I can to stop communism spreading, even if that means cooperating with the KGB over ORCHESTRA."

"There's a now a counter-culture in America."

"American sheep in different clothing," said Alan. "Whether you're wearing a flowery shirt and hand-made clogs on a commune, or sneakers at work." He glanced at the agent's discarded sneakers next to the chair. "Nothing's unique. Someone, somewhere did it before you."

"Are you sure you don't want a game?" asked the agent. He felt like he was already in a contest with the man from the White House.

"Johnson's Daisy ad in sixty-four created fear that Goldwater winning would end in nuclear holocaust. People were taken in by it. And so-called intelligent liberals at that."

"And it worked."

"It was better than Soviet propaganda," said Alan.

"My generation isn't so easily led," suggested the agent.

"If a fire alarm goes off and I tell you with enough authority to follow me, you will do, even if the smoke's thicker up ahead."

"I guess we'll wait for an alarm to go off."

"Kids don't vote," added Alan, "for Nixon or anyone else. They pointlessly protest instead. When they get jobs, cut their hair, and take an interest in who occupies the building next door, they'll vote for someone like Nixon."

"When they have something material to lose?"

"Exactly," said Alan. He gulped down the remainder of the coke. "We're conditioned to preserve the rewards given to us."

"Even though Nixon'll accept the same peace deal in Vietnam that LBJ turned down in sixty-eight? Nixon sabotaged it then as he needed the war to continue, but he'll accept it now as he needs the war to end."

"We all need enemies."

"Americans in glasshouses?" suggested the agent.

"Are you sure you're with us on ORCHESTRA?" asked Alan.

"Even the die-hard Democrats are voting for Nixon," he replied. "I don't wanna jeopardise my standard of living."

"Is everything in place for the hockey match?" asked Alan. He looked at his watch. The president expected him upstairs in the hideaway office.

"The assassin from London has been approached. The contact came from an old source he trusted." The agent pulled on his well-worn Adidas sneakers.

"No loose ends," said Alan. He stood and buttoned his jacket.

"The Englishman won't be leaving Moscow once he's done what we ask."

"And Cooper Bain?" asked Alan quietly. "The president needs deniability if anything goes wrong."

"This isn't our first rodeo." The agent patted Alan on the shoulder then left.

Once the CIA agent had gone Alan loosened his tie and removed his jacket.

Moscow

Saturday 2nd September

Moscow

Saturday 2nd September

11

COOPER BAIN had woken from a restless night's sleep. He'd lain on the bed fully dressed, expecting his hotel room door to be broken down and him arrested by the KGB.

But the early September morning had arrived, and he was surprisingly unmolested by the security services. The alias of Chesney Hoyt seemed safe.

On the pillowcase there was a small smear from the residue black hair dye that he'd rinsed out before bed. He stripped the pillow and took the case with him to put down the laundry chute on his way out. He exchanged the pillow for the spare one in the wardrobe.

This morning he expected to receive a message from CONDUCTOR, if the barber had done as he was told and made contact the evening before.

He left the hotel and walked in the opposite direction than he needed to go.

At the Komsomolskaya metro station he took his time to pay the five-kopek charge at the kiosk, ensuring anyone following him would also have to linger. He didn't see any shadows.

He disembarked at Lermontovskaya, having only gone one stop on the train. He pretended to be confused by the different subway lines. When no one else who had disembarked with him was left on the platform, he got on the next train and carried on to his actual destination of Sportivnaya.

He was confident of being free from surveillance.

By the time he'd walked to the over-ground rail line by the Moskva river and climbed the steps to the pre-Revolutionary Krasnoluzhsky Bridge, he was sweating and out of breath. After thirty years of operations, Cooper was glad this would be his last. He was no longer fit enough for field work.

The footpath was narrow. Each time a train sped past the gust of air made him nervous and unsteady. It was a good location for a drop site as visibility in front and behind was excellent. Only if the Soviets had him in a pincer movement would escape be difficult. Then he would have to jump into the river and hope for a lucky landing.

As he approached the stone pillars he glanced behind. There was no one else on the bridge.

He removed a piece of asphalt debris wedged into the stonework, behind which was a crevice small enough for a message to be left in.

It was empty.

The second drop site was nearby.

He leant on the railings and lit a cigarette. Below, Cooper watched the people, trying to detect anyone who might not be what they pretended to be. It was a great vantage point.

The bridge's steps were easier to take on the descent.

Novodevichy cemetery was only a short walk away.

He bought a bunch of flowers from a stand located by the entrance gates.

Cooper was not pretending to be a tourist so there was no need to amble around the cemetery. He knew which area to go to.

Between two empty graves with fictitious names on there was a dead rat. This was not an uncommon sight in such a place.

Cooper knelt and laid the flowers on one of the graves. He checked no one else was in sight. The rat had been doused in Tabasco sauce to dissuade any cemetery cat from taking it for dinner. Cooper quickly unsealed the Velcro strip in the rat's abdomen and removed the plastic capsule from inside. He slid out the piece of paper with the message and replaced the capsule.

Now he was in danger. Being caught with a coded message was a death-sentence.

He walked casually to the lake situated behind the cemetery. Tourists who'd fallen for the lie that this was the inspiration for Tchaikovsky's Swan Lake wandered the paths and crossed the little bridges.

A young couple seemed to be following him. He didn't panic. He maintained a casual strolling pace and didn't look back.

He crossed a bridge. The couple crossed it moments later. He tied his shoelace, and the couple stopped to take a picture of the lake.

The message hadn't been read yet. To destroy it now would ruin ORCHESTRA. But to be caught with it would mean arrest and execution.

He wanted to run but knew he mustn't.

A newspaper had been left on an unoccupied bench, so he sat down and pretended to read the paper. Inside he'd unfolded the message taken from the dead rat and quickly read it.

CONDUCTOR assured him that ORCHESTRA was safe. Another KGB dupe had been found to take Vassily's place. Cooper was to proceed as previously planned.

Cooper walked towards the young couple. They didn't acknowledge him. They were waiting on a small bridge. As Cooper walked past, he knocked into them and dropped the newspaper into the lake.

"Excuse me," said the young woman in English. She had a Scandinavian accent.

"*дура!*" exclaimed Cooper. He was not going to be caught out replying in English. The KGB had used that trick many times before on less experienced agents.

Inside the dropped newspaper was the message, which had been written on water-soluble carbon paper. Even if someone were able to get the paper out of the water, the message inside would already have dissolved.

This was old-school field craft, but Cooper preferred it to microdots. He and CONDUCTOR had used it ten years before. Cooper was pleased that it still worked.

Neither the bridge nor the cemetery could be used again for several years, but Cooper knew the location of the next drop site if needed.

He made his way back to the Metro station. The young couple were no longer following him. There was just enough time to get to the seminar on electrochemistry near Soviet Square which was necessary to legitimise the cover of Chesney Hoyt. His attendance would reassure the authorities that Chesney really was an electrochemist from Lubbock, Texas.

After the seminar, he could leave Moscow for a few weeks to stay in West Berlin and wait for phase two of the ORCHESTRA plan.

12

ALEXEI DIDN'T know he was ORCHESTRA's new fall guy. In betraying Vassily, Alexei had positioned himself to take his lover's place in the secret plot being run by hard-line elements in the CIA and KGB to re-freeze the Cold War.

The Centre, the Lubyanka building, was where the phone call that morning had told him to report, even though it was a Saturday.

He'd been unable to sleep the night before. Memories of Vassily's torture terrorised him. Almost a full bottle of Vodka had numbed the pain, but only slightly.

The joke told to every new KGB agent was that the neo-Baroque Lubyanka building was the tallest in the country because even the gulags of Siberia could be seen from its ground-floor prison cells.

Alexei found the building to be an unwelcome reminder of the mercurial power of the Soviet state, even more so this morning. It was the ideology Alexei believed in, not the government. As he passed through one of the pedestrian gates, Alexei worried if that belief had been lost along with his relationship with Vassily.

He should have been more nervous at receiving a weekend summons to the Centre than he was. He expected punishment. He welcomed justice for what he'd done to Vassily.

The sentry checked his papers, saluted, and opened the gate for him.

Being early, Alexei crossed to the main building. On the eighth floor, breakfast was being served in the restaurant. He needed food to soak up the vodka.

"Morning Alexei Ivanovich," said one colleague. "You don't look good."

"Night surveillance," lied Alexei. He knew that no mention would be made of Vassily, even if other agents knew about the events of the day before. Any trace of Vassily Petrovich Grekov would by now have been expunged from the KGB. His colleagues would have been given a false story which they would pretend to believe. Vassily wouldn't become a warning to others. He would simply be erased. No one ever leaves the KGB, and Alexei knew that.

He wondered if his memories of Vassily, the good ones, would also be lost one day.

After breakfast he went to the third-floor office as instructed. It was a few minutes before nine o'clock.

The secretary broke the wax seal on the safe. This was being supervised by a man with a clipboard whose job it was to patrol the offices and witness the sealing and unsealing of the safes each morning and night.

"It's so inconvenient," explained the young secretary once the man had left. "Even if I need a document urgently, I have to wait my turn for him to arrive."

Her outer office had scuffed unpolished parquet flooring, industrial-toned light green walls, and furniture that was twice her age. Her youth and beauty didn't match her surroundings.

She smiled coyly at Alexei. As she checked the teletype read-outs, she moved her body in such a way that Alexei recognised as flirting. He gave her an apologetic smile and looked away. He was used to such behaviour from his young female colleagues.

His legs were bouncing impatiently, and he fidgeted in the chair. Being summoned to the Centre was rare, and almost never welcome. Whatever was going to happen, he just wanted it to be over.

A red light illuminated above the internal door.

"Please follow me, comrade," said the secretary. She smoothed down her skirt and sashayed in front of Alexei to lead the way.

In another office a large woman dressed in the green uniform of an army major sat at a desk in front of a bank of phones.

"Wait!" she barked. She scowled at Alexei then waved him and the young secretary onwards through a set of double doors into a large luxurious office.

"Sorry," whispered the young secretary. "The comrade-major can be abrupt sometimes but she's really rather nice."

"I certainly wouldn't want to arm-wrestle her," replied Alexei. The secretary laughed harder than the joke deserved.

He'd never been in this office before. From the view through the tall windows he could see that it straddled the old and new sections of the building. The walls were panelled in mahogany, the furnishings were plush, and there was a portrait of Felix Dzerzhinsky on the wall.

"Is this the office of the …" He didn't finish his question as the secretary smiled and nodded. "And is that the …" He pointed to the red phone on the desk.

"Don't pick it up!" interrupted the secretary. It'll be answered by you-know-who at the Kremlin rather than the switchboard.

"I wasn't planning on making any phone calls." He took a few more tentative steps into the office. "Do you know why I'm here?" he asked.

The outer doors were flung open.

Alexei and the secretary stood to attention, expecting the KGB chairman.

"Relax, Alexei Ivanovich," said Vladimir. "The chairman will not be joining us." The secretary left quickly. "The comrade-chairman is a family friend so I'm borrowing his office for the day."

Alexei disliked those who exploited their influence for personal gain. In the Soviet Union he was proud that the son of a farmer and the son of a politician should have equal access to the ladders of opportunity. This belief was fundamental to who Alexei had become. But after Serbsky he despised Vladimir anyway.

Vladimir indicated one of the sofas and they both sat down.

"Alexei Ivanovich I am rescuing you from the boredom of the Seventh Directorate," said Vladimir.

"But I …"

"Please don't thank me," he interrupted. "It is only a fraction of the reward you deserve."

Alexei wasn't going to offer thanks, but rather a plea to be left alone where he was.

"Let me tell you more about ORCHESTRA," said Vladimir.

ALEXEI WORKED well into the late afternoon. He'd been locked in a small sparsely furnished office with the only copy of a dossier on ORCHESTRA. From now, he reported only to Vladimir.

Vladimir had told him the slim file contained everything the KGB knew about ORCHESTRA. Alexei doubted this was the truth. He couldn't believe anything the KGB told him anymore. The dossier's contents were mostly guess work and fear mongering.

Alexei sifted through the bureaucratic nonsense from other officers who'd been reluctant to submit names and reports admitting their enquiries had been dead ends. Finding out about Vassily was all that interested Alexei. It was why he'd agreed to work for Vladimir. He wanted answers, and this was the only route to get them.

He'd wanted to ask about Vassily's fate, fearing the answer. But he couldn't. The colonel had to become Alexei's ally if he was to find out what Vassily had become ensnared in.

No notes could be taken. The dossier would have to be handed back, and the numbered pages checked against the contents list. Once sealed in the safe Alexei would not be permitted to see it again.

Almost nothing of value had been established about what or who ORCHESTRA was. It involved the Americans, but those in the CIA working as double-agents for the KGB had been unable to find out anything about it in Washington.

Was being assigned to this a reward, as Vladimir had said, wondered Alexei. Or was it a punishment for the crime of being a *stukach* and informing on a fellow agent?

Alexei had seen the face of the American Vassily had met at the railway station. It seemed to be the only actionable lead in the investigation so far.

A document dated two days before reported that an unknown KGB agent was due to meet with an American in Moscow, and that the American was staying at Hotel Mir. Alexei saw his own name amongst the list of surveillance teams Vladimir had requisitioned to follow every American staying at that hotel.

That directive from Vladimir had led Yukalov to re-assign Alexei the day before. It had been luck, bad luck, that the American his team had been assigned to follow, Jeffrey Johnson, was the one involved in ORCHESTRA. There had been dozens of surveillance teams deployed that day, any one of which could have been randomly assigned to this specific American. Any other team might have lost the American in the streets of Moscow. They might not have recognised Vassily at the railway station. Alexei's life could have been different.

A tap at the door indicated Alexei's guardianship of the file was finished. He checked his watch and was surprised by the time.

"THE MAIN door's locked," said the doorman.

"But I'm running late," implored Alexei.

"So?" replied the insolent security guard.

Alexei ran to the basement and emerged through one of the covert doors leading to a subway tunnel under the road by Detsky Mir children's store.

He walked quickly.

At Soviet Square, and despite being late, he took a moment to acknowledge the red granite statue of Lenin. More than the mummified body in the mausoleum, this depiction was where Alexei felt most inspired by his hero. Returning from Egypt after the betrayal of his father and his murder, this had been where Alexei spent hours as a teenager in contemplation. Lenin's writing had given Alexei a purpose. This statue had replaced his father.

He looked at the face of Lenin, staring down at him. Alexei needed a sign that what he'd done to Vassily the day before had been justified. He knew that for Lenin there had been no middle ground, only right and wrong. He'd learnt from Lenin's writings that the pure of faith could not waver in their devotion to the political ideals, as Vassily had done.

For Comrade Lenin the only question that had mattered was whether the action taken advanced the cause of the Revolution. This had to be Alexei's only consideration now about what he'd done, and in the work for Vladimir he was going to do.

Lenin had always acted for the Party. He'd expressed no remorse for those killed in the revolutionary cause. Would Lenin not have condemned even his wife, Comrade Krupskaya, had she committed a betrayal such as Vassily had against the political cause?

He wanted to stay and ponder, but his twin sister would be waiting for him.

Being here, in the shadow of the Moscow Soviet building's balcony where Lenin had addressed gatherings in the street, Alexei felt the only easing of his pain in two days.

Alexei had trusted Vassily in a way he'd never allowed himself to since his father's death.

Alexei had been betrayed.

AS LENIN'S statue was providing Alexei with some reassurance, the delegates of an electrochemical seminar emerged from a nearby building.

Cooper Bain turned left, to cross the square in front of the red granite statue of Lenin.

Alexei checked his watch again. He stood up and turned away from the Lenin statue.

It was only a flicker. A subconscious brain response.

Each man looked at the other and there was recognition.

The moment of perception passed, quickly dismissed.

"There you are Alyosha!" exclaimed Tara.

Alexei ignored his sister. He began to turn his head to look again at the old man.

Tara turned his face towards hers. She stood on tiptoe and kissed his cheek.

13

EVEN WHEN giving her brother an affectionate peck on the cheek, Tara kissed men as if she were trying to possess them. The female Dimichenko sibling was always enthusiastic about life.

"You've curled your hair," observed Alexei, reaching to touch a strand of his twin sister's wavy raven-black hair.

"Don't you dare!" rebuked Tara, slapping her brother's hand away. "It took me over eight hours to set these in for the party tonight."

"Do I have to go?" wined Alexei, as if he was ten years old again and hoping his sister would help get him out of a loathsome chore.

"Yes Alyosha, you do," she said. "If I have to suffer another one of mama's gatherings then you do too. Anyway, you haven't visited us for ages, and you'll enjoy the hockey."

"Here, let me carry those." Alexei took the bags heaving with food that Tara was struggling to carry.

"Quick!" she cried, "the bus is leaving."

Alexei usually enjoyed taking the bus. The smell of garlic from home potions the city's poor still used for medicine was overpowering on a hot city bus, but it was the smell of real Russian life.

On this journey he was uncomfortable. The other passengers looked at him with scorn and envy, noticing the amount of food he was carrying. Alexei knew these passengers had empty shopping bags stuffed in their pockets and were going home with empty stomachs.

"They think I'm your girlfriend, Alyosha," whispered Tara. "Look at them watching us." She moved in closer to her brother, but Alexei edged away in discomfort.

"No, Tara," he replied. "They're looking at us like we're a pair of privileged bourgeois elitists."

"How I wish *that* were true," she joked.

"You and mama want for nothing."

"That's not so," replied Tara, "I'd love to have longer legs." She giggled. Alexei frowned.

"Oh little Alyosha's angry with me again." Tara rolled her eyes.

"I'm not going tonight," said Alexei. He stood.

Tara pulled at his arm to make him sit back down.

"I'm sorry," she said. "Don't make me go to this party alone."

Alexei sat down again.

They both looked out of the window.

Tara watched the city-scape. The streets were busy with people. The neon lights of various restaurants were illuminated, making the linden trees lining the boulevards sparkle.

Alexei stared at his and his sister's reflections. They were twins but so different. He tried to find physical similarities.

Alexei's slender features and far-away look gave his face a brooding, romantic quality. He'd been told he could convincingly portray a young hero from a Tolstoy novel. He wished he looked less European and more Slavic.

Whereas Alexei appeared timeless, he noticed his sister could only be recognised as someone from her own modern era. Her violet eyes, porcelain skin, heart-shaped lips and cheekbones set her apart from some of the other young Russian women with oval features. Alexei could never imagine his sister dressed in a smock and headscarf digging potatoes out of the hard ground in a village.

Tara's vivaciousness covered a core of steel that both he and his sister shared. In Alexei, others often interpreted this trait as an intellectual superiority, a piety that people respected but which made them feel inferior and sometimes resentful.

Alexei had seen how young men behaved around his sister; how that same confident core in Tara attracted these men but scared them also. It seemed to make her desirable but untouchable; dangerous, but deliciously so. He'd seen Tara cultivate this formidable attractiveness with those young men. She was amused to be nicknamed 'the tsarina'; the name suited her.

Alexei disliked coming back to where he'd grown up. The family home occupied an entire floor of a pastel-green pre-Revolutionary building in an elite neighbourhood of the city. He was ashamed of it.

"My little wolf is here!" called Raisa when she saw her son in the hallway. She was barefoot and dressed in a bohemian kaftan. She was smoking a cigarette through a long amber holder. "Come, come, Alyosha my darling." She dragged Alexei into the centre of the main salon where other guests had gathered.

She ignored Tara.

Raisa squeezed her son's cheeks and inspected him and his clothes. The guests cringed in sympathy with Alexei's embarrassment.

"This suit looks like it was made for a revolutionary," she said.

"I am a revolutionary, Mama," replied Alexei, "we all are, aren't we?" Several of the guests in their imported evening wear and expensive jewellery took long gulps from their crystal champagne flutes and started to talk amongst themselves about insignificant matters, turning away from Alexei's censorious eyes.

"You know what I mean, Alyosha," said Raisa. "We all admire you for your steadfastness. I just wish you dressed better, darling. Why don't you make use of the special KGB stores like Tara? And she's not even in the Service."

Alexei knew his sister didn't really work for the Novosti press agency. His spies working in various hotels had reported his sister entertaining foreign businessmen. Their mother must also have known how Tara really came by her expensive wardrobe, thought Alexei. But theirs was a family of secrets and pretence. In that respect he had much in common with his mother and sister.

"Give your mama a kiss."

Alexei noticed how much older his mother seemed than when he'd last visited. Her face was becoming jowly. Her eyes were cloudy with too much alcohol, and her voice raspy from too many cigarettes. Nevertheless, his mother shared with Tara a sparkle of adventure that attracted people to her, despite the danger that feistiness suggested.

One of his mother's lovers had described Raisa Dimichenko to Alexei as having the temperament of a gypsy in the body of an ageing Hollywood movie star.

Alexei condemned his mother's longing for acceptance. He'd felt ashamed seeing her submit to the husband who'd betrayed Russia, her fawning to the lovers before and after her widowhood that had not been hidden from her children, and the suffocating relationship she tried to maintain with Alexei. All these men had rejected her, even her son.

"I'll go and help Tara," said Alexei.

"Oleg Grigorevich, will you play host please? I must get myself ready." Raisa shouted this back into the salon as she topped up her glass and hurried past Alexei. "And it takes longer than it used to," she added.

"She's on form," said Alexei, lifting the shopping bags onto the kitchen table. "Oleg Zhirov's here I see."

"He's mama's new *companion*," replied Tara. "Do you know him?"

"Unfortunately," said Alexei.

"He's so old, and fat."

"Any man of noble birth who's survived the Revolution, the purges of both Stalin and Khrushchev, and secured a senior place for himself amongst Brezhnev's gerontocracy is someone I don't trust."

"Oh you and your ideological purity!" said Tara, swiping her brother across the arm with a tea towel. "If he's managed to adapt to the political climate then so be it."

"You must have queued for hours to get all this," said Alexei, removing items from the bags one at a time.

"Don't be silly Alyosha, I just telephoned the lovely man who runs the store. He had everything packed and ready when I left Novosti." She took a bag from Alexei and tipped out the contents in one go. "It hardly cost me anything."

Alexei could guess what she'd done for such favours.

"If the farmers have toiled to harvest the produce," said Alexei catching items before they rolled off the table, "then the least that the decadent city dweller can do is to wait patiently to receive the fruits of others' labours."

Alexei thought of Veera Sergeevna from his apartment, spending hours queuing outside an ill-stocked shop, leaning on the walking stick she used to ease the pain in her back. Often since moving into his apartment, Alexei had taken her place in the line for her and felt a great sense of comradery with the others patiently waiting for their allocation, regardless of their occupation or the amount of money in their pockets.

"You don't have to eat it then *Little* Lenin," snapped Tara.

"I shan't," replied Alexei. "*Tsarina*," he added.

"We'll see. The commentary for the hockey in Montreal won't be broadcast until much later. Don't complain to me when you're hungry."

"I need a drink," said Alexei. He left his sister to prepare the food.

He declined the offer of champagne from a guest and found a bottle of inexpensive vodka instead.

"We shall soon have Pepsi-Cola on sale here in the Soviet Union, Alexei Ivanovich," said Oleg. "I negotiated with the Americans." He addressed all of Raisa's guests. "You may have read in Pravda that Stolichnaya and PepsiCo have made a deal, well I was the one who arranged it." The guests clapped. "It will be the first American consumer item to be produced, marketed and sold in the Soviet Union. That's détente, comrades!"

The vodka now tasted bitter to Alexei.

"Will we win tonight, Alyosha?" asked Raisa.

Alexei shrugged.

"After defeat at chess, we need to win all eight of the hockey matches with Canada to recover our pride," said one of the guests. "This is now more than just sport. It's politics."

Tara carried in a buffet of pickled vegetables, fish in aspic, caviar, and borsch. The guests started to make toasts, dedicating their words to more and more ridiculous purposes with each new bottle of wine that was opened.

"How is work?" asked Alexei of Tara, helping her carry the food. "At Novosti." The clarification was unnecessary as his sister had never spoken to him about the extra work he knew she undertook. Alexei considered it to be prostitution.

"Well, that Philby character has joined us in the tenth section at Novosti," said Tara. She flipped some other concoction preserved in aspic onto a large plate.

"What's he like?" asked Alexei with genuine interest.

"Surprisingly, very charming, in a boyish way. He hates Moscow. How can anyone hate this city?" She arranged the food on the plate.

"He got married recently, didn't he?" asked Alexei.

"Well, it hasn't helped. Depressed alcoholic is how someone at the agency described him to me. Carry these out please, Alyosha, that's the last of the food."

"You're not going to leave me in there alone are you?" he asked.

"Of course not." She stood on her toes to kiss him, but he stepped away with the plate of food before her lips could touch his. "I'm just going to get changed."

"*Another* new dress?" he asked. Tara smiled.

"Alexei, what do you call a musical Soviet trio?" asked Oleg, slightly drunk, and gesticulating wildly as if he was conducting an orchestra. Alexei knew the punchline to this old joke but decided to play along anyway to please his mother.

"I don't know, Oleg Grigorevich," he replied, putting a plate of mushrooms down for the guests. "What *do* you call a musical Soviet trio?"

"A quartet returning from an overseas tour!" bellowed Oleg, as others joined in the laughter. "Listen, I've got another one I heard this week from someone in the Politburo: How do you deal with mice in the Kremlin?" Guests smiled and shrugged. "Put up a sign saying: 'collective farm', then half the mice will starve, and the rest will run away!" Everyone except Alexei laughed.

Such jokes, if told amongst anyone other than the elite of the city, would have sent them straight to the cells at the Lubyanka. Alexei had arrested and interrogated dozens of people for much less.

"Did you hear about the train?" asked another of Raisa's friends. A series of encouraging smiles urged the woman with hair that was now slightly dishevelled, and make-up smudged, to tell her joke. "Lenin, Stalin, Khrushchev, and Brezhnev are all on a train that has broken down. Comrade Lenin steps forward with a solution, and declares a subbotnik, asking the peasant train crew to solve the problem. Then Stalin comes forward and has the train crew shot. Khrushchev rehabilitates the dead men..."

"And Comrade Brezhnev?" interrupted another quest.

"Oh, he just pulls down the window shade and pretends the train is still moving!" The guests roared with laughter. Several of whom would return to work on Monday to carry out the instructions of the man they now made fun of.

"Watch out, Yulia Simonovna," warned Oleg, putting his arm around Alexei's shoulders. "Young Alexei Ivanovich here might start taking notes and you'll find yourself reduced in status."

"We're all equal, Oleg Grigorevich," replied Alexei with a bristle in his voice as he stepped out from under the old man's arm "here in the Soviet Union."

"Don't be naive, boy." Oleg's response was not in a tone of levity. "Those in the West have never been free, and those here in the East are certainly not equal."

Alexei looked around the room and considered whether anyone in attendance had ever done a day's manual work in a factory, much less understand what life on the collective farms was really like. He spent a few weeks every year helping with the harvest, but even so Alexei felt a certain shame at being a city dweller, seeing himself now as one of the white-collar intellectual class. He feared becoming one of the petty-bourgeois that diluted the true character of the state, undermining the Revolution. He didn't want to become an Oleg.

"We are the unacknowledged heroes of the Revolution," said Oleg. "We are the hidden class who have made everything work and who sustain the rest of the public idealism that is riddled with inefficiency."

Alexei could see from the attitude of his mother's guests, that they agreed with Oleg, seeing themselves as apart from the masses, but the saviours of the system, a system their jokes mocked.

"Saving the Revolution while you eat from my mother's imperial kuznetsov porcelain dinner service?" asked Alexei.

It was dangerous for him, a junior KGB officer, to be so insolent towards a senior Party official. Oleg was a possible heir to Brezhnev. But he thought of those in his own apartment on Gorky Street. Nine families occupied a space smaller than his mother's entire residence and used strips of the daily Pravda newspaper in the toilet to clean themselves.

"You're just an angry young man," said Oleg. "Playing at being a revolutionary."

"So speaks *Count* Oleg Zhirov," replied Alexei.

"Alyosha, have you met Doctor Sorokin?" Raisa interrupted the argument, pulling Alexei away by the sleeve of his jacket. Her drunken voice was loud as she declared her faith in the latest Rasputin-like miracle cure. "Where's she gone? The doctor's an expert in bio-rhythms."

"It was para-psychology last time," said Alexei. He had often criticised his mother for the extravagance of indulging in such expensive hobbies whilst pretending they were genuine medical treatments. Vodka was the only medicine available to those in his apartment, as it had been for his fellow soldiers in the Guards.

"Natalya Nikolaevna met her at the Botkin," said Raisa, ignoring her son's disapproval.

"Your friends treat that hospital like a spa," said Alexei. "It was founded on the principle of classless health provision."

"You're tiresome Alyosha," said Tara. "Always searching for people undermining a revolution that happened over fifty years ago."

"The task of the revolutionary proletariat is not yet complete," said Alexei. He indicated towards the room full of his mother's guests to prove his point.

"Come along Mama," said Tara, "let's leave *Little* Lenin and join the party. *I* intend to enjoy myself."

Alexei remained on his own watching the guests. He was sure, if he looked hard enough, he would find a connection between ORCHESTRA and this Soviet elite.

Perhaps his betrayal of Vassily would ultimately help to protect the Revolution in an era where dinner party jokes about the Party leadership were made freely over a sumptuous banquet, he thought. It may be that the odious career-centred Vladimir had given Alexei an opportunity to serve the Party in a great capacity.

Alexei, the favoured son who could do no wrong in his mother's eyes, was ashamed even of his own mother as he watched her getting drunk and embarrassing herself. It was Tara, the forgotten twin, who rescued Raisa from herself. It was Tara who turned the volume on the radio up to distract the guests with the hockey commentary coming live from Canada.

After Prime Minister Trudeau had dropped the puck signalling the start the first match of the eight-game series, there had been two quick goals to give Canada an early lead.

Raisa's guests objected loudly as Team Canada adopted violent tactics to disrupt the play of the disciplined Soviets.

The dinner party guests in the Dimichenko apartment listened noisily as the better form of the Soviets led them to a 7-3 victory. The Canadians didn't even shake hands with their opponents after the defeat.

Alexei, listening from the kitchen, was pleased with the result. The Bolshevik body-check had caused the most significant national institution in Canada to crumble in the first match, and it looked as if the humiliation at the chess tournament would now be compensated for. Vassily would have been ecstatic with the result, he thought.

14

THE LAST of Raisa's guests had gone.

"Alyosha you behaved appallingly tonight," said Tara. "Poor mama was so embarrassed by your rudeness." She collected empty glasses.

"Tara don't…" mumbled Raisa, half conscious on the sofa.

"She'll pass out soon," said Alexei. "As usual." He helped his sister tidy up.

They'd all had too much to drink.

"Why can't you just…" Tara struggled for the right word. "Participate?"

"Participate?" Alexei spat the word out. "In this? This grotesque show?"

"Alyosha's just …" Raisa tried to sit up but fell back. She waved a hand in the air. "Alyosha's just serious."

"Alyosha's not serious, Mama," said Tara. Her mother was already asleep. "He's a cut-out, Alyosha's a cardboard cut-out."

"Why are you attacking me, Tara?"

"Because you risk everything for us in being so damned orthodox."

"I'm a communist."

"You're a zealot." She put the glasses and plates back down. "Don't you see? You provoke people, important people here tonight. People who could take all this away."

"Would that be so bad?" asked Alexei.

"Yes!" exclaimed Tara. "I like champagne." She took a swig from a glass that had some champagne left in it. "I like nice clothes." She twirled to show her new dress. "And I love Russia, just as much as you."

"You don't," replied Alexei.

"And you're the authority? Why? Because of Egypt?"

"Tara, no!" Raisa stirred from her drunkenness. "Dance with me Alyosha," said Raisa, hearing a favourite tune on the radio.

"This again!" exclaimed Alexei. "Egypt?"

"Yes, Egypt." Tara stumbled with her mother, trying to get her to another chair.

"Here, let me help." Alexei tried to help move Raisa.

"No, Alexei!" exclaimed Tara. "We don't need you."

"We?" he asked.

"No one needs you," said Tara.

"It was papa's choice to betray his country…"

"I miss him," interrupted Tara.

"Our father was a traitor."

"Not to me!"

"I saw him, Tara," implored Alexei. "I had to tell."

"You wanted to tell. You wanted to prove something, and you didn't care what that did to him, to us, to anyone else!"

"Trust me, Tara…"

"I don't trust you, Alexei!"

"Why?" he asked.

"Because you scare me, Alexei."

He reached forwards to pull his sister into a hug. She pushed him away.

"I hate you!" She threw a glass against the wall, just missing Alexei's head. "And you're disgusting. I know what you are."

"Alyosha…" mumbled Raisa, stumbling towards her son.

"Mama, leave him." Tara took hold of her mother and eased her back onto the sofa.

"I love you, little wolf," mumbled Raisa to her son.

"Mama." Tara started to cry at the rejection.

"I did it for the family," begged Alyosha.

"Are you getting upset, Little Wolf?" taunted Tara.

120

"Do you think it was easy to denounce my own father?" implored Alexei. "I was just a boy."

"You did it for yourself, Alexei. You're not part of this family. You gave that up in Egypt."

"At least I was honest about what papa did."

"You've got many faces, Alyosha, and all of them a damn lie."

"You're just jealous," he said.

"There are things you just don't do, no matter what. This is life, Alyosha. Real life. Not a fifty-year-old manifesto." She pointed to their drunk mother, passed out on the sofa. "You did this," she accused. "It's family life. You took away my father. There are rules, higher rules than what your fantasy of Lenin says."

"You're a fine one to talk about morals, Tara."

"You see *this* doctrine Alyosha?" She stepped closer to him and threw her arms out wide. "It's called a fucking family."

"There are more important things, Tara."

"I didn't want a comrade, Alyosha! I wanted a brother. I wanted a father. I wanted a family. And you took that away!"

"I did what was right, Tara."

"You broke me, Alyosha! You took everything." She looked at her mother asleep on the sofa, someone who adored her son and ignored her daughter. "You still take it away Alyosha, without even realising!"

Tara slapped Alexei.

He touched his cheek, feeling the heat rise to the surface.

"You think your political belief will save you Alyosha."

"You're my sister," said Alexei. He thought of Vassily. "My twin."

"To you we're just a biological co-incidence. You always destroy those who love you.""

He slapped her face hard.

She fell against the table on which were the remains of the buffet. Food smeared itself over her new dress, her face and hair.

Tara stood up slowly. She scooped food off her dress. She wiped her hand on the tablecloth.

"Tara," said Alexei. "Please. I'm sorry."

"About what?" Tara asked quietly. "I don't think you know."

Tara quietly closed the door as she left the apartment.

"I know," he said, to himself. "I do know."

Alexei scooped his mother up and carried her to her bedroom.

IT WAS the middle of the night. Alexei was in his childhood bed but couldn't sleep.

Every time his eyes closed with tiredness, one of many horrific memories from Serbsky entered his head. He thought about Vassily, wishing he'd passed the loyalty test in the bath, hoping that he would have then been redeemed, and his treachery with the Americans forgiven. If the Party could forgive Vassily, so too could Alexei.

It was his own conscience, as much as Vassily's unknown fate, that troubled Alexei. He was horrified with himself that he could, so easily, have given up the man he loved to suffer inhuman torture whilst he, the Judas, stood watching on the other side of the glass.

Tara had never forgiven Alexei for informing on their own father when the family had been living abroad in Egypt. He'd never considered forgiveness was needed. His father was the transgressor. His death was a just punishment for the crimes against the Soviet Union. The family had been fortunate that the government covered the scandal up, but Alexei had understood his sister's resentment.

He doubted ever being able to forgive himself for what he'd done to Vassily.

Both men had been traitors. But Alexei now considered himself the villain.

The interrogation from those at the Serbsky Institute, and the defiance of Vassily under torture, had been powerful. Alexei questioned his faith in what had, until yesterday, been the most valuable thing he owned: his commitment to the Party.

In choosing the Party he worshipped and the ideology he defined himself by, over the man he loved and the sexuality he was becoming less ashamed of due to that influence from Vassily, Alexei felt a deep sense of grief. He knew he had now lost something of great value. As yet, he wasn't clear whether that greater loss was the Party or the lover.

He left his mother's apartment and walked through the city.

He found himself outside the Bolshoi Theatre in Sverdlov Square at four o'clock in the morning. The walk down Gorky and Pushkin Streets had been taken in a trance.

He sat down and leant against the monument to Karl Marx. This is where he'd come in his teenage years.

When assigned back to Moscow, after the happy years in the Border Guards, he'd come here in the night again. It was where he'd paid the effeminate young men loitering around the theatre for the use of their bodies.

He hated these young men.

It had been sordid but necessary.

He'd used them for a few minutes to satisfy the sexual desire which otherwise would have overcome him. For only a few roubles, they would let him make use of their bodies. Ashamed of himself but having released what he had considered to be the sexual perversion he was cursed with, he could return to the life he had created for himself dedicated to communism.

He'd treated the late-night visits to the square by the Bolshoi like going to the toilet, a necessary bodily function.

An elderly man standing above Alexei coughed, jolting him from the melancholic reflections.

Some roubles were thrust into Alexei's shirt pocket, and the man took a firm grip of his upper arm. Alexei allowed himself to be stood up, not understanding why he consented.

This was not the reason he'd come there. He wasn't sure why he'd come to this area of the city, perhaps just to remind himself what Vassily had saved him from, but Alexei was no male prostitute.

He reached into his pocket to hand back the money, but the elderly man then grabbed Alexei's crotch. Alexei only had that very second to rebut the molestation, after which he'd have consented to whatever service the elderly man expected for his money.

A second passed.

The elderly man's grip tightened.

Alexei didn't refuse him.

Leaning against one of the trees nearer to the Ivan Vitali fountain, the elderly man pulled down Alexei's trousers and underwear. Alexei estimated the man to be aged sixty. He was wearing expensive clothes. Alexei noticed a wedding ring.

Not a single word had been spoken between them, nor would it be. Alexei had never spoken to the contemptible bodies he'd paid for the use of. He'd hated them for their depravity and for allowing themselves to be used by strangers, as he was now being used.

A Militsya police siren spooked the customer. He stood quickly and hurried off into the protective darkness of the trees. Alexei stayed where he was, not even covering himself up.

A few tears broke from the corner of his eyes and rolled down his cheeks. He wanted to be found by the police. He deserved to be found, and the truth about him exposed.

The sirens faded along Marx Prospekt. The customer didn't return.

Absurdly, at that moment, he remembered that he'd planned to mop the floors of the communal areas in the apartment that morning. It was still his week on duty, and he didn't want to risk a rebuke from Maria, the apartment steward. Ending up in the Comrade's Court for not being a good neighbour, like the accordionist in the apartment before him, seemed like the wrong punishment for what Alexei felt were the serious crimes he'd committed the previous day.

Another man approached out of the darkness, then stopped a few feet away and looked around nervously. This one was young, perhaps only a teenager, as Alexei had once been when first coming to the square at night.

The customer jangled some loose change in his hand, offering a few kopeks at best. Alexei wiped the tears away from his face. The teenager stepped closer with an expression of hatred and contempt. He turned Alexei around aggressively to face the tree and pushed his body forwards against the trunk.

Alexei decided that he would also clean Veera Sergeevna's cooker after mopping the floors. She'd appreciate that kindness, he thought.

Moscow

Thursday 21st September
(three weeks later)

15

THE AEROFLOT Tupolev TU-134 aircraft from Stockholm to Moscow's Sheremetyevo airport was full.

'Wild Bill' Yaxley disembarked with the Canadian hockey fans. He stretched out his back. The aircraft was an improvement on the bone-shaking models he'd endured for many years across east and central Europe. Nevertheless, it was still deserving of its NATO reporting name of *crusty*, thought Bill.

He was alert for any faces he might recognise.

The coded message from a long-dormant Moscow contact in the spurious invoice for furniture not ordered had led to an offer of work too lucrative to ignore. He usually only did one or two jobs a year, and certainly wouldn't usually have considered anything only weeks after the Dutch drug case.

CONDUCTOR had been a good source of work during the fifties. When contact had ceased in sixty-two, he assumed CONDUCTOR, an anonymous source, to be either dead or in prison. Ten years later CONDUCTOR had woken up with a job that Bill could retire on. It intrigued him.

Margaret hadn't asked any questions. She assumed the new job had been commissioned by Sir Hilary for the British. Bill decided not to enlighten her. She preferred his government-sanctioned jobs. He suggested she visit her sister Rose. He would be back in England before Margaret returned from France.

He wanted to retire. He wanted rid of the guilt and melancholy. The long suicide of Bill Yaxley might yet have a happy ending, he thought.

The courtesy bus brought the Stockholm passengers from the plane to the fluted modernist terminal building that looked like a shot glass.

Bill took his time.

He browsed the display cabinets outside the Beriozka souvenir shop. More Canadians were arriving every hour on flights from various locations. He wanted to wait until the airport was so busy that the border checks would be less thorough.

The shop attendant was glad of Bill's foreign currency. While she gift-wrapped the Palekh lacquer cigarette case he'd bought for Margaret, she didn't notice Bill slip the only piece of espionage equipment he'd brought with him in the box of the Soviet camera he'd also just bought.

"Could you gift wrap the camera also please?" asked Bill.

"With pleasure, sir," replied the attendant.

Both items, wrapped by the airport's own attendant, were unlikely to be checked by the customs officers. Bill had used this trick on previous missions to smuggle small items through security checks. It had never failed.

At the post office he collected the hotel reservation confirmation and a ticket for the following day's hockey match. So far, CONDUCTOR was meeting all his promises. The three thousand Canadian hockey fans flooding Moscow for the four games in the series to be played in Russia made Bill's task easier than would be the case otherwise. But he was not complacent.

His shoes were new. The leather soles struggled to get traction on the polished floor of the arrivals lounge. Bill joined the line to get his passport stamped.

The short notice from CONDUCTOR had proved problematic for his false passport. Bill's contacts in Canada had, only a few days before, managed to send him the details of a genuine British-born man of fifty-four years who'd been living in Canada for thirty years. The London forger had finished the passport only on the morning of Bill's flight.

Bill knew that should the KGB in Ottawa check, they would find the details in Bill's passport to be those of a genuine person who was away from his home address for a couple of weeks. His neighbours, if asked, would not be able to say for sure where he had gone. Bill knew the man to be on a cruise that he'd mysteriously won despite not remembering having entered a competition.

On too many occasions Bill had found his work almost compromised by a poorly established legend that was easily disproved by the security service or private investigator of whomever he'd been paid to disrupt. Things had become much more complicated than the old days when a duplicate birth certificate of someone who'd died in infancy was sufficient. He looked forward to not doing any of this again after tomorrow.

His passport was checked, stamped, and handed back.

Bill stepped into the Soviet Union.

The queue at the Intourist desk was long. He was tempted to bypass this and catch a taxi to his hotel. But he wasn't pretending to be a businessman who'd visited the city before. He was supposed to be a tourist, a hockey fan from Canada. This was supposed to be his first visit to Moscow. He would have to register with the Intourist service, just like the other visitors.

Bill knew the Intourist staff were not just there to help foreigners enjoy a care-free holiday. Most, if not all, worked for the KGB. With so many foreigners in the city for the hockey, the KGB would only be able to check those who stood out. He had to blend in. That meant waiting in line.

"Are you booking a city tour?" asked the man behind Bill. Bill knew Moscow almost as well as he did London, but the idea from the Canadian seemed like a good one to help blend in.

"I sure am," replied Bill.

Bill noticed a young man walking down the line of tourists. Bill knew him. The face was a little older, but recognisable from the photos.

This was someone Bill had hoped to see. But it was someone he had not expected to be at the airport.

Bill wanted to study the young man as he moved down the line. He knew he mustn't. He looked away.

"The team had better recover their form," said Bill to keep the tourist in conversation while the Russian walked past.

"I didn't think we should have booed our own team," said the tourist. He leaned closer to Bill and, in a whisper, he added, "We are at war after all. It's like booing our army."

"To Russia with luck," joked Bill.

"It felt more like good riddance than good luck after the Vancouver humiliation."

"Winning three out of the four remaining games will be tough though."

"I don't trust the Russians," said the tourist. "You never know with them; dirty tricks."

"The Soviets know the world's watching," said Bill. "They'll want to put on a good show and make their city seem as good as ours in the West."

"Still, don't drink the water," advised the tourist. "It'll give you the …" He struggled for a polite term to use.

"The Trotskis?" suggested Bill jokingly.

"I like that!"

The Russian continued to walk down the line as Bill and the Canadian tourist moved up by a few spaces.

ALEXEI WALKED slowly down the line of Canadian tourists queuing for the Intourist desk.

He studied the huddles of Canadians who'd arrived from Paris, London, or Stockholm on whatever flight they could find a seat on.

An older middle-aged man returned his stare. It made Alexei look twice. The man was then in conversation with another tourist. Alexei thought no more of it.

Alexei was looking for three specific people: Ren Kaplan, a young agent with the Royal Canadian Mounted Police Security Service. Gisela Bauer, an East German Stasi agent. And the American who'd met Vassily.

These were the people he needed to find.

These were part of ORCHESTRA.

132

These were the reason the chairman of the KGB, on Vladimir's recommendation, had given Alexei authority over unlimited resources and had assigned ORCHESTRA top priority status.

Analysis of every piece of coded communication Alexei could get access to had, eventually, paid off. After weeks of relentless work Alexei had connected the pieces of the jigsaw that others, perhaps except for Vassily, had missed.

At the first hockey match in Moscow the following day a document would be exchanged between the Canadian and East German assuring each other's countries that they were leaving the east and west alliances to join the non-aligned movement of states.

The Kremlin had been briefed. One of its satellite states could not be allowed to leave the Warsaw Pact.

The documents must be intercepted.

Kaplan and Bauer were due to arrive by air that day, but Alexei's research had not given him a time. He'd been planning this airport surveillance operation for days.

Alexei was proud of his discovery.

When his thoughts darkened, and he thought about Vassily he came close to asking Vladimir about Vassily's fate. When he questioned the legitimacy of the Brezhnev government's interpretation of Lenin's doctrine, he shifted his mind back to ORCHESTRA for comfort.

He'd been promised promotion. That elevation would not be based on his mother's connections, nor on the heroic myth of his father that a few senior Soviets had created to cover-up the treachery. He would become an important defender of the Revolution based on merit. A Soviet new man. A hero.

The more serious the work and the higher the stakes, the less guilt he felt about Vassily.

KGB officers had been deployed throughout the airport terminal on his order. They had to find and follow Kaplan and Bauer.

Alexei was looking for the American.

ORCHESTRA had to be stopped at any and all costs.

COOPER BAIN knew which flights Kaplan and Bauer were on.

It was early evening at the airport terminal.

He'd been back in Moscow since the day before, arriving with a tour group of Canadian hockey fans.

He was wandering the bays of the airport car park looking for the number plate the message from CONDUCTOR had told him to find.

The weather was dreary, and so was Bain's mood. He disliked having to meet Oleg in person. It seemed an unnecessary risk.

He found the car and got in the rear seat.

"I'm not happy about this meeting," said Oleg to Cooper, looking out at the car park with concern. Cooper raised a finger to his mouth in a gesture of caution, to which Oleg rolled his eyes. Cooper used a small device that emitted a burst of intense voltage to destroy any bugs that might be present in the car, or on Oleg.

"Neither am I," replied Cooper, satisfied that he could speak freely. "But CONDUCTOR's instructions were quite clear that we should meet."

"Well, let's get things over with quickly, the place is crawling with fucking gebists."

"I thought you were KGB too," commented Cooper. Oleg shrugged. "What's the latest with Vassily?" asked the American.

"He's currently lying in an unquiet grave," advised Oleg. He offered Cooper a cigarette. The American declined; he never accepted anything a KGB officer offered him, just in case.

"Dead?" asked Cooper.

"As good as. There are damp lettuce leaves with more brain function." Oleg cracked a window open for the smoke.

"I'm surprised he held out. Serbsky's a tough call."

"Lucky we had a back-up plan really, isn't it?" chuckled Oleg. "Is he in there?" he asked with disdain.

"I thought he was basically your step-son?" asked Cooper.

"Like hell he is. He's certainly no son of mine. I'm just fucking his slut of a mother."

134

"Seems like a very driven young chap to me. Very faithful to the Party, thankfully so for us. Appears to be the perfect son material to me."

"Let's just say that, for an ex-Border Guard, Alexei Ivanovich has a very light touch on the balalaika." Oleg took a long drag on his cigarette and let the smoke out slowly. "Sodomy is a bourgeois vice. Stalin would have ensured he spent five years breaking rocks in Siberia for it."

"Seems like you've designed an even worse punishment for him," replied Cooper. Oleg didn't comment further. "Anyway, our patsy idealist has commandeered most of the Moscow Oblast KGB resources for this, as we'd hoped he would."

"I left a trail of false evidence, and the little queer followed it."

"The two red herrings are due in the arrivals hall anytime soon," said Cooper. "Yaxley's already passed through and is currently losing himself in Moscow."

"Vladimir has been running around the Lubyanka telling all the seniors his man, Alexei, has uncovered a plot revealing Canada and the DDR's intentions to join the Non-Aligned Movement of states. After Prague, the idea of East Germany leaving is unconscionable. He's been given a blank cheque for the next two weeks while the hockey series is on."

"Thankfully so," replied Cooper. "I'm glad he took the bait."

"I'll do what I can from the Politburo to make sure the KGB are running all over Moscow following the red herrings as soon as their flights land." Oleg coughed on the cigarette. "Leaving our man from London to get on with things undetected?"

"Exactly," confirmed Cooper.

"And Nixon's still on board?" asked Oleg.

"As soon as Brezhnev's dead, he'll make cancelling the arms treaties a core part of the November election campaign. Things should re-freeze between our two governments faster than Lake Ladoga in January."

"Good. You know I can't help if anything goes wrong from this point on," warned Oleg.

"CONDUCTOR's made that quite clear."

"Well, seems like everything's as it should be. Good luck." Oleg offered his hand, which Cooper shook. "I don't suppose we'll meet again, comrade."

"Hopefully not, *comrade*, no offence," replied Cooper. He scanned the car park to make sure there weren't any KGB agents loitering around before getting out of the vehicle.

OLEG'S CAR pulled out of the parking space. Cooper Bain walked off quickly towards the bus stop.

The driver of another vehicle nearby refolded the newspaper he'd been glancing through; it was a copy of the London Independent.

"Up to speed on the cricket?" asked his passenger.

"It's one of the few luxuries I can afford with the eight-hundred roubles a month the Soviets give me," replied the driver. "This and Frank Sinatra records."

The passenger next to him put down the long-lens camera used to photograph the two men meeting in the car they were watching.

"You have what you need?" asked the driver. He pulled the cuffs of his sports-jacket down to cover the self-harm scars that he was so ashamed of on those occasions when he was sober enough to notice them, as he was now.

"A very nice insurance policy if he becomes the next leader as predicted," said the passenger.

"Assuming everything goes to plan tomorrow at the stadium."

"It will," replied the passenger.

"We're idealists, you and I," said the driver of the car.

"And we've both made sacrifices. All the instruments are now playing to a tune we're conducting."

The driver turned the key and pressed his suede desert boot on the pedal, which eased the vehicle forward.

"Things haven't worked this smoothly since sixty-two," commented the driver. "I'm glad you're back in charge."

"No one ever leaves the KGB," replied the passenger with a smile, enjoying having returned to the long-dormant role as CONDUCTOR for one last mission.

136

Friday 22nd September

16

"ALEXEI IVANOVICH, there are over four hundred acres to patrol," pleaded Pavel.

"I've requisitioned as many officers as I can, Pavel Fedorovich," replied Alexei.

"I'm not worried about inside the stadium during the match. It's the lawns, parkland, stalls and pavilions that concern me while we wait for the hockey to begin."

"We know what Kaplan and Bauer look like. We have agents following them. Just keep the net around them close but not too tight," advised Alexei. "No one has to worry about anything other than those two."

"That's what I'm worried about, Alyosha," added Pavel. "The other foreigners are under minimal security. We're not paying attention elsewhere."

"There's no need to. We'll watch the document being exchanged, Pasha, then we'll intercept and arrest them both; You and I." Alexei patted Pavel on the shoulder. "We'll be Soviet heroes."

"If you think so," said Pavel.

"I'm right about this," insisted Alexei. "I'll be at the Yunost for a while."

He left Pavel, who was quickly lost in the crowd.

Alexei zigzagged his way to the ferro-concrete Yunost Hotel where he'd set-up a command centre, and where he'd stayed the night before.

Restlessness kept Alexei alert. He glanced at every face he passed. He was still looking for the American.

Every fragment of evidence he'd pieced together since being in charge of the KGB's ORCHESTRA investigation had led him to Ren Kaplan, Gisela Bauer, and the document exchange at the hockey match due to take place later that chilly evening.

The pieces were fragile, some had been brave enough to say they were too tenuous to justify the enormous scale of the surveillance operation to the exclusion of all other lines of enquiry. But Alexei's betrayal of Vassily was known by all, but unmentioned; that made him credible.

Uncovering the plot eased his guilt about Vassily. But he needed to find the American to truly understand what part his lover had played in ORCHESTRA.

Only once had Alexei doubted himself in the last three weeks. Vladimir had reassured him. If the information had come from a defector, an easy source, then there would have been more scepticism. Such information was generally mistrusted. But Alexei had followed a trail of evidence. The sources were mostly intercepted communications.

Hard work. Core intelligence skills. Determination to solve the puzzle of ORCHESTRA had led to success.

Alexei had reported only to Vladimir during that time, briefing him away from the Lubyanka at the new First Chief Directorate building off the circumferential highway. He shared the names of anyone being critical of the plans for this first hockey match. Vladimir made sure those naysayers were quickly transferred to ignominious duties in inhospitable parts of the Soviet Union.

Isolated. Zealous. Obsessed. Alexei had hardly slept for two weeks.

For both Alexei and Vladimir, their conclusions now had to be true. Everything had been gambled on them being right.

In the control room at the hotel Alexei looked again at the photos of Ren Kaplan and Gisela Bauer. Copies had been given to all security officers on duty at the Luzhniki sports complex. Even the Navy had been commanded to patrol the

Moskva river surrounding the promontory of land to stop the foreign agents escaping by boat.

Alexei read the latest telex messages. These had been coming in every hour for the last twenty-four updating him on everything Kaplan and Bauer did. He also listened in on the surveillance frequencies being used by those officers following the two subjects.

The fear of Kaplan or Bauer being spooked and not going through with the exchange dominated Alexei's thoughts. He switched entire surveillance teams every half an hour to ensure the same agents weren't noticed by the two foreign spies.

He'd ordered female agents who'd recently given birth to push their prams along routes the Canadian and East German were taking. Long-since-retired agents were reactivated to munch toothlessly on a snack in a café opposite the hotels where Kaplan and Bauer were staying.

The greater the cost, and the more unprecedented the resource commitment, then the more credible the operation seemed.

The radio confirmed to Alexei that Kaplan and Bauer had arrived at the complex.

He was too agitated to stay in the control room.

The dark-blond hair and bushy sideburns of Ren Kaplan were as familiar to Alexei now as if the Canadian were his brother or best friend. But the two had never met. In a wide-collared paisley shirt and a blue denim suit, the bottoms of which flared out over a pair of heeled boots, Kaplan was not trying to blend in.

The Canadian spy mingled in the Luzhniki market with a small group of other young Canadians he'd become friendly with at the hotel where he was staying.

Gisela Bauer was only metres away from Ren Kaplan.

Alexei was excited. This could be the exchange.

Bauer hadn't associated with anyone since her arrival.

Alexei held back. The crocheted beanie hat Bauer was wearing made her easy to follow. She was nervously fiddling with a hand-made wooden necklace. She was chewing on her lip. She adjusted the strap on one of her cork sandals and straightened out the pleats of her frayed corduroy skirt.

She looked to be waiting for something or someone.

Alexei was more interested in Kaplan. He moved closer to the Canadian.

He'd personally examined the Canadian's luggage. He knew everything about this young man, even how long he spent in the toilet.

The female's heading to the stadium.

The update over the radio was a disappointment for Alexei. Bauer was walking away from Kaplan.

He approached Kaplan in the market.

Their shoulders brushed against each other.

"I'm sorry," apologised Kaplan.

The two young men smiled at each other. It was the first time Alexei had allowed himself to get close to the target of his obsession. The touch of their arms gave Alexei a renewed zeal to succeed. He now knew the document would be exchanged during the hockey match. The next time he met Kaplan, Alexei thought, would be at the Lubyanka, or maybe Serbsky. He wanted the Canadian to suffer, to know what this plot had forced Vassily into, what Alexei had been made to do. Kaplan would have to pay the debt.

Alexei's heart was beating fast. His limbs quivered with either excitement or nerves. The uncertainty of what would take place inside the stadium felt like a coming storm that might break into a torrent or rain or pass by anticlimactically. Either the document would be exchanged, and he would be a hero, or the foreign spies would reconsider, and Alexei would be a failure.

She's in the stadium

The voice in his earpiece was reassurance. Bauer hadn't noticed the surveillance on her, he thought.

The earpiece had been made specifically for Alexei by the technicians of the Eleventh Department. The silicone used had been dyed to match exactly with his complexion and replicated the contours and shadows of his own ear. On anyone else it would be obvious, but in the ear of the agent it had been made for the device was almost undetectable. The wireless transmitter and receiver were on a sling under his armpit.

Under the other arm was a gun he was prepared to use if necessary.

Kaplan joined the queue for entry to the sports palace.

Alexei backed off to find a side entrance.

"Only those designated are to enter the stadium," Alexei clarified over the radio. "Everyone else remain outside. Cover the escape routes. I don't want the stadium full of agents in case the spies get scared off."

His palms were sweaty, and his heart was still racing. All his sacrifices for the Party would soon be rewarded and justified.

COOPER BAIN walked through the stadium gate with a group of Canadian fans.

He'd received a message from CONDUCTOR that morning confirming everything was to proceed as planned.

The Canadian fans were jubilant, despite their team coming to the Soviet-hosted leg of the series having only won one match and tied another. The Soviets had won two, but the three thousand Canadian fans in Moscow had rallied.

Cooper, as a Texan, had no interest in ice hockey. At the hotel he'd been staying at in West Berlin for the last few weeks recordings of the matches so far had been sent to him so he could convincingly talk about them with the fan group he was now part of.

Team Canada had been humiliated on their home ice. Over-confidence and a lackadaisical approach from players had let them down. Cooper hoped he had not been guilty of the same misstep with ORCHESTRA. The plan was working. Oleg's trail of evidence had been found by Alexei and believed by his superiors.

Cooper had ensured he got an aisle seat in the stadium.

He was pleased to see very few uniformed police and military inside the stadium.

The Canadian fans were more boisterous now, corralled into the small area set aside for them. Cooper joined in with the noise and liveliness. This contest had been reframed as a middle-ranking country taking on the mighty Soviet Union superpower.

Cooper located Kaplan and Bauer, each sitting with opposing supporters.

He took one end of a 'Canada Go' sign and waved it.

Sitting several rows below him, Cooper saw Bill Yaxley.

Cooper was confident history would be made in the stadium that night, but he knew it wouldn't happen on the ice.

AS THE music of the Canadian national anthem played the few thousand Canadian fans sang "O Canada".

"They're loud," said Vladimir, standing next to Alexei in the stadium control room.

"David thinks he can scare Goliath by singing," said Alexei.

"I met your sister here earlier," said Vladimir. "Does she enjoy hockey?"

"We're very different," replied Alexei. He hadn't seen Tara since the fight at his mother's apartment. The shame of hitting her was not something he wanted to be reminded of.

"You're twins though aren't ..."

"Comrade-colonel," interrupted Alexei, "our anthem is about to start."

The sound of nearly fifteen thousand home team supporters singing the Soviet national anthem shook the walls of the stadium.

A ballerina skated onto the ice and presented the Canadian team captain with the traditional goodwill gesture of a loaf of bread. Alexei wiped a patriotic tear from his eye. This match was going to be a great moment for the Soviet Union. When that national anthem was next sung it would be at an honours ceremony for him, thought Alexei. He was defending the Party of Lenin.

"Are you sure about this?" asked Vladimir. "We've hardly got any security personnel inside the stadium."

"I'm sure, comrade colonel," said Alexei without hesitation.

"Good luck then, Alexei Ivanovich," said Vladimir. He shook Alexei's hand. "They're expecting me in the VIP box."

"Enjoy the match," joked Alexei with a wink.

17

NEITHER OF the surveillance targets moved from their seats during the first period of play.

It was a hard-fought first period on the ice. The Canadians tried to get the puck out of their end, while the Soviet long forward pass wasn't paying off.

Both Vladislav Tretiak and Tony Esposito guarding the respective team goals proved that the post can be the goalie's best friend. Parise for Canada buried the puck between Tretiak's legs to give the Canadians the first goal and break the tension.

"Watch the targets," advised Alexei over the radio, reminding those agents who'd been allocated positions inside the arena to focus on ensuring neither Kaplan nor Bauer made a move without being watched. "Don't get distracted by the match," he added.

Most agents were being kept outside to ensure neither foreign agent could escape after the document handover, and to make sure that neither agent was spooked by seeing too many KGB inside the stadium.

Alexei didn't watch any of the hockey. He stared at the monitors in the control room that showed the crowd.

By the end of the second period, Clarke and Henderson for Canada had made the score 3-0 to the western visitors.

On the monitors Alexei could see it was getting more difficult for the smaller-than-usual cohort of KGB agents in the stadium not to become so caught up by the match and the damage being done to their national pride.

"Tretiak's consistently too far back in the goal," said one of the agents in the control room with Alexei.

"What?" asked Alexei.

"Our team doesn't look as invincible as they did in Canada. Team Canada has brought the game to the Soviets," added the agent.

"I don't care," replied Alexei. He was becoming nervous.

During the breaks in play Ren Kaplan and Gisela Bauer both left their seats, causing Alexei's surveillance operation to mobilise. Neither foreigner came anywhere near the other.

"I need sections one to three to leave the stadium," ordered Alexei over the radio.

"Comrade, that's madness," said the agent in the control room with Alexei.

"They know we're watching their every move," said Alexei. "Let them think we're distracted."

On the ice the pace picked up in the third period.

Alexei now doubted his own judgment, questioning his conclusions and decisions from the last two weeks. He was too agitated to remain in the control room listening to his agents' hushed reports and watching the surveillance footage.

A Soviet goal in the fourth minute by Blinov, following a pass from Petrov, was followed by a Canadian goal one minute later; these goals foreshadowed an unexpected resurgence by the Soviets.

Alexei wanted play to slow down. He needed Kaplan and Bauer to show some sign they intended to meet and exchange the document.

Ten minutes of play remained.

Time was running out for Alexei.

The home nation scored three goals in quick time, levelling up the score. The Soviet pressure on the ice forced the Canadians into a defensive position, allowing the trouble to come to their end of the ice.

Alexei felt a similar pressure in his own match being played out off the ice. Neither Kaplan nor Bauer had shown any signs of trying to contact, or even search, for each other.

Vladimir Vikulov, one of the classiest Soviet forwards, edged the home team into the lead with a goal. It was fourteen minutes into the final period of play.

Alexei was now sure the document exchange would take place after the match.

"All agents leave the arena," he ordered over the radio. "The exchange will be after the match. Cover every exit route from the stands through the stadium and the streets to the metro station."

He heard hurried footsteps behind him.

"Comrade, we can't clear the stadium," said one of the senior KGB agents. "Not until Brezhnev has left."

Alexei couldn't falter in his commitment now.

"Clear the arena," he said over the radio, confirming the order.

"You don't have the authority!" implored the other agent.

"Tonight, I do," replied Alexei.

"We'll see." The other agent hurried off.

The crowd were cheering. Around the arena Alexei saw KGB agents begin to leave their positions and redeploy.

He couldn't let Kaplan and Bauer escape after the exchange.

Alexei checked his gun. He re-holstered it under his arm and made his way to the VIP box to update Vladimir.

'WILD BILL' didn't return to his seat for the third period of play. Layouts of the arena sent to him by CONDUCTOR indicated what would be the best position for his task.

The lack of KGB agents at any of the access doors surprised him, pleasantly so.

Bill tuned his radio into the KGB frequency the message from CONDUCTOR had advised him to use. He heard the order for all final resources inside the arena to leave their positions.

From his hiding place, Bill watched as the KGB officers in the VIP box began to leave.

Bill didn't like this. He was unsettled by the lack of anticipated security measures. He'd expected heavy monitoring whilst in Moscow over the last twenty-four hours, but he hadn't even been followed. His description should have been circulated when he didn't return to his seat for the final period, but it hadn't been.

It should have been more difficult, perhaps even resulting in him having to kill agents, to get to the hiding place inside the stadium. And there should have been more eyes scanning the arena from the VIP area, looking for threats.

It was all too easy, and the gentle voice on the radio seemed to be in control, inexplicably making everything much simpler for Bill than it should have been.

The range indicator on his weapon confirmed that the target was within two-hundred and fifty feet.

He fixed the shoulder stock to the modified Colt .45 and slotted the telescopic sight in place. That single ocular device became his eyes.

He loaded a toxin-tipped dart into the modified weapon. It was a single-shot weapon, but one shot was all Bill needed. Bill brought Brezhnev into sight. He knew the shot would be silent, and the hair-sized dart would be undetectable at the autopsy. For a man such as Brezhnev, who had been declared clinically dead but resuscitated by his doctors more than once already, no one was likely to consider foul play, especially as Bill's presence had been so unnoticed.

The Soviet hockey team edged in the lead with their fifth goal, to Canada's four. The Soviet's had made a comeback, with two goals seconds apart.

The gentle voice on the radio directed his officers to leave the inside of the arena. The voice reminded all KGB agents to not let either suspect out of their sights once they left the stands, whilst not spooking them either; the voice directed that the document exchange had to now take place after the match.

Listening to the KGB commentary, Bill realised why his own path had been so easy.

He scanned the faces of the VIPs in the box out of curiosity. His movement stopped when he saw the face of the young man standing at the stairwell entrance trying to attract someone's attention. It was the same face he'd recognised when in the queue at the airport. It was a face he knew well from photos.

Watching the young man through the telescopic sight, Bill was distracted, emotionally so. When he saw the young man's mouth moving, corresponding to the instructions being relayed over the radio he was listening to, Bill's mouth went dry and beads of sweat appeared on his forehead.

Alexei was the fall-guy for Bill's assassination, for the whole ORCHESTRA plot.

The game had three seconds left.

A final face off.

The puck rolled back to Tony Esposito.

The game was over.

The Soviets had another win.

Brezhnev stood and clapped.

Bill moved the aim of his weapon back to the Soviet leader, but he was fractionally too slow in his movement.

At that moment, one of the few remaining KGB agents, a young soldier who'd heard the order to redeploy, but decided to ignore it until the match was over, looked up from his position. He saw the barrel of a gun.

The warning was raised just as the shot made a pffft noise that was unheard even by those spectators immediately below it.

The follicle-sized dart had been the only piece of equipment Bill had brought with him, having been made in Stockholm. Everything else for the weapon had been sourced from old contacts in Moscow.

There was only one dart.

The radio channel was interrupted by the word 'gun' repeated over and over again.

Bill saw Alexei pushed out of the way as Brezhnev and the other dignitaries were almost lifted off the ground by the remaining close protection officers and hurried down the stairs and through the corridors of the arena by the KGB who'd heard the warning.

The dart, being aimed at the Soviet leader's neck, had brushed past the lapel of Brezhnev's jacket just before he was out of view. It had landed on the concrete floor.

Bill had failed, for the first time in his career.

THE CLARITY of the situation dawned on Alexei and Vladimir at the same time. The officer in the control room took command and ordered all KGB personnel back into the stadium from their redeployed positions outside the sports venue.

Alexei edged slowly down the stairwell into the corridor behind the seats in disbelief.

Vladimir, his gun in his hand, caught up with the man he now thought who had deceived him into ordering a surveillance operation on a document drop, when the actual plan was an assassination.

From the capture of Vassily, the apparent credibility of Alexei, the discovery of ORCHESTRA plot details that no one else had been able to find, and the redeployment of KGB officers both before and during the match Alexei had cleared a path for the assassin, and Vladimir had authorised it all on trust.

Alexei knew he would seem to have been the traitor from the very beginning.

He was in too much disbelief to run.

Vladimir thrust the barrel of his gun into Alexei's ribs. Alexei didn't resist or attempt to grab for his own weapon in self-defence.

Alexei wondered if he'd even reach Serbsky, or whether Vladimir would ensure the dead body of a traitor would be cremated without ceremony before any interrogation could implicate the KGB officer who had authorised all of Alexei's requests.

The gun barrel pressed harder into his body indicating he should start walking, which he did.

BILL KNEW that fire extinguishers can save your life in a fire. That they had other life-saving characteristics was a revelation.

The canister came crashing down on the back of Vladimir's head as soon as the KGB colonel had pushed Alexei into a quieter corridor not being used by the fans exiting the stadium.

Bill, an expert at combat with everyday items, then proved that the pen is indeed mightier than the sword as he rammed the biro from Vladimir's tunic pocket into the KGB colonel's left eye, disorientating him long enough to enable Bill to loop his leather belt round Vladimir's thick neck.

He pulled the strap through the buckle until the metal locked tightly. Bill attached the strap to a cabinet door handle and swiped Vladimir's legs from under him. The weight of Vladimir's body falling to the floor further tightened the belt around his neck to the extent that, even if he could remain conscious long enough to get his feet back underneath him, he'd be unable to loosen the make-shift noose.

The whole manoeuvre had taken barely five seconds to execute and was conducted with the fluidity and ease of someone well used to such activity, despite his fifty-four years.

"Let's get outta here a bit fuckin' sharpish, like," said Bill to Alexei, whose book-learned English didn't immediately understand what was being said to him. But, as with Vladimir, he put up no resistance as the two men joined the crowd in the main corridor.

Alexei's mind had gone into shock.

Bill hurried Alexei along with the hundreds of others flooding out of the stadium. They crossed the street, heading towards the metro station. Bill tugged on Alexei's arm and led him off to the left; he knew the KGB would already have the entire area and transport hubs locked down to trap them inside the cordon.

Bill led Alexei through the gatehouse of what used to be the Novodevichy Monastery. Once inside the irregular rectangle of blood-red high walls and white religious buildings, Bill paused.

"Breathe son," he ordered. Alexei took a deep breath.

Bill took a few seconds to get his bearings then guided Alexei down one of the paths through the complex of sixteenth and seventeenth century buildings.

"Who are you?" asked Alexei. "Why are we here?"

Bill didn't answer.

A plain-looking woman opened the door they'd approached. She was dressed in a long black cassock with a leather belt round her small waist.

"Stay here," said Bill. He went inside the building with the woman. The heavy wooden door closed behind them, leaving Alexei on his own waiting outside.

He started to walk back the way he'd come, not being comfortable in the company of the Englishman who had just killed Vladimir.

Alexei needed time to think and plan his next move.

He took a few steps further along the path, and he realised he had nowhere to go. The KGB would be swarming the streets outside the former convent and would arrest him within minutes. Once arrested, he'd be given no opportunity to explain the mistake and prove his innocence.

The door's hinges creaked as it opened, and Bill walked past Alexei, giving him a friendly tap on the arm as he went. It was clear that Alexei was not being invited to go with the Englishman, which suited him.

"You're to wait here, with us, at least for now," said the woman by the door. She had a gentle voice.

"Us?" asked Alexei.

"Come inside," she replied, pointing inside the dark room.

"Are you a nun?" asked Alexei, stepping through the doorway into a room that seemed even colder than it had been outside.

"We both are," replied the woman. "Abbess Barbara is sleeping."

Alexei looked across at the elderly woman in the only bed that was in the room.

"I'm Sister Juliana." Once the door was closed and bolted, she tied a ribbon around her body on which was attached a wooden cross with the three distinctive horizontal cross beams of the orthodox faith. Sister Juliana went over to the abbess.

"She was tonsured in nineteen-eighteen, on the day news was received that Sister Barbara, a friend of hers, had been killed by the Bolsheviks. In fact, she was clubbed, thrown down a mineshaft, and left to starve whilst singing hymns. The abbess took her name as her own in tribute."

152

"I didn't think this place was a monastery anymore," said Alexei.

"And you're right, it isn't. Officially, this is a theological institute. But the Abbess is not well and, after many months spent entreating the government, she has been allowed to return here, to the monastery where she took her vows, to…" her voice trailed off.

"To die?" suggested Alexei.

"To prepare herself to meet Him." Sister Juliana's soft voice corrected Alexei, as a favourite teacher might gently nudge a young pupil towards the right answer.

She walked through another door to the only other room in the apartment.

"I should tell you that I'm a communist," declared Alexei.

"And as such, your beliefs cannot co-exist with ours? Are you going to throw me down a mineshaft?" Sister Juliana placed some bread and a glass of water on the table, indicating for Alexei to sit down and refresh himself. "I'm named after Saint Juliana of Lazarevo, a sixteenth century woman from Moscow who devoted her life to helping the needy and the poor." She pushed the bread and water further towards her visitor. "Twenty-five years ago, I was tonsured into the sisterhood by the abbess, taking a vow of chastity, hard work, obedience, and charity…even towards communists." She smiled at the young man. "Saint Juliana didn't ask people's political beliefs before offering them help, and neither shall I."

"That man, the one who brought me here, he told you I need help?"

"Don't you, young man?" Her manner was calm and comforting.

"You're putting yourselves in danger, having me here." Alexei stood up. "I should go."

"Where to?" asked the nun, not getting up from her chair to try and stop him.

Alexei didn't reply, but neither did he carry on towards the door.

"We may be superstitious and backward, in your eyes," added the nun, "but neither your atheism, nor the danger of

153

whoever you're hiding from scares me. So, rest, for a while at least." She went back into the main room.

After a few seconds, Alexei sat back down to eat and drink what had been offered to him.

Once finished, he washed up the other plates and glasses that were by the cracked sink in the corner of the room.

"Oh, excuse me," he apologised in a whisper, stepping into the main room and disturbing Sister Juliana in prayer as she prostrated herself on the floor next to the sleeping abbess.

"That's all right," replied Sister Juliana standing up, "you won't disturb her. Sit for a while with us."

Alexei and Sister Juliana sat on small wooden stools next to the bed. Were it not for the occasional rising and falling of her chest, the ancient abbess had the sunken cheeks and pallid skin of someone already dead.

"I'm sorry for disturbing your prayer."

"It's hard not to, we do a lot of it," joked the friendly nun. "Even whilst everyone else is sleeping, we are praying for them."

"Do you mean that literally or metaphorically?" asked Alexei.

"I suppose it fits both," she replied with a knowing smile. "Would you stay with Mother Barbara for a few minutes?" She glanced at the clock on the wall. "I prefer not to leave her alone." Alexei nodded his agreement.

Sister Juliana closed the heavy door behind her as she went outside into the walled compound.

The room was cold and silent, the thick ancient walls not even letting the noise of the city penetrate the room.

Alexei reflected on what had happened at the stadium, shuddering with more than just the chill of the room as he realised the sequence of events over the last few weeks that had led him to be unknowingly complicit in an assassination attempt of the Soviet leader.

He cursed his stupidity, recognising now all the intelligence clues for their deliberately misleading misdirection. He tried to find somewhere in his memory a document, person, or substantive fact that could be used to prove he had been duped, but everything indicating the Canadian and East

German plot would seem, to someone not blinded by the need for success, as obvious misdirection.

At best he would be found guilty of complete neglect and stupidity, at worst he would be seen as complicit in the actual plot.

The abbess took an unexpected deep breath. A dry, bony hand clasped his. She coughed and tried to raise herself up but struggled to do so. Alexei leaned over and helped her shoulders onto the second pillow, which eased her coughing.

She moved into consciousness and watched him adjusting the bedding.

"Sister Juliana?" she asked in a meek voice.

"I'll get her," he said, but the bony hand held his with unexpected strength, preventing him from leaving her bedside.

"No, stay," she urged. Alexei obeyed, and sat down on the stool closest to the bed. The frail woman blinked into wakefulness, and smiled at Alexei, studying his face as if she were reading on it answers to the questions her muddled mind was asking.

"I don't think she's gone far," said Alexei, feeling uncomfortable.

"She works very hard for me," replied the abbess, but still not releasing Alexei's warm hand. "She could have been elevated to the Schema by now, but she has chosen to remain a novice out of humility."

The comment prompted Alexei to think of his own refusal to progress his career through the higher echelons his mother had tried to facilitate for him. It wasn't just his career that was now in jeopardy after the fiasco at the sports palace.

The abbess clasped his hand in both of hers as she drew him nearer to her.

"Join me in praying for forgiveness," she said, immediately starting a recital which Alexei couldn't accompany her in, even if he'd wanted to. He'd never been inside an orthodox church, let alone heard a prayer.

"God, my good and loving Lord, I acknowledge all the sins which I have committed…" she said.

His hand was released as the abbess faded back into unconsciousness.

Sister Juliana came back into the room.

"Is she...?" asked Alexei. He couldn't complete the sentence but didn't need to.

"She's just sleeping." The nun tucked the old abbess' bony hands under the warm blanket. "I've had a message. You're to join William."

"Who?" asked Alexei.

"The Englishman who brought you here. He said the metro is now safe, and that you're to join him in Lenin Hills. Do you know the observation point?"

18

"IT WAS a set-up," said Bill. He offered Alexei a hip flask of brandy. Alexei was looking across the river to Moscow and hadn't noticed Bill approach.

Alexei didn't react.

Bill shook the canister.

"You need a drink, trust me, sonny-boy." Alexei still didn't respond. "Anton Chekhov said: 'anyone who wants to understand Russia should come here and look at Moscow'; I'm inclined to agree with him," said Bill, taking a sip from the flask.

"Who are you?" asked Alexei in uncertain English.

"I speak pretty decent Russian," replied Bill in Alexei's own language. The colloquial East-end phraseology and estuary accent was forced into a more disciplined form of speech by the Russian language and pronunciation, both of which Bill was surprisingly good at.

"Then, in Russian, I ask again, who are you?" Alexei looked across at the Olympic ski jump, and away from Bill. He leant on the balustrade of polished granite.

A couple of hundred feet below Alexei the city stretched out boundlessly. The foreground was dominated by the sports complex where his life had changed only an hour or so beforehand. The panorama was a colour palette of pre-revolutionary brick-red, Stalinist-era dark-grey, and the yellow of more recent building works. Alexei had never noticed how distinguishable each period was from the other simply by colours.

"I wouldn't expect you to remember me, Alyosha. You were a child last time I spoke to you," said Bill. "I think we were chatting about a Plastic Man comic book when Tara interrupted us because she wanted me to take her swimming." Alexei didn't turn around. "What was the real name of Plastic Man, I've forgotten?" asked Bill.

Alexei looked quizzically, suspiciously, at the Englishman who had such an accomplished command of the Russian language. Alexei didn't reply.

"I knew your father," clarified Bill.

Alexei considered this new information but, far from easing his worry, being rescued by an English spy made him feel trapped once again, particularly when the spy knew so much about him. Their meeting felt by design rather than accident. He was tired of feeling imprisoned by circumstances, whether that be his elite family, his sexuality, the ORCHESTRA plot, and now potential abduction by the enemy. Both personal and imposed demons kept him stuck in situations not of his own making.

He considered escaping, violently resisting if necessary. He'd seen how easily the wrinkle-faced man had decommissioned the bear-like Vladimir, but the Comrade-Colonel had been surprised, Alexei would remain vigilant for an opportunity to get away if things became more uncomfortable.

"You're thinking of escape," said Bill. He stood to one side. "We're still in central Moscow, the metro's a short walk away, feel free to leave."

Bill turned his back. He heard Alexei start to walk away, slowly, as if expecting to be stopped.

"Do you have a plan, by the way?" asked Bill, not turning around. Alexei stopped walking but didn't reply. "Thought not," said Bill. "Why not stick with me until you think of one, unless suicide is the intention, because I can guarantee several thousand KGB officers are now turning over every rock to find you." Bill turned to face Alexei. "I dare say that's the nature of the commentary you can hear on that clever ear-piece of yours." Alexei didn't make the rookie mistake of touching the device to confirm it was there, but he didn't need to; the Soviets had stolen the technology from the CIA, so Bill knew what to look for.

"Perhaps I will catch my breath," said Alexei, walking back a few steps towards the balustrade. Trust was slowly being built. Everything Bill had said was right, the radio frequency had been disabled quickly after his arrival at the convent, but before that he'd heard the instruction for every available officer to search for him, although he hadn't yet been named as a traitor. The radio channel was now silent. He clenched his arm against his sides to check the gun was still in place, but it had gone.

"You have a stronger moral compass than the people you work for," said Bill.

"And who do you work for?" asked Alexei, after a pause. "Another deluded British spy thinking your country still matters?"

"Thanks for the politics lesson. We're all socialists, comrade, but unfortunately it can't ever work in practise, surely the last fifty years of your country's history has shown you that?"

"Is this why you took me? It's a long way to come from London to debate the doctrines of Marx and Engels with a kid you apparently knew fifteen years ago in Egypt."

"Indeed it is. And I think *saved* rather than *took* is more accurate." Bill used his hands to smooth down the wispy white hair that had become disorganised by the early evening breeze.

"You said I was set-up," commented Alexei after a period of silence.

"As you have been," confirmed Bill. "I know, because you were set up to help me."

"Help you? How?" asked Alexei.

"How's your mother?" enquired Bill; it was a habit to answer a question with another.

"You must know that I'm not going to answer any questions," replied Alexei.

"Quite so, I'm not expecting trust, even though you'd be dead by now were it not for me, but I'll indulge you, after all I know who you are, but you don't remember me."

"I'm not going to tell you anything, particularly if you really were a friend of my father's," said Alexei adamantly.

"I'm well aware that you're not a traitor, Alyosha." Bill leant backwards and took out a cigarette, offering one to Alexei. "That's why they chose you." The mention of treachery made Alexei wonder whether the Englishman knew the truth about his father and the events in Egypt, perhaps he was even part of it.

As they smoked, Bill told Alexei everything he knew about ORCHESTRA, about CONDUCTOR, the commission Bill had received to assassinate Brezhnev, and what he'd realised seconds before taking the shot. The confession was a declaration of trust, one Bill hoped would be reciprocated by the young man he'd last spoken to on a sun terrace in the suburbs of Cairo fifteen years before.

"So you see, ORCHESTRA needed you to believe the two spectators were actually spies about to exchange a document. Everything you've done over the last two weeks has made my path more likely to succeed."

"Then all I have to do is hand you over." There was no menace in Alexei's voice; his comment sounded more like a suggestion than an intention.

"Naivety is only a virtue in little girls," replied Bill. "If you know anything about the organisation you work for then you'll realise that if I hadn't saved you, they'd have thrown you in the Lubyanka. You'd take the blame for an almighty screw-up, one of the biggest. Now that I have saved you, you'll be branded a traitor. Truth is a concept, not a reality."

"And you have a plan?" asked Alexei.

"Not yet, but I have somewhere to hide, which is more than you have." Bill indicated they should start walking. "There's a quick stop I need to make first".

Bill walked off. After a second of hesitation Alexei followed him.

"Patrick O'Brian," said Alexei incongruously. He didn't trust Bill, but he had no other option than to follow the Englishman.

"I'm sorry?" asked Bill.

"Plastic Man's real name was Patrick O'Brian."

"So it was," replied Bill with a smile. They walked off towards the university.

19

IT WAS a long walk, but Bill had advised against the bus.

Alexei was struggling against the fatigue of the last few days, having barely slept since the Canadian and East German had arrived in Moscow.

They approached the new building for the Moscow Circus. Bill resisted the urge to keep checking behind to see if they were being followed. Despite the decades of spy work, looking back for any shadows when about to meet a contact was an impulse still difficult to resist. People going about their daily business never check behind themselves; one might just as well be wearing a sign confirming they were a spy.

There were enough bureaucrats milling around the circus to make Alexei nervous.

"They're not looking for you," said Bill. "They're here to ensure none of the performances hint at mockery of the Soviet Union."

Bill led Alexei past the tumbling acrobats and cages with exotic animals pacing up and down, the smell of which seemed incongruous for the city centre of Moscow. Bill asked one of the bureaucrats for directions, even though he knew where to find the man he'd come to see. Foreign spies rarely engage voluntarily with any locals, especially not government officials; this was yet another of Bill's tricks learnt over many years of espionage work. He was an advocate of hiding in plain sight.

"That's who we're here to see," said Bill, pointing to a poster with a picture of a bald clown on it. His whole head was painted white, with the addition of a ludicrously small orange hat kept in place at a jaunty angle by a piece of elastic under his fat chin.

"Boris Pankov?" asked Alexei.

"He was recruited by the American magician and CIA agent John Mulholland in fifty-four when he was a student with the Moscow State College of Circus and Variety Arts. Pankov supplemented his studies of magic tricks and juggling with those of Mulholland's CIA manual," said Bill.

"Seems a strange choice for a spy," said Alexei.

"It's a perfect choice," said Bill. "On tour with the Circus across Europe and China throughout the fifties and sixties, Pankov was famous, even named People's Artist of the USSR."

"As a clown," said Alexei.

"Clownery was a perfect cover for the passing of messages between East and West. His character played the fool for the audiences who loved him, whilst Pankov continued to fool the Soviet government that honoured him." Bill stopped and smiled at another of the posters. "The red nose, polka-dot bowtie, and over-sized floppy shoes have protected Pankov from suspicion for nearly twenty-five years. The obvious deception of his clownery and magic tricks perfectly disguised the subtle acts of betrayal against his government." Bill walked on. "Against your government," he added.

"It's a risk telling me this," said Alexei. "I'm KGB."

"Not anymore," suggested Bill. "And I need you to trust me."

"Hello, comrade, I have the tickets you asked for," said Pankov as Bill and Alexei entered the dressing room. Pankov shared the room with two other clowns, both of whom had finished applying their make-up, and were getting dressed into comedic trousers and blouse-like shirts for the evening performance. Pankov was only wearing his underwear, his make-up half applied.

"Thank you, Boris Gavrilovich," said Bill. "My young comrade here is very much looking forward to seeing this evening's performance."

"Don't be late, Pankov," snapped one of the younger clowns, having finished getting dressed. Bill disliked the lack of respect, but his friend didn't seem to care, and just waved an acknowledgement as the other two clowns picked up their remaining props and hurried out of the small dressing room.

Middle-aged and overweight, Pankov's hand noticeably shook as he tried to finish applying his make-up.

Bill waited for the other two clowns to walk out of earshot.

Pankov fought against a persistent cough as he tried to apply the large red dot to the end of his nose. He looked cautiously in the mirror at Alexei.

"He's one of us," reassured Bill. "You don't seem well, Boris," he added. Bill took the brush out of his friend's hand and helped to apply the thick paste to his face.

"It's the chemicals in the face paint the government gives us." Pankov pushed Bill's hand away to cough again. "All this time when I thought I was fighting against *them*, *they've* been killing me without even realising it." He smiled, which made the sad mouth he'd already painted on his own thin lips seem sinister. He took a long drag on a cigarette and then stubbed it out with difficulty. He leant against the mirrored table to steady himself.

"Here, let me help," said Alexei, coming to the clown's aid and helping the old man get dressed into his costume.

"Have you asked your contacts for help?" asked Bill.

"You're the first to ask for anything in nearly two years," replied Pankov dejectedly. "My communications remain unanswered and have done ever since Mulholland died to join his friend Houdini up there." Pankov made the sign of the cross on himself and looked to the ceiling.

"I'll see what I can do," promised Bill, making sure the pom-poms on the front of Pankov's shirt were all aligned.

"The hand is no longer quicker than the eye," said the clown, clumsily snapping a fifty-kopek coin from behind Alexei's ear. "And so old Pankov's no longer useful. He now risks being seen for what he truly is in the wilderness of mirrors." He tossed the coin in the air towards Alexei, who caught it and went to hand it back. "Keep it," said Pankov. "I need to finish."

Bill and Alexei took the dismissal.

"Have a good performance, my friend," said Bill.

The clown put the little orange hat on his bald head and exaggeratedly snapped the elastic under his chin. As he left, Bill saw in another mirror that Pankov was pouring himself a large glass of vodka.

"I remember seeing Pankov the clown when I was a teenager," said Alexei. He and Bill made their way back to the street.

"He's delivered pills and potions laced with shellfish poison or crocodile bile to more Soviet officials than any espionage agent I've known. He's a magician, not a clown, and a first-class spy," replied Bill. "And if you ever betray him, I'll make damn sure a dose of botulinum finds its way into your tea."

Bill pocketed the letter that had been hidden in-between the two circus tickets.

"Let's split-up," suggested Bill. "We need to make sure neither of us has been spotted." Bill checked the street signs. "Slowly walk a circuitous route along Lomonosov Prospekt," he instructed. "I'll take the trolleybus towards the city, get off after only a few minutes, and walk to meet you."

"I might run off," suggested Alexei.

"You're not my prisoner," replied Bill. "Meet me at the dormitory closest to the botanical gardens. It's being renovated so there's no one living there for the next few weeks."

Minutes later, Bill found Alexei waiting outside the dormitory. He hadn't expected Alexei to follow the instructions but was pleased the young man seemed to be willing to trust him.

"Is this safe?" asked Alexei as they went inside.

"The university has nearly forty-five thousand rooms. Even if the KGB officers look for you here, and even if they only spent one minute in each room, it would still take them thirty-one days to complete the search."

Bill had been living in one room on an upper floor of the half-renovated student accommodation block.

"I don't remember you," said Alexei.

"That's not a surprise to me," replied Bill. He lit a paraffin camping stove to make some tea. "But that doesn't mean I'm lying, does it?"

"To take my sister swimming, my mother would have to have trusted you, which means I'd remember you."

"Raisa does trust me," said Bill.

"Does?" asked Alexei.

"Your scepticism does you credit; it might yet save you," replied Bill. The water was taking a long time to boil. "I was trusted by your parents. Ivan and I had been allies during the war. When I heard what happened, I came to visit Raisa. The comic book earned me your trust pretty quickly, but Tara became jealous."

"How do you mean *what happened*?" asked Alexei for clarification; he was giving nothing away voluntarily.

"To your father." Bill poured the tea, having to use a cup for Alexei and a bowl for himself as these were the only two receptacles he'd sourced for his brief stay in Moscow. Alexei was already sitting on the only chair in the room, so Bill turned a bucket over and perched on that; it didn't help his knees.

"Ivan was an unfortunate casualty of the Syria crisis," said Bill. "The Soviets shouldn't have got so close politically to Damascus, and he'd have known that himself. Ivan was a good man."

"Did you kill him?" asked Alexei.

"You know I didn't," replied Bill.

"It seems unlikely that my mother would invite a British spy to visit her weeks after widowhood though."

"You don't give up, do you?" joked Bill. "I admire your mistrust, I really do." Bill drank some tea. "But you're the one who said I was a British spy, not me. Am I a spy? Sort of I suppose. Am I British? Guilty. But am I a British spy? No. I work only for myself, and I'm very good at what I do."

"You missed the shot today." Alexei took a gulp of tea. "Deliberately?"

"I don't think so," replied Bill. "But I've never missed before." He studied the young man opposite him. Alexei had grown into someone Bill's old friend from the war would have been proud of. The boy Bill had known didn't deserve the burden of denouncing his father as a traitor, and the young man before him now didn't deserve to take the fall for ORCHESTRA. But getting out of central Moscow with no foreign government assistance was about the most difficult extraction to perform.

"What did the clown give you?" asked Alexei.

"Let's find out," replied Bill.

Bill dragged the chair that he made Alexei vacate under the ceiling light. He slowly rubbed the letter hidden between the tickets back and forth across the bulb, the heat from which would act as a reagent to reveal a second line of text interspersed with the original writing.

"What does it say?" asked Alexei.

"See for yourself," replied Bill, getting down from the chair. Alexei looked at the piece of paper, being a schedule for the circus performances.

"Shouldn't there be something else written on here?" asked Alexei, concerned that they had both been betrayed by the clown, as the leaflet had no new text aside from the schedule.

"There should be," replied Bill, wondering also if his friend had betrayed them, his ears listening for sounds of anyone entering the building. He walked to the window and peered down into the street to check for any unusual activity. Nothing seemed out of place. He went out to the corridor and returned a few seconds later after discovering no footsteps on the staircase.

"Crafty bugger," muttered Bill to himself in English after a thought occurred to him. "He didn't trust you," said Bill to Alexei, returning to Russian.

"So what now?" asked the younger man.

"But Pankov would have trusted me, and I trust you," said Bill. A thought occurred to him. "Give me the coin Pankov tossed to you." Alexei fished the fifty-kopek coin out of the pocket of his suit and gave it to Bill, which the older man studied carefully. Pressing on the edge, the coin flipped open to reveal a small piece of paper inside.

Bill read the message quickly, then leant over Alexei and touched the paper to the stove's flame. The flash-paper ignited instantly, and Bill threw it on the floor, stamping it into ashes and dust.

"Well?" asked Alexei. "If it's from CONDUCTOR, then I need to find him," said Alexei. "It's my only chance." Not sharing the contents of the note was a gesture that made Alexei question the trustworthiness of his rescuer.

"That's not such a sure thing," warned Bill, sitting down on the chair.

"What do you mean? If I find CONDUCTOR, then the KGB might believe I wasn't responsible for Luzhniki."

"But you don't know who he is. What makes you think they'll believe you over him?"

"Who is he then?" asked Alexei. Bill didn't reply. Alexei's face showed the disappointment in Bill's lack of cooperation. "You risked yourself to save me; is that just because of my father?"

"Are you sure that CONDUCTOR is your enemy here?" asked Bill, ignoring Alexei's last question.

"Of course," replied Alexei with certainty. Bill didn't add his own comment to the young man's reply. He kicked the upturned bucket towards Alexei, who was now sitting cross-legged on the dusty floor by the camping stove. "A friend was duped into cooperating with this damn conspiracy, and I stepped forward as the replacement fool to take the blame for him, for you. I'd say that makes whoever's in control my enemy." There was a hint in Alexei's tone and choice of words that suggested he suspected Bill of being CONDUCTOR.

"It's clear that CONDUCTOR has put you in harm's way, but you seem to think exposing him to the KGB, or the Party, or whatever state apparatus you think will listen, might somehow help you. What I mean is that CONDUCTOR, and what he represents, might just be what you also believe." Bill poured himself a second cup of tea.

"Who is CONDUCTOR?" asked Alexei, for a second time, showing he was not giving up. Bill sipped his tea without answering immediately.

"He's trying to preserve something, I think. He's a believer, like you."

"Believer? In what?" asked Alexei.

"In communism, I suppose."

"But you're the person he asked to kill Brezhnev. That can hardly be for the furtherance of communism?"

"Strangely, I think it was. Not to me, but to him it was a solution to a problem." Bill sipped some more tea and took time to finish his answer. "CONDUCTOR wants the Soviet Union to be a superpower, to oppose the West, not become its friend. Brezhnev is détente, and détente is peace. But communism needs war."

"Communism is about international peace," said Alexei. "Only the West brings war.

"In London, I can stand in the street and say pretty much anything I like. At best, a few people will pause and listen with bored expressions on their faces. The odd one might criticise my comments, but even the police officers will stroll casually by, even if I call the Prime Minister an incompetent flabby fool. In every communist country I've visited, in fact every socialist one even, political oppression is systemic."

"Then why help CONDUCTOR?" After the events of the last few days, Alexei didn't feel the usual fervour to defend such accusations of state tyranny, he was also physically and emotionally exhausted.

"Because I was paid to."

"Capitalist." Alexei almost spat the rebuke at Bill.

"I never claimed to be a saint. That label I leave for people like your father, one of the few good Russians I've met."

"Then you didn't know him as well as you think," replied Alexei quickly, immediately regretting what he'd said. The careless disclosure was because of his tiredness.

"What do you mean?" asked Bill, with anger in his voice.

"He was Ukrainian," replied Alexei after too long a pause for the answer to seem plausible.

"That's not what you meant," insisted Bill. Alexei stood and looked out of the window into the darkness. "Your grandfather was Ukrainian," said Bill, coming to stand behind Alexei. "Ivan was born here in Moscow." Alexei didn't look up. "But I think you already knew that."

Bill had interrogated enough people to know that leaving silence open for a confession, a silence that eventually became too uncomfortable to resist, was much more effective than filling that space with more questions. But Alexei was not someone with a weak mind. Alexei made eye contact with Bill through the reflection in the window only once, fleetingly, but his expression was such that Bill knew Alexei had something more he wanted, or perhaps needed, to say.

Bill took the opportunity to really study the young man, someone he'd watched grow into manhood only through the occasional family photo Raisa sent via the diplomatic bag through the embassy.

"I think you know more than you pretend," said Alexei, bringing Bill out of his wandering thoughts. Bill stopped himself from replying; let Alexei fill the silence again, he thought.

Alexei wanted to say more. He could tell this friend of his father's about what he'd seen in Egypt, of his father killing the embassy secretary who'd threatened to expose him as a traitor, of the complicity his mother had in covering the murder up to protect her status and privilege, and the threats from his sister whenever Alexei had tried to speak about what the twins had witnessed as children, and what Alexei had said to the government officials. The truth needed to be spoken out loud, and it needed to be told to someone who knew Ivan, his father. But Alexei didn't fully trust the Englishman who seemed to answer a different question to whichever one he was asked.

"You need to get some rest," suggested Bill after the silence had become too uncomfortable for him. From the flash-paper communication from Pankov he now had the location of CONDUCTOR'S next message. To save Alexei, only CONDUCTOR could help.

"Will you try again?" asked Alexei, bringing the conversation back to the ORCHESTRA plot. "To kill Brezhnev?"

"That depends."

"On what?"

"On whether it will get you out of this mess." Bill stood up carefully before his knees seized up.

"This seems like a lot of trouble to go to for a kid you read a comic with a long time ago."

"A thank you would suffice," replied Bill sarcastically. "I know how much you meant to your father, and it doesn't seem all that long ago to me." He said this in a more sincere tone.

"After today, Brezhnev's going to be hard to get to."

"Possibly," said Bill. "You might even try to stop me yourself."

"Best not tell me your plan then," said Alexei draining the tea in his cup.

"But I need your help, Alyosha."

"I won't betray my country, and my name's Alexei," he insisted.

"I'm not asking you to betray anyone, yet. First, I need to contact CONDUCTOR to find out some information. If there's a way to get you to safety, I'll find it."

"Then why do you need me. I've no idea how to get in touch with anyone from ORCHESTRA. Who is CONDUCTOR?"

"I don't know; we've only ever dealt by message and codenames. I need to write a note, a note that others won't read. Which means I need you to rinse that cup out and masturbate into it." Alexei looked quizzically at Bill, wondering if he'd heard the old man correctly, considering whether Bill's Russian had lost its meaning in translation. Bill saw the young man's expression. "I admit it sounds a little kinky, but I need invisible ink and, if I try, we might be waiting several days. A young virile chap like you should have no trouble. It doesn't need to be full, just enough for a few lines in between the visible one's I'll write."

"Aren't you supposed to use lemon juice for that?" asked Alexei.

"Look around, do you see any fruit? You've been sitting on a bucket and drinking from a cereal bowl. I hadn't expected to return here after the match, so I'm not fully equipped for espionage, or guests." Bill rummaged through the items he'd left behind, trying to find something to write on. "Trust me, semen's just as good, better even. There's a bathroom next door, but don't take too long."

Alexei stood up with the cup, moving hesitantly. Bill threw a magazine at him.

"Here's a five-year-old imported copy of Playboy. One of the builders must have found it and left it here for later; it might hurry things along." Alexei knew that a Plastic Man comic would have been more help.

Bill waited for five minutes. When he went to the bathroom to check on progress, he found the door open.

The cup and magazine were by the sink, but Alexei had gone.

Bill was disappointed that the young man had not trusted him after all. He picked up the cup and was surprised to find some of Alexei's semen inside.

Saturday 23rd September

20

WHEN THE doorbell rang Raisa still had a cold cloth pressed to her bruised cheek. Oleg had slapped her before he'd left for work. He didn't usually hit her in the face.

She opened the door and was dumfounded.

Bill was standing in the hallway. He looked tense.

Bill smiled and Raisa burst into an uncontrolled torrent of tears.

The friendly gesture from someone she loved, but hadn't seen for nearly three years, was like a valve opening. A pressure that had been building since the night before when Oleg had arrived was released in a gust.

Bill was surprised. He didn't resist when Raisa threw her arms around him.

"I wish you'd warned me," she said. She tried to cover up the bruise with her hair as she showed her guest inside, "I've not got ready for the day yet." The crying was short-lived, and she recovered herself quickly from the pleasant shock.

"Leave it out," replied Bill in his cockney accent. Years before Raisa had forbidden him from speaking Russian with her, and her English was good enough to follow his colloquialisms. "You're still beautiful."

"But morally I stink," she replied. Bill didn't contradict her; he knew she liked to think of herself as having the soul of a gypsy. "But what do you expect from someone raised by wolves, hey Bill darling?"

She offered him a cigarette, which he accepted. She placed another in the end of her cigarette holder and took a light from him. She was relaxing into the familiar flirty, sassy person Bill had always known her to be. Bill's presence always reminded her of the thirty-year old gutsy broad she'd once been, someone being thrown out of hotels just after the war. Her husband had condemned her for such behaviour, but Bill had always understood it, and she loved him for that.

"Well, I think the wolves did a pretty sweet job of it," joked Bill, sitting down where Raisa indicated.

"How's Margaret?" asked Raisa.

"Kind of you to ask; she's fine."

"Well, now you've seen me in my nightdress you can report back to your darling wife that the erect nipples she once said could seduce any man in Europe, aren't quite as…what's the word she used?"

"Perky?" said Bill with a broad smile. "And I don't think Margaret spends too much time thinking about your nipples now."

"I was always jealous of her you know?"

"She's a fine woman," said Bill, uncomfortable talking about his wife when with Raisa.

"Beauty was never my own possession." Raisa was getting lost in her own thoughts. The melancholy of the morning hadn't quite shifted. "It distracted men, the beauty, but I never owned it. It made people forgive me for things they never should have."

"Like Ivan?"

"Yes, just like Ivan. I always wonder if it was because of me that he…" Raisa was momentarily haunted by memories that hurt her to remember. She jumped up to break the thoughts. "Let me get you some coffee, come into the kitchen and tell me why you're in Moscow…or shouldn't I ask?"

"Funny you should say that, I am caught by the short and curlies." Raisa looked at him, clearly not understanding the idiom. "In a pickle? Up shit creak? Fucked?" he clarified.

"That word I understand," she replied with a smile. "How can I help? Ask for anything." In the kitchen she laid out a fresh cup and filled it with imported Italian coffee.

"Is one of these Oleg's?" asked Bill, nodding towards the two used cups already on the table.

"Of course you'd know about him," said Raisa. "Darling Bill's always one step ahead. I suppose you saw him leave?" Raisa sounded embarrassed.

"Looked like he's got loads of charm."

"Fists full," she replied sarcastically, a skill Bill had taught her decades before.

She took Bill's coffee cup over to another cabinet and poured a generous glug of whiskey in; he smiled in appreciation.

"Have the KGB visited yet, I mean aside from Oleg?" he asked. The whiskey in the coffee caught the back of his throat. It was a welcome boost after a night spent roaming the city and waiting outside the building to make sure it was safe to meet Raisa.

"No. Why?" She was about to claim Oleg wasn't KGB but knew as much as Bill did that Oleg's job with the Politburo had a wider remit than government legislation.

"It's Alyosha." Bill took hold of Raisa's hand as he spoke the name. He felt the blood in her veins go cold, and he supported her into a chair, forcing her to take a sip of his whiskey-laced coffee.

"You've seen him?" she asked.

"I was with him yesterday."

"With him? How do you mean?"

"You didn't tell him –"

"No," interrupted Bill. "He's in trouble with the KGB."

Bill hurriedly told Raisa as much as he felt necessary about the day before, knowing there wasn't much time. Raisa felt a similar weight of grief in her chest to that when she'd left Bill in Cairo to return to Moscow as a single mother and widow years before.

"I don't believe it, Bill," she cried. "How could they do that to him? To my little wolf."

"As hard as it will be, if he comes here, Alyosha I mean, you have to turn him away immediately," warned Bill. "Oleg already has a team outside watching. If they see him arrive, they'll be in here seconds behind him. Is there another way out of here?"

"The backstairs, they go up to the roof, or down to the alleyway." Raisa was in shock as she answered the question distantly.

"It's important to keep in mind that you can't protect him, as much as you want to. Tell him I'm a trusted friend and send him back to me. He'll know where to find me," said Bill. "I'll protect your son."

"Our son," clarified Raisa proudly. She was grateful for Bill's presence in the city where her son was now being hunted. Bill looked guilty, remembering his friend Ivan, the betrayal, and the secret about the children he and Raisa had kept all these years.

There was a loud knock at the door. Raisa gave Bill a look of alarm. He patted her hand calmly.

"Answer it, invite them in, there's nothing wrong here, is there?" After a second or two Raisa shook her head, having begun to compose herself.

By the time the two KGB officers had been invited into the kitchen by Raisa, trying to behave as surprised by their arrival as she could, Bill was already on the roof. He crossed to the external fire escape stairwell, and the coffee mug with his fingerprints on was cast aside, smashed into several pieces.

He heard the footsteps hurriedly coming up the metal staircase on the side of the building before he saw the KGB agent they belonged to.

To return up the stairs would have been pointless. If the agent was not there for him, but just taking up a surveillance position on the roof, running away would make him look suspicious. There was also no other escape route. He slowed down and gave a nod of greeting to the agent as their paths crossed in the middle landing, hoping this would deceive the KGB agent into thinking they were both there for the same reason.

He thought he'd got away with it, until the gun barrel was pressed against his spine.

"*Podnimite ruki!*" ordered the agent. Bill couldn't risk a bullet that would shatter his spine, so he complied and raised his hands, hoping there was only this one agent. Bill would wait until he sensed the young man's grip on the gun loosen.

From behind him, the agent ran his free hand up and down Bill's torso, coming across the gun Bill had taken off Alexei the day before. The agent spun Bill around and held up the gun he'd found, noticing it as a KGB-issued weapon, which confused him.

That second of confusion was all Bill needed.

Smiling, as if to say that the agent had made a mistake, he brought his knee up smartly into the agent's crotch with as much force as the onset of arthritis would allow. The KGB agent fell backwards, dropping the guns in each hand as he did so; these clattered down the rest of the metal staircase. After recovering, the young agent smiled, knowing he'd easily be able to overpower his ageing attacker.

Bill quickly dropped into a crouch and produced a small revolver from an ankle holster under his trouser leg.

"Always check for a second gun, son," he said in English.

Bill fired. He was a good enough shooter to aim for the face rather than the larger torso.

The bullet entered the agent's mouth just as he opened it wide to shout for help; it was like a funfair shooting range with water pistols, thought Bill. The confirmation of a perfect hit on this occasion was an explosion not of water from a balloon on the end of a hose at the fair, but a spray of the agent's blood, brain matter, skull and hair, followed by the plunging of his limp body over the railings to the alleyway below.

The noise of the shot would immediately alert the other agents and anyone else who happened to be nearby, so Bill had to put the excruciating pain in his knee out of his mind and sprint down the remaining stairs. He took two or three steps at a time in a series of jumps that he knew he'd pay the price for later in both knees.

He limped across Marx Prospekt, past the Metropole Hotel. A team of early morning workers clad in grey burlap outfits were washing down and scrubbing the benches in the square. A truck drove past hosing the road before another day of heavy traffic arrived in the city.

Bill crossed Sverdlov Square to the metro station tucked next to the Lenin Museum.

He realised he was being followed.

The man walking towards him from the fountain on his right-hand side seemed too purposeful to be on an early morning stroll, and he was dressed too smartly for a Saturday. The metro would be too difficult to evade him in.

He could turn back, head through the passageway in the old Kitai-Gorod wall and try to make a run for it once on the other side, but a sudden change in direction might prompt his arrest by the man closing in on him now. Alternatively, he could try and lose himself in the corridors of the huge Moskva Hotel, but the KGB could quickly mobilise every member of hotel staff to look for him.

Bill walked up the steps of the portico to the Lenin Museum and pulled on the door handle.

It was locked.

There was no time to pretend he was a regular tourist, disappointed by the museum being closed. He hurried down the steps and swung left past the building towards Red Square. He hoped there would be enough tourists in the square this early to lose himself amongst.

Red Square was almost empty, but there was a queue of people with empty shopping bags in their hands, waiting for the doors of GUM, the state department store, to open. This three-storey building stretched along the length of Red Square opposite the Kremlin. Bill wouldn't have time to go around it. He had to go through.

Bill joined the queue of people waiting outside the main entrance opposite the Lenin Mausoleum. Bill saw the agent join the queue behind a few people further back. Bill was confident that even the KGB wouldn't risk causing a scene in front of a queue of shoppers and a dozen or so tourists taking pictures of the iconic Moscow landmarks in Red Square. But his description would already have been transmitted on the KGB frequency, and agents would be hurrying towards the department store.

He needed to disappear quickly.

An attendant opened the door. Bill took a swipe at the Achilles tendon of the young woman standing in front of him. Her scream of pain drew the attention of others. They broke from their formation in a line to find out the cause. Bill slipped forwards and into the building. The manoeuvre gave him an extra second or two to choose his path and get ahead of the agent who was following close behind him.

Under its huge glass roof the building consisted of three vertical levels and three rows of shops separated by ornate archways, and all connected by bridges and stairwells into a labyrinth of passageways.

Bill crossed the floor and ran up the first stairwell. He emerged on the middle landing. He saw the agent on the landing opposite. A look of surprise and annoyance was on the Russian's face. The two watched each other across the divide of the first row of shops. Bill winked, smiled, and darted through a nearby alleyway further into the maze.

When Bill next emerged to get his bearings, he was still on the middle landing but overlooking the fountain in the central octagonal section. The agent was on the ground floor talking to another agent. He pointed up to identify Bill who, a second later, had disappeared back into the network of access routes.

Bill couldn't overthink things, there was no real strategy, just luck or bad luck to his route out of the building. He also couldn't run, otherwise the increasing numbers of shoppers would betray him to the agents due to his suspicious behaviour. His knees also couldn't be relied upon to sustain a fast-enough pace.

There were six bridges across each of the three rows, and the pattern was replicated on each floor. He went back the way he'd come, hoping the agents wouldn't expect him to return to Red Square.

As he crossed a bridge to the final stairwell, he saw the second agent on the next bridge along. They looked at each other trying to determine which way to advance. Bill turned back, and he saw the agent communicate his position to whoever else might be in the building looking for him.

When Bill's next surfaced from the stairwells he saw the original agent further along the same row.

The longer he took to escape from the building the higher the risk of it being flooded by KGB agents. He went back to the central octagon on the middle floor to wait. Let them come to him, he thought.

Women in headscarves and overcoats, carrying their purchases wrapped in the distinctive GUM paper and string pushed past him as he tried to assess the best location for him to wait. A headscarf that had accidentally been dropped gave him an idea.

When the original agent walked past the stairwell, he gave no more than a cursory glance inside, taking no notice of the figure sitting down on the stairs wearing a headscarf, with their back to him. As the agent took two more steps past the stairwell, Bill stood up. In one swift move he'd wound the scarf into a rope and looped it across the agent's neck, pulling him backwards into the stairwell as he choked him.

The agent was strong, clawing against the makeshift garrotte, and trying to shout for help. Bill knew he wouldn't be able to strangle the man before the alarm was raised and his location betrayed. He thought fast and reversed the direction, now pushing the agent forwards out onto the landing. He tightened the noose.

Bill took them both up to a running pace and, as they approached the iron-work railing, suddenly released the scarf and firmly thrust a shoulder into the agent's strong back.

To screams of horror from the shoppers watching, the agent fell, his limbs windmilling in panic. He landed half inside the fountain, breaking his back across the stonework of the water basin. By instinct everyone ran to the balustrade and looked down at the body, allowing Bill to hurry across the building using the bridges, and disappear back down the nearest stairwell.

Bill emerged at a casual walking pace a few seconds later onto October 25th Street. He tried to lose whatever shadows he might still have by weaving his way through the streets and alleyways, emerging into Dzerzhinsky Square. The looming site of the KGB headquarters opposite him was an unwelcome landmark, so he quickly descended into the metro to get away from the evil stare of the forty-foot bronze statue of Felix

Dzerzhinsky, the father of the state security apparatus, which dominated the circular flower bed in the centre of the square that was already busy with traffic.

Bill realised that, in trying to help Alexei by speaking to Raisa, he may have only made things worse. Alexei's gun would be found next to the dead agent, and it would be concluded that Alexei killed him en route to see his mother, with the help of Bill, who would eventually be identified from any description already relayed to the KGB's information services department.

He had to sort the mess out, and he needed CONDUCTOR's help.

The letter he'd delivered to the apartment post-box of an intermediary that morning wouldn't be replied to by CONDUCTOR until the following day. Until then, he'd have to wait at the university, and hope Alexei, his son, returned to him.

Shologda

Monday 25th September

21

ALEXEI'S ESCAPE from Moscow two days before had been easier than he'd expected.

He was trained in surveillance.

Alexei knew that the main transport hubs, his friends and family, even the foreign embassies would have overt and covert KGB agents watching them. So he stole a car.

The borders would be on high alert, so he'd driven deeper into Russia and abandoned the car where it was unlikely to raise suspicion.

It had been a long walk from where he'd left the car, then a bus ride, to reach the kolkhoz village where he spent a few weeks every year helping with the harvest.

The KGB were unlikely to cast their net this wide this quickly, Alexei hoped. He knew how they operated.

In the village two years before he'd first met Vassily. During that hot late summer with Vassily, Alexei had discovered a different life. Honesty. Simplicity. Happiness. Events in Moscow had now snatched that chance of happiness away. But Shologda was again a temporary refuge.

The forest of oak, linden, maple, and ash were a fence.

The meadows and farms were a sanctuary.

The Pakhra River was a border separating him from the city.

Two days in Shologda had given Alexei time to think.

He trudged up a hill following overgrown paths through the village. The large milk pail of water he was carrying from the well was cumbersome to carry. He rested against a broken handcart, flexing his shoulders.

"You're from the city."

Alexei turned sharply towards the voice behind him. In the long grass a middle-aged man was lying. He nudged a tattered hat away from his eyes.

"You lost?" asked the man.

"No," replied Alexei. He didn't want to encourage more questions.

The man struggled to stand up. Alexei didn't offer any assistance.

The tramp approached and Alexei could smell alcohol. The stains on the villager's trousers showed where urine had dried. There had been more than one such soaking it seemed.

"Fancy clothes," said the tramp. He stood next to Alexei and reached a dirty hand towards the wide lapel of Alexei's denim jacket. Alexei had bought the denim suit especially for the hockey match so that he would look less like a KGB agent.

"Cigarette?" asked the tramp.

Alexei held out the red box of Prima cigarettes. With shaking hands the tramp removed a few and handed the packet back. Alexei lit the cigarette the tramp held in his mouth, he also lit one for himself.

"This village was awarded the Order of the Red Banner of Labour for over-production many years ago," said the tramp. He spoke unexpectedly well.

"Where is everyone?" asked Alexei.

"The village has been classified as *neperspektivnie*."

"Meaning?"

"Deemed to be *without merit*," replied the man. He inhaled deeply on his cigarette as if it might be taken away from him. "The region wants agro-industrial towns instead of patchwork villages like ours."

"Ours?" asked Alexei. "You live here?"

The tramp chuckled. "Live here! Comrade, I'm the kolkhoz chairman!"

Alexei now recognised him, barely.

"But I was here last year," said Alexei. "The harvest was good."

"The government doesn't care. They cut off the electricity and water supply two weeks ago. Everyone's leaving for the concrete flats in the new town."

"And you?" asked Alexei.

"No," said the man. "Thanks for this." He inhaled on the last few embers of the cigarette stub.

Alexei watched the man stumble down the hill through the long grass that was already reclaiming what once had been a path.

Alexei picked up the pail and walked onwards.

When he'd last been in the village the many young workers helping with the harvest had made Shologda seem active and appealing.

Alexei now saw it as it truly was.

The village was haunting in its collapsing, neglected state. The decay which now seemed so evident had, during the height of those summer weeks, seemed like quaint charm.

The only noise in the village now was that of a loose shutter banging against a wall in the breeze.

The post-office was boarded-up, and the small library where Alexei had led political talks for the young workers was now empty of any books.

The shop had a note in the window informing customers that it would only open for two hours each week. Alexei peered inside. The few customers left to buy anything from it could purchase a brand-new piano or expensive dress, but there was no food for sale.

Behind the shop the wheat fields were ready to be harvested but this year's crop would die.

Alexei had happy memories of working in the fields, of sitting in a circle with the other workers and Vassily in the summer sun. With a large picnic cloth draped over the freshly mown ground, and the bundles of hay stacked around them like temporary trees they'd built themselves through hard manual work, it had seemed like paradise.

Nadezhda and Lev, his hosts then as now, made the young people feel welcome. Nadezhda would bring around baskets of

189

food, and Lev would stroll from group to group with his hands behind his strong back, surveying the work, satisfied by their collective achievements.

Alexei couldn't stay in the village but returning to Moscow didn't seem like an option either.

He remembered the moment three weeks before, at Kiev station, when he'd seen Vassily's guilty expression after watching him meet the American. So much of what he believed in had changed since then.

Two days of distance in Shologda hadn't settled his confusion, but it had proved that running away was not a solution.

He had to return to Moscow. He knew his way around the hotels there. He could make a discreet approach to a western businessman. He could defect.

But he was not like his father, not like Vassily; he was not a traitor.

The only escape was to prove his innocence.

The American who'd met Vassily needed to be found. The British assassin must be arrested. The ORCHESTRA plot must be exposed.

Alexei would redeem himself.

He would return to the city. He would fight.

"WE CAN start the harvest next week," said Lev. He was counting the money earned in town that day from selling the puppies he'd bred. "When the other young people arrive."

"There won't be a harvest this year," said Nadezhda. She was inspecting the clothes bought at the rag fair in town, deciding which could be made into something useful for her husband to wear.

"I shall see to it that there is," said Lev. He put the coins he'd counted into a purse.

"I'm not staying," said Alexei. He spooned servings of the mushroom soup he'd prepared into three bowls.

"I can't stay," clarified Alexei.

"Can't?" asked Nadezhda. "I know the house is a little run down, but –"

"I'm in trouble," interrupted Alexei.

"Can we help?" asked Lev.

"What sort of trouble?" asked Nadezhda at the same time as her husband.

"It's not fair to tell you," said Alexei. He wasn't going to lie, not to them. He wanted to protect them also. "It's government trouble."

Lev looked across at his wife.

Alexei knew saying even this much was a risk. Lev, who'd returned with his wife to his childhood village in 1953 as a mechanisation expert, had often spoken of the glory of socialism on previous visits. He was a former chairman of the kolkhoz. Reporting Alexei would bring them favour, and they needed such an advantage.

"Perhaps I should leave now," said Alexei. He stood up. "I'm sorry. I shouldn't have come here."

"Collectivisation has only led to famine," said Lev. It was a brave declaration to make to a KGB agent.

"I don't understand," said Alexei.

"Alyosha, sit down," instructed Nadezhda. She looked across at her husband and smiled. "In return for our bountiful harvest every year, each villager only received five hundred grams of grain as payment. Barely enough to survive on."

"I'd always admired your commitment to socialised farming," said Alexei. He didn't understand. "You both led the work brigades each harvest."

"Those in the towns and cities ate well off our toil," added Lev. "We're not communists, Alyosha."

"We're not even socialists," said Nadezhda in a whisper.

"But you've stayed here," said Alexei. "I don't understand." For a boy of strong ideological faith growing up in the city, the kolkhoz had seemed to him like the romantic triumph of socialism, a conquest over the landed estates and serfdom of the pre-revolutionary era. Lev and Nadezhda had seemed to Alexei the embodiment of that communist success.

"We're prisoners," said Lev. He stood up and re-fixed a sheet of newspaper that had come away from the wall. The newspaper was being used to cover the increasing number of cracks. "We're hostages who've made the best of their captivity," he added.

"Most villagers are denied internal passports. We couldn't leave," said Nadezhda. "It's a second serfdom."

"Central planning has only ever led to starvation," said Lev.

After a few seconds of reflection Alexei said, "I think I admire you both even more now." These people he trusted had been honest with him. And it had come at a time when his faith in all that he'd previously believed was at its most unsettled anyway. Their honesty gave him hope.

"Tell us more about your trouble, Alyosha," said Nadezhda. "Perhaps we can help?"

"Thank you," said Alexei. "But I mustn't."

"Nadia, leave the boy alone," said Lev. "It's his business."

"Did you get what you needed in town?" asked Alexei. He wanted to change the subject now that he'd announced his intention. He didn't want to discuss the decision to go back to Moscow in case they tried to talk him out of it, which wouldn't be hard to do.

"We could have brought the cart back loaded with chemical fertiliser, which is no use," said Nadezhda, "but there was no sugar." She spoke with the indifference of someone who'd survived the Stalin years and long-since realised that the promises of Khrushchev and Brezhnev had been empty ones.

"There won't be sugar for another two days. By the time we make it back all of it will have gone," added Lev.

"Do you think it's perhaps time to accept the offer of an apartment and move to town?" asked Alexei, his voice one of concern not criticism.

"This can't last," said Lev, sitting down to his soup, and fighting against a persistent cough. "We just have to wait things out." He held up the bowl with dirty hands and slurped the thick liquid through an overgrown moustache and beard that completely hid his mouth.

Lev coughed as he spoke, "This is an administrative reform to avoid the much-needed political reforms. They're industrializing farming to distract the bureaucracy and keep it busy." Lev checked the handkerchief he'd put to his mouth for blood. "Someone'll see the folly of losing places like Shologda before too long."

"It's the nature of eternal Russia," said Nadezhda. "We move from order to chaos and back again to order on the surface, but underneath things sort themselves out eventually." She'd stopped eating and was stirring into her husband's soup an herbal paste she'd made to ease his cough.

"How else do you explain the nonsense of a train from Moscow crossing the path of a train from Leningrad, when both are carrying the same items to opposite cities?" asked Lev.

Alexei looked across at Lev, and realised his host was a man caught on a spinning wheel from which he couldn't get off. Eventually he'd either be thrown off, or the wheel would stop turning.

Lev brushed aside his wife's ministrations as unwanted irritations. He turned the volume on the radio up so he could hear the deep voice of Yuri Levitan more clearly. He poured out more vodka.

"*Nichevo*," said Nadezhda disconsolately as she put to her lips the vodka her husband had passed over. It was a phrase of apathetic acceptance that Alexei had become used to hearing, more so over the last few years, especially from those far removed from Brezhnev's gerontocratic bureaucracy.

Nadezhda returned to her soup and listened to the velvety radio announcements that she'd tuned into regularly ever since the familiar voice of Levitan had brought comfort to her nation through loudspeakers in the street during the Great Patriotic War.

"He announced the first international race I won," said Nadezhda, remembering the running competitions of her youth. Yuri Levitan's voice continued to announce the day's news "Although that was many years ago now," she added.

Her overweight, ruddy-faced appearance bore very little resemblance to the black and white picture of her as a slender twenty-year old middle-distance athlete. The picture of her triumph had pride of place on a shelf which had been repaired too many times to make it trustworthy. One end of the shelf was now propped up by the old accordion that Lev had played

193

on summer evenings. The bellows were now torn, and the instrument rendered useless other than as a support structure.

"Is it possible to solve a problem that has no solution?" asked Lev. It was the set-up to a joke Alexei had heard before.

"We don't answer questions about agriculture," replied Alexei with the punchline. He collected up the empty soup bowls. Lev smiled to himself and leant back in his chair.

At bedtime Alexei fastened the pyjama bottoms of Lev's that had been loaned to him, but which didn't even remotely fit. He turned down the lamp in the small room he'd been given the use of. The single bed he'd slept on during the harvest had long since been broken up and used for other, more essential, purposes, but Nadezhda had kept the old mattress, which Alexei made himself as comfortable as possible on. He'd slept in worse conditions when with the Guards in the Baltic region, and his immediate surroundings had never been a high priority for him.

There was a tap at his door.

"Alyosha, we're so worried," said Nadezhda. Alexei could see she'd been crying. "Stay here with us."

"I want to, babulya," said Alexei. He used the affectionate term for grandmother to demonstrate his love. "It will only put you in danger if I stay."

"You're all that's important, Alyosha," she replied. She held both of his hands together clasped inside her bent arthritic fingers.

"I can only do what I must if I know you and didulya are safe," said Alexei.

Nadezhda kissed his hands.

"Goodnight Lyoshka." She closed the door herself.

Alexei had been rewarded with unguarded companionship from Lev and Nadezhda. He felt safe in Shologda. He knew he couldn't stay.

Tuesday 26th September

22

IT WAS early.

Alexei lit the stove to take the morning chill out of the little house that Lev and Nadezhda tried to maintain as best they could.

He tucked some money under a broken jug on the table as a parting gift, despite knowing it wasn't a lack of roubles, but a scarcity of useful things to buy that caused his hosts their difficulties. Most of the potatoes from that year's crop were already spoiled due to the poor conditions available for storage, the rest were unlikely to get the few remaining villagers through the winter. But he had nothing else to leave them as thanks for their hospitality.

A floorboard creaked under Nadezhda's weight as she entered the kitchen.

Alexei was already in the doorway on his way out. He felt ashamed at being caught leaving without saying goodbye.

"I didn't want to wake you," he lied.

"You're a kind boy," replied Nadezhda, not believing his explanation. She leant on the gnarled wooden table to steady herself and waved him towards her.

She embraced him in a firm hug. He could smell the mustard flour and garlic that she covered herself with to treat whatever latest ailment was troubling her. Nadezhda's mother had been a folk healer, and so the little house her daughter now lived in was full of potions to remedy any medical complaint someone in the village might have.

She released her grip and held Alexei at arms' length. He expected her to ask him to stay.

"Remember," she said seriously, fixing her cloudy eyes on Alexei, "the same pan of boiling water that softens a potato, hardens an egg." He looked at her quizzically. "It's what you're made of," she clarified, "not the circumstance you find yourself in, that determines what happens to you."

The hunch-backed old woman didn't wait for a reply. She turned to the stove to warm her cold hands against the fire.

Alexei stepped backwards and walked out through the door, already feeling stronger.

The early morning walk to the bus stop was chilly, but Alexei shoved his hands deep into his denim trouser pockets and whistled a happy tune to try and distract himself from the gravity of the journey he was taking back into the arena of danger.

The bundle of money which he'd left on the table had been slipped back in his pocket by Nadezhda. She'd realised Alexei would need it more for the return to Moscow than she would in a village where there was nothing to buy. If he survived the return to Moscow and cleared his name, Alexei promised himself that he'd use whatever political capital he might restore to his reputation to help his two friends in Shologda.

MAXIM PAUSED before scooping the ice-cold water out of the bucket.

"One, two, three…" He held his breath and splashed handfuls of water over his face and torso.

He dried himself with his shirt and collected the rest of his clothes from the long-disused barn where he'd bedded down for the night. It had been too late to drive into Shologda itself the evening before when he turned off the main road.

He lit a cigarette. Before the match ran out, he touched it to the corner of a piece of paper. He watched as the note from the day before curled and burnt. The written summons from one of the bored married women he regularly met for sex and cash to top-up his low pay had delayed him leaving Moscow.

The bundle of roubles she'd given him after sex now made a bulge in the back pocket of his tight jeans. The money had been left by the housewife's husband for her to buy a new sewing machine with, having heard that a much-needed delivery had been made to the city. But she'd preferred to spend the afternoon and the money on sex with her rough toy-boy rather than queueing for hours with other women outside one of the few stores in Moscow that could reliably have sufficient stocks of such consumer goods. Maxim knew he'd given her more satisfaction than a sewing machine ever could.

In his other rear pocket Maxim had a ticket for the seventh match of the hockey series with Canada for later that day. He didn't want to waste time in Shologda.

Maxim had played hockey for the Soviet Union as a teenager. He loved hockey more than he did women. And Maxim really loved women.

The dramatic opening game on the Moscow leg, when the Soviet hockey players had produced an impressive win had been better than an orgasm for Maxim. But that had been followed by a Canadian victory the previous Sunday. If Canada won tonight's match, they'd level the series score, with the final, deciding, match to be played in Moscow on Thursday. Maxim needed to get back to the city.

In the KGB Maxim drifted from task to task based on need rather than any specific team or directorate that he was linked to. He was difficult to control. A rebel with a cause was how someone in the KGB had described him. He preferred it this way, and his bosses in the KGB did too.

He'd enjoyed spending the last few days disrupting the Canadian team as much as possible.

He cut their practise sessions at Dvoretz Sporta short with bureaucratic explanations about staff hours. He bribed the referees chosen for the match-games. He instructed the goal judges to be hesitant when turning their red lights on after the Canadian team scored.

The threat made while the Canadians were in Sweden preparing for their journey to Moscow, to keep the players and their wives in separate hotels, had forced an ultimatum which, eventually, Maxim had backed down on. Nevertheless, at the Intourist Hotel, Maxim had arranged for the player's wives to receive almost inedible food. Cases of Canadian beer accompanying the squad had been deliberately lost at the airport. Their imported steaks arrived half the size originally intended.

Maxim was determined to make sure his enquiries in the village didn't force him to spend another night in the dilapidated barn.

Being in Shologda reminded him of his childhood. They were not happy memories.

He had no interest in finding Alexei Ivanovich Dimichenko. He'd only agreed to the journey to Shologda because the senior officer who asked him was attractive and he hoped to be rewarded by her with sex if he found the fugitive.

He'd been trained in the spetsnaz.

He was a soldier, not a policeman.

The western cultural influences of the late 1960s creeping into the Soviet Union had become more attractive to him than the discipline of life as a conscientious KGB agent. His refusal to adopt the conservative hair-cut and sombre tie that agents were expected to embrace also made him an outsider amongst his peers. That non-conformity made him attractive to the bored housewives of central Moscow, and they had money to spend on him.

His dark Georgian skin, thick black tousled hair and unshaven face were reminiscent of a young Joseph Stalin.

He chose to dress like an American and preferred to listen to *The Kinks* or Bob Dylan on western radio channels that weren't being jammed, rather than Russian folk music on vinyl or cassette. It was his hope that his superiors would recommend him for foreign operations in the USA, not least to remove an annoyance from their ranks.

Maxim put the crumpled safari-style shirt and tan-coloured corduroy bomber-jacket back on. He tucked the scout knife into one of his unpolished biker boots and zipped up his jacket against the early morning chill.

He slid the Malysh 9mm semi-automatic pistol in one of the jacket pockets. His bosses told him not to use the Malysh, but he preferred it. Whilst the Malysh only took five rounds, its small size and lack of protrusions, having an internal hammer, facilitated rapid withdrawal from his pocket.

Such tactical considerations were left over from his brief time with the special forces. He'd seen many agents hindered by under-arm pistol holsters, or the sharp mechanical features of their weapons getting caught on clothes. Maxim sacrificed both shooting distance and bullets for a less cumbersome weapon from the armoury of the Technical Operations Directorate. Despite his scruffy appearance, Maxim was a professional killer.

He walked into the village, leaving outside the barn the unreliable pale green zaporozhets supermini car he'd been given for the trip. The vehicle was the type given by the government for free to invalids. It was impossible to get successfully around a tight corner at any sort of speed. The designers had apparently been aiming for the Fiat 500 but had missed that ambition by quite some margin. He left the keys in the ignition, hoping a villager might steal it; the bus back to Moscow was preferable.

Had Maxim left the barn thirty minutes earlier, or had he turned right towards the main road, he'd have recognised the denim-suited man waiting for a bus to Moscow from the crumpled photo which was in the opposite jacket pocket to the pistol. Instead, Maxim walked into Shologda and made his way to the house of Lev Yegorovich Filatov.

The Filatov house looked like it would collapse under the weight of the first snowstorm when winter arrived. The plaster was coming away from the walls, and the corrugated roof was rusted beyond effective use.

Maxim was about to knock on the door, wondering if it would stand up to the impact of his fist, when a plump lady rounded the corner of the building carrying a basket of eggs.

Neither spoke.

The woman's expression showed both a realisation that the scruffy young man was not welcome, and fear that he was a threat. To Maxim the old woman's reaction revealed she had something to hide, most likely the traitor he'd been sent to the village to find.

Nadezhda dropped the basket of eggs.

She turned and ran behind the house.

Despite her weight, she still had the mind of the competitive runner who'd won international prizes in her youth.

Maxim walked around the corner of the crumbling building. He was surprised by the distance she'd managed to put between them; he ran after her.

Putting a hand on her shoulder, Maxim pulled the woman to the ground. She had a small knife in her podgy hand, which she swiped upwards. It sliced across Maxim's thigh.

He cried out in pain, and his injured leg gave way underneath him.

Nadezhda clumsily regained her feet and faced him with the small weapon in her hand. She was ready for another strike against her attacker, whom she'd guessed had come for information on Alexei.

Maxim remained on the ground trying to stem the bleeding from the gash on his leg.

Nadezhda ran back towards the house. She screamed for her husband.

Reluctant to chase after her and risk another close-quarters injury, Maxim took out the pistol from his jacket pocket. Without pausing to shout a warning for her to surrender, he fired two quick shots at the target. Policemen gave warnings, the KGB did not. He was trained to only draw a gun when intending to shoot, and to make sure two quick shots were fired, otherwise risk the second shot missing when the target was thrown off balance by the first impact.

Maxim didn't miss.

Nadezhda's body tumbled in the mud.

She was dead.

Maxim grabbed the bleeding leg wound with one hand, and kept the small pistol aimed towards the house, knowing that the two shots would alert anyone else inside. He struggled to his feet.

The bushy-face and bare barrel-chest of Lev appeared next to the building. He was carrying a Hungarian made AK-47 by his side.

Maxim knew his own gun was out of range, but he fired two shots at his new target, more in hope than expectation. He limped forwards.

Both bullets missed, kicking up clods of mud way short of the house.

Had Lev's facial hair not been so abundant, Maxim would have seen the former kolkhoz chairman smile as he lined up the AK-47 to shoot the young man. Maxim continued to hobble forwards as fast as he could, knowing he had only one bullet left.

Lev's weapon jammed.

The old man didn't panic, the habits learnt during the war nearly thirty years before were instinctive. He checked the magazine, reloaded, aimed, and fired again.

Nothing.

During the combat of Stalingrad in 1942 the weapon he had back then had been the only thing Lev could trust. It had never jammed during six months of fighting against the Nazis. The Kalashnikov was supposed to be a superior weapon to anything he'd had in the war, yet it had now failed him at the critical moment.

Lev removed the magazine, pulled back the charging handle to the rear, and visually checked the chamber to make sure there wasn't a round in there.

Maxim saw Lev's weapon jam twice. He had gained some ground. He fired the final shot from his pistol.

The shot still fell short, but only by a few inches.

Maxim threw the gun away. He knew he couldn't close the distance that remained fast enough to get to the kolkhoz chairman before the AK-47 was cleared and fired. Maxim took a few more paces, then stopped and pulled out the scout knife from his boot.

The technique of knife throwing was something Maxim had been taught with the special forces but had never put into practise. Lev was a large enough target so that accuracy was less of a concern. It would be making sure the rotations were correct that might save Maxim's life before the old man corrected his weapon malfunction.

Maxim stood up as straight as he could, putting the uninjured right leg forward slightly. He positioned both arms towards the target to perfect his aim. He carefully nestled the blade against his palm whilst grasping it between two fingers and his thumb. He raised his throwing arm behind his head. He stared at Lev.

The chairman pushed the magazine back into his weapon.

Maxim snapped his throwing arm forward quickly. He moved his weight headlong with it and kept both shoulders still. He relaxed the pinch-grip on the blade at the optimal release point, just as Lev raised the AK-47.

The blade embedded itself in Lev's chest. It severed the left anterior descending coronary artery, an injury which ensured rapid death.

Both the rifle and the half-naked man fell to the ground.

For a scruffy, womanising, disinterested KGB agent, the throw had been perfection. It had saved Maxim's life.

Maxim hadn't heard the noise of the approaching car, nor had he noticed the group of people getting out. When the adrenalin rush subsided after the knife's release, his legs turned to jelly. He slumped to the ground.

Even the sight of his attractive new boss striding towards him, the tails of her long black leather coat fluttering behind her, didn't give him the energy to stand back up.

Tara, pacing across the garden towards Maxim, was scanning the area for signs of her brother. The long black leather coat and boots gave her the appearance of a dominatrix. Her voluminous hair was tied up. She had her Makarov pistol drawn and ready to fire.

The three officers that had travelled with her obeyed her orders to search the house.

"Where is he?" she asked of Maxim. She stood over the injured agent but didn't offer any assistance.

She wanted to be told that her twin brother, the traitor, was dead inside the house.

23

ALEXEI DISEMBARKED from the second bus he'd taken. He got off before it travelled too far into the heart of Moscow.

He knew where he would go first, and it wasn't far.

The spare key to Vassily's old flat was still under a loose brick in the garden outside the drab concrete apartment block. Assuming no new tenant had yet been moved in to replace Vassily, Alexei reasoned that it would probably be the safest place to hide.

If he kept quiet and made sure no neighbour saw him enter or leave, he'd be able to get some rest. There were details he needed to plan out to try and clear his name. H also needed a change of clothes.

The lock on the communal door was broken again. As the autumn chill descended across the city warning of the approaching winter freeze the tramps had been congregating inside at night for warmth. The narrow stairwell smelt of stale urine.

The wall-mounted radiator in the communal hallway, fixed above his head, was making the usual gurgling noise. By habit, Alexei slapped it hard as he walked past. The noise stopped. He was very familiar with this block of flats.

He opened the door to Vassily's old flat. The fetid smell struck Alexei instantly. He put his hand over his mouth. He hurried through the varnished pine wood-panelled hallway into the kitchen and flung the window open to let some fresh air

205

into the stale flat. The kitchen cabinets were covered in the same dark brown pine veneer as the hallway, and Alexei searched through them for the air freshener aerosol that he was sure he'd brought round for Vassily a few weeks before.

The aerosol was where he'd left it. He walked through the small flat spraying the air freshener.

Alexei walked into the bedroom.

Vassily was lying on the unmade bed. His head was propped up against the floral headboard.

On the bus journey back to Moscow Alexei had prepared himself to confront the reminders of the life he'd once had in Vassily's old flat. He expected that Vassily's ghost would haunt him, as the Ghost did Hamlet, torturing Alexei about the spectral character's eternity in purgatory due to the manner of his death.

What Alexei hadn't strengthened his mind to was finding Vassily there in person.

The man who had once been Alexei's strength and saviour was grinning inanely at the intruder; it was the smile of an uncomprehending simpleton.

Vassily's shaven scalp showed burn scars. His stained clothes explained the overpowering smell of faeces that had permeated throughout the small apartment. Alexei stopped spraying the aerosol, but otherwise he couldn't move.

Vassily, satisfied that the visitor had not come to harm him, returned to the chessboard on the bed next to him. Chess had been Vassily's favourite game, but the man on the bed was not meticulously recreating Spassky's King's Gambit opening moves against Bronstein in 1960. Instead Vassily was randomly moving the pieces around pretending they were attacking each other, as a child might do with toy soldiers.

He could run away, he thought. Pretend he hadn't seen this. This was dismissed just as swiftly as it had entered his thought process.

Alexei's instinct was to cry. This was followed immediately by the desire to help.

The man-child that Vassily had become offered no resistance to being undressed. Alexei led him into the bathroom. Vassily's body hadn't yet lost its muscularity, but it was as if the skeleton underneath had lost its density; he was like a ragdoll in both his posture and shuffling gait.

Alexei knew enough about the drug tortures at Serbsky to assume that Vladimir, the vivisectionist, had ordered a heavy dose of a drug combination that would explain the yellowing of Vassily's skin, early signs of physical collapse, and brain damage.

There was a disgusting perversity in Vassily's broken wrist having been put in a cast to heal, whilst his mind had been degraded by drug treatments. It was painful for Vassily to move. He had a high temperature. Alexei knew that aminazin, sulfazin, and reserpine in sufficient quantities could easily have the effects he was seeing.

Either Vassily had somehow escaped, or he'd been sent home. It made no difference how Vassily had got there. The treatment received at Serbsky, a result of Alexei's denunciation, had left Vassily buried alive in his own body.

Once he'd been bathed, and the sheets changed, Alexei helped Vassily back to the bed.

Alexei tried to talk to Vassily. He tried to offer comfort and investigate if any vestiges of the Vassily he knew were still present. His questions were met either by rambling or animal noises. Throughout his bath, Vassily hadn't stopped grinning as if he recognised the man who was helping him but couldn't quite place from where.

Alexei cleaned the flat in its entirety. This distracted his mind from both the man-child in the bed playing with the chess pieces, and the worry about his own survival. If capture for him meant the same fate as Vassily's, then Alexei was minded to take an overdose of whatever pills he could find in the apartment that night.

Alexei cleaned everything. The soiled clothes and bedding were bagged up and disposed of. The windows were closed against the cold air. Only then was the magnitude of his discovery felt by Alexei.

Heartbreak was a concept he was familiar with from novels and melodramatic movies, it had even been something he thought had been experienced earlier that month when taking the most difficult decision in his life to betray Vassily to protect the Party. But none of that experience had prepared Alexei for the process of grief he now underwent, witnessing the spiritual death of the man he loved.

Knowing he had been the cause made that aching of sorrow seem unbearable. He felt as if someone was wringing his heart in their hands like a wet towel. The pain couldn't be worse even if someone had thrust a knife deep in his chest. One torrent of the darkest, heaviest sadness was quickly followed by another, like waves in a storm that rolled in on top of each other as the first was absorbed by the beach.

And yet, Vassily was still there, still alive. But was it him anymore?

Alexei lay down on the bed next to Vassily, something he had done so many times before. It felt natural to be there. Perhaps that same sensation struck Vassily, rather like a subconscious muscle-memory, because he stopped playing with the chess pieces and reached across for Alexei's crotch.

Alexei knew he should stop what was happening, but he wanted everything to be all right again, so much so that he let Vassily continue. As with the chess, Vassily could remember what he liked to do, but not how to do it. He was still grinning inanely.

Alexei brushed the hands away and drew Vassily back up towards him on the bed. He put his arms around the man whose expression was now one of confusion. Alexei closed his eyes, trying to pretend that everything was as it had once been, but the constant muscle spasms Vassily suffered because of the drug damage left him fidgeting in Alexei's arms. The dampness of Vassily's dribble reached Alexei's skin through his shirt.

Alexei felt repulsed and overcome with grief at the same moment.

Only then did Alexei tune his ears into the radio commentary of the latest hockey match in the Soviet-Canada series. It had been playing unnoticed by him during his cleaning of the flat. He needed a distraction.

The game was in the third period, tied at three goals each. Canada needed to win this, the penultimate match, to level the overall score going into the final game. The commentator reminded listeners that the Soviets needed to win this to take the series with a match in hand.

Three minutes and thirty-four seconds of the game were left. The commentary reported that a fight had broken out on the ice. Players from both sides skated over to join in, as the referees tried to separate the teams. The commentator described how Esposito had Yakushev by the neck in a headlock.

Alexei had heard about the dirty tricks of the Canadian players. He thought about his own country's dishonesty towards him and Vassily.

Mikhailov and Bergman were each given a five-minute penalty for roughing, and the game recommenced with five players on each team.

Two minutes fifty seconds were left.

Maltsev took a shot on goal. He missed. Lapointe gave Mishakov a jolt in front of the Canadian goal-net. The teams faced-off. The puck went into the Canadian zone.

Alexei wiped more dribble away from Vassily's chin.

The score was level at three apiece; the Soviets just had to hold their position.

Henderson got the puck for Canada and went down the ice. He lost his balance in a Soviet attempt to intercept, close to the Soviet goal, Henderson aimed. Tretiak had no chance to save it.

Despite the goal judge being slow to put the light on, Canada had taken the lead with four goals to the Soviet's three.

Alexei knew he couldn't leave Vassily in this condition of indignity.

The puck was back in the Canadian zone. Petrov took a shot. It was wide.

The Soviets needed to bring the game back level.

Liapkin took a shot. It was unsuccessfully.

Yakushev was stopped by Esposito in front of the net.

Ellis, with some distance from the Soviet goal, took a swing and propelled the puck forwards. It struck Tretiak hard on the shoulder, sending him down onto the ice.

Fifty-eight seconds were left.

Team Canada were trying to keep control of the puck, and the match.

Matsev intercepted, got the puck, and took a shot. Esposito saved it.

Alexei needed to take control of matters, as the Canadians were on the ice. He'd returned to Moscow with a purpose.

Twenty-one seconds left.

Alexei clung tightly to the twitching shoulders of Vassily, who looked at him. Vassily didn't understand; his was the look of someone Alexei no longer recognised.

Team Canada had the puck. It was intercepted by the Soviets, their last chance to score.

One second left. Not enough time.

The match was over, won by Canada with four points to the Soviet's three. The series was tied, with one match left, and all to play for on Thursday.

Without giving his decision any more than a moment's thought, Alexei swung himself on top of Vassily. He clamped Vassily's arms to his side between Alexei's own legs. He covered Vassily's face with a pillow and pushed the weight of his upper body down on the soft object. He would finish what the Serbsky torturers had started.

The body underneath Alexei tried to thrash around in panic. Vassily hyperventilated beneath the pillow, expelling breath in panic, but unable to replenish it with oxygen into his airwave. Carbon dioxide was quickly building up in his bloodstream.

The thrashing underneath Alexei became less consistent as Vassily faded in and out of consciousness.

Despite the effects of the drugs, Vassily was a strong man. It was that former person of physical power who was now struggling to survive; it almost made Alexei want to remove the pillow just to see the Vassily he knew one last time.

Alexei pushed down harder.

Three minutes had passed. They felt like more than an hour to Alexei. He was sodden with sweat. His arms and legs were aching with lactic acid from the exertion.

Two more minutes. The writhing stopped. Alexei relaxed his legs.

But the man underneath the pillow was not yet dead, just unconscious.

Alexei kept the pillow over Vassily's mouth and nose to make sure the airwaves could not re-open. Alexei cried a torrent of tears. He buried his own face into the thin pillow. He could feel the facial features of the man he'd just smothered through the pillow fibres. He used his mouth to feel for the lips he'd touched so many times before.

In a tender embrace, and with their mouths as close to each other as the material of the pillow would allow, he sent Vassily off to that next place with one last kiss goodbye.

Alexei wrestled control over his torrential thoughts. He was exhausted but in charge of his own mind.

Everything had now changed.

He and Vassily had been unwitting players in a game between officials either side of the Atlantic.

It was a long-standing fraud. Alexei realised he'd been the victim of a confidence trick. It had all been a lie.

He'd murdered his lover because of it.

It must be destroyed also.

Alexei switched off the radio.

Wednesday 27th September

24

COOPER BAIN felt safer hiding in plain sight.

He hoped the Palace of Congresses auditorium, inside the Kremlin wall, would be the last place the KGB would look for him.

Oleg would be there at the ballet, and Cooper wanted to talk to him. It was less than twenty-four hours before another attempt would be made to assassinate Brezhnev at the final hockey match of the series. Cooper needed Oleg's assurance that Alexei was not going cause any problems.

The story of Spartacus seemed an odd choice for a ballet, Cooper thought. As he watched two men in Roman armour ridiculously leaping and springing around the stage pretending to fight, Cooper was even less convinced the subject matter was appropriate. Spartacus, having been sent into the gladiatorial ring to fight for the entertainment of Crassus, killed his friend, before inciting his fellow slaves to rebel, so aghast is he at what Crassus had made him do.

The music stopped. The curtain closed for the interval. Cooper reflected on how much more appealing the Kirk Douglas movie version was, the premier of which he'd crossed anti-communist picket lines to see with newly elected President Kennedy at the Warner Theatre in downtown Washington eleven years before. And now he was watching a rendition inside the heart of world communism.

He shuffled along the line of seats, smiling politely at his fellow audience members. He kept Oleg in view. All senior Politburo members were given the best seats, so Cooper had found the man he was looking for quite easily amongst the other grey balding heads. Everyone is equal, but some are more equal than others he thought.

There was another important reason for him needing to speak with Oleg urgently. With the high alert in the city, his original exfiltration plan with the Canadian hockey fans was too risky. Nor could he go to the American Embassy. Oleg was the only man who might be able to help him leave Moscow.

The interval was his opportunity to make contact amid the bustle of spectators jostling for drinks. The crush of bodies jostling against each other formed a frustrating barrier. Being made of white marble pylons, glass, and aluminium, the Palace of Congresses was an expressive but austere architectural Soviet addition to the medieval fortress complex of the Kremlin, but it was not designed to easily facilitate finding a needle in a haystack.

Oleg saw Cooper first.

The meeting in the airport carpark had been an unacceptable risk but had been ordered by CONDUCTOR. Oleg considered that meeting an American CIA agent in the Kremlin, surrounded by colleagues from the Politburo and KGB, was beyond reckless.

Oleg had survived the regime of a tsar, two revolutions, three Soviet leaders, and Stalin's purges. He was not going to allow carelessness now to jeopardise all that, not least as he was poised to take over the leadership of the Party if the assassin succeeded in his task at the final hockey match.

"We need to leave," Oleg said to Raisa.

"Are you unwell?" She pretended to sound concerned for his health. She hated him.

"No," he replied curtly.

He grabbed her firmly by the elbow and led her away from the American, who was still pushing through the crowd looking furtively from face to face.

"It's time to go," added Oleg.

"I think there's a second half…" she started to explain. Her feet could barely keep up with the pace Oleg was setting.

Oleg strode with purpose towards a side door.

Once out of the main building and in a corridor, he let go of Raisa's arm. He hurried on ahead to ensure he was out of sight, leaving her to catch up. He used the connecting walkway to cross over from the austere Ural-marble modernist structure of the Palace of Congresses to the small domed seventeenth century Patriarch's Palace.

A MIDDLE-AGED usherette in a utilitarian blue suit and with her hair tied back in a neat bun barked at Cooper, ordering him back to his seat.

He had not found Oleg during the interval.

The lights were dimmed in the wood-panelled auditorium. The final few patrons took their seats.

Cooper could see that Oleg and his female companion had not returned.

Pretending he'd forgotten something, and before the dancers came back on stage, Cooper apologised to his neighbours. He shuffled back along the row to the aisle and hurried out of the auditorium.

He didn't notice two people get up from their seats two rows behind and follow him.

Copper didn't collect his coat from the cloakroom in the level below. He hurried through the empty Hall of Soviet Emblems, being the lobby of the building that minutes ago had been full of people.

He heard other footsteps on the polished marble floor behind him. He looked back, hoping it might be Oleg coming to speak to him. Seeing that it wasn't, Cooper knew that pretending he was anything other than an American spy would be futile. He was being followed. But he also realised the KGB were unlikely to kill someone within the concert hall, or within the walls of the Kremlin complex for that matter, so he ran.

Cooper's first thought was to weave his way through the fortress, through the Patriarch's Palace, across Cathedral Square and past the Grand Kremlin Palace to exit via

217

Borovitsky Tower. If he hadn't lost his two shadows, he knew taxis would be passing along the embankment. But it was a long route to take through the medieval complex that was the beating heart of the Soviet Union.

He could also head across the complex past the corniced building used as government offices to the Spassky Tower, which would bring him out into Red Square and near the Rossiya Hotel. He had a room there booked under one of his pseudonyms.

But the only gate which he definitely knew would be open at night was the main public entrance next to the former arsenal, and closest to the concert hall.

His nerves got the better of him for once and he didn't want to take the risk of finding the other Kremlin exits all locked. When out of the concert hall, he headed for the Troitsky public exit only a short distance away, but which it would be easy for his pursuers to follow him to. Once out in the streets of Moscow he would try and disappear, although the evening suit he was wearing for the ballet was a hindrance to him blending in.

He ran with as much pace as he could towards the north-west Kremlin wall. He then walked casually through the archway. He smiled at the two sentries by the first gate, who he hoped would assume him to be the first of thousands of audience members who were about to exit through the gate after the evening's performance.

As soon as he started to walk across the Troitsky Bridge, Cooper realised his mistake. He was completely exposed until he passed through the Kutafya Tower on the other side of the bridge over the Alexandrovsky Gardens. Only then would he be free from the Kremlin.

He couldn't run because the uniformed guards would become suspicious; instead, he had to hope that the two agents who he knew would be close behind would try to apprehend him only when out of the government complex. They were unlikely to know he was on non-official cover. Assassinating an American spy within the Kremlin was likely to be an unwise diplomatic move even for the KGB.

Getting arrested was a more significant concern than being shot for Cooper. Détente had to count for something.

The red star atop the Troitsky Tower was reflected in the puddles left by early evening rain. Cooper noticed this as he put his chin to his chest and quickened his pace. He walked as fast as was reasonable along the ancient cobblestones.

He didn't look back. He knew the agents would be there.

He focussed on every step taken. He rehearsed what he'd do once through the outer gateway at the bottom of the slope, exploding into an escape attempt that had little chance of success. A taxi, even though the driver would later report back to the KGB about the destination of his American passenger, would be the best option.

Cooper passed a lamppost. He was still far away from the white Kutafya Tower.

His body was tensed to take the impact of a bullet, just in case his pursuers didn't care for diplomatic protocol, but his legs kept moving forwards.

In the sixteenth century, the tower had been a bridgehead against attack, protecting the citadel from those seeking to besiege the fortress. It had played a similar role against Napoleon. Cooper hoped it would be his own bridgehead and gateway to safety now.

The drizzle turned to heavy rain.

Copper heard creaking metal and the slam of the wrought-iron gates closing at the Kutafya Tower, forbidding him exit.

He turned back. The young female KGB officer was sheltering from the rain under the protection of the Troitsky Gate. She was smiling, knowing her prey was trapped. There was no need for her to get wet.

Cooper smiled back at her, acknowledging that he knew she'd won.

He tightened his evening jacket across his chest as protection from the rain. He took a few slow steps back the way he'd come.

His grey hair was now sodden.

He still believed in ORCHESTRA and had hope that the assassin would succeed during the final game of the hockey series. The risks had been worth it, but only if the mission succeeded, and he couldn't be the one who betrayed that plan under interrogation.

He stopped walking.

He looked over the edge of the bridge. It was a long way down; perhaps too far.

MAXIM DISLIKED the ballet. He also loathed wearing smart clothes but Tara had ordered him to wear a suit so they wouldn't stand out at the Palace of Congresses.

Tara had recognised the American first.

The limp from his bandaged leg had slowed Maxim down. Tara rushed on ahead.

"What are you doing?" asked Maxim once he'd caught her up.

"Waiting," said Tara.

"For what?"

"For the American to realise he's trapped."

"Are you sure he'll know where your brother is?" asked Maxim.

"We'll soon find out," said Tara. "We found Vassily's body today so Alexei's still in Moscow."

"But he's your brother," said Maxim.

"He's a traitor," replied Tara. "Traitor's must die. Alexei taught me that himself when we lived in Egypt." She watched the American, knowing the CIA agent couldn't escape.

FARTHER ALONG the north-western wall of the Kremlin from the bridge, Alexei stood in the Alexandrovsky Gardens grotto made from the rubble of buildings destroyed by Napoleon's occupation of Moscow. He was smoking a cheap cigarette, sheltering from the rain, and waiting for the performance in the concert hall to finish.

He'd followed his mother and Oleg to the Kremlin from her apartment. After the performance he hoped to speak to her. His family were the only people left whom he trusted.

Before he declared war on the system that had betrayed him, he had to explain everything to his mother and sister, and to tell them to leave the city. The family name had survived his father's treachery; it was unlikely to survive in good repute a second time.

Alexei heard a fleshy thump and a cry of agony further along the gardens by the Troitsky Bridge. He stepped out into the shadow of the Romanov obelisk that Lenin had ordered modified to replace the names of tsars with those of Lenin's chosen world thinkers. He hurried past what looked like an ancient altar but was actually a ventilation shaft for the hidden grimy-brown Neglinnaya river which used to be a moat to the fortress.

Alexei recognised the American he'd seen Vassily meet at the Kiev rail station. Caution stopped him from approaching further.

The height of the stone bridge had been significant enough to break the American's leg from the fall. A fractured shard of bone had torn through the American's evening trousers. His lower leg was bent forwards at the knee joint. The American was screaming in agony as he dragged himself away from where he'd landed.

He saw Alexei and stopped.

"Help me," he pleaded in English. His face was smeared with blood from a head wound.

Alexei looked up to where the man had fallen from.

Tara was looking down at him. Her head and upper body were poking through the sawtooth pattern of embrasures and stone merlons that formed the crenelations on top of the bridge wall.

Two sets of the same eyes looked at each other.

Alexei noticed the gun. She'd been aiming it at the injured American but moved it in Alexei's direction.

He opened his mouth to call to her. Her expression was quite clear. She meant him harm.

Alexei turned and ran away.

Tara aimed the weapon at her brother. It was an easy shot. She couldn't pull the trigger.

Maxim joined her, with his weapon drawn, but Alexei was out of range, hurrying past the tomb of the unknown soldier.

"Was that him?" asked Maxim. Tara didn't reply. Instead she hurried down the walkway, ordering the guards to open the gate.

Once outside the Kremlin complex she paused. To her right was her brother, perhaps she could still catch up with him. To her left was the injured American.

The American had made it to the bronze bas-relief in the lower part of the Alexandrovsky Gardens. Tara approached him slowly, angry with herself for not having the strength to shoot her brother, the traitor.

The blood stream from the American's body mixed and diluted with the rain collecting in the area of the monument to Alexander I. The large monument now looked like a tombstone for the American spy.

Tara kicked over the American's body.

She'd made the wrong choice.

The American was dead.

Thursday 28th September

25

TARA WAS awake first. Maxim was still asleep in the other single bed.

She got up and walked naked around the room in the Rossiya Hotel. The room had been the American's.

The modern hotel, the largest in the world, was a place she knew well from her years spent as a swallow, the name given to girls used by the KGB to entice men into honey-traps. This room was like all the others she'd spent time in.

She drew back the heavy green velvet curtains and stood framed in the large window that had a view across towards the Kremlin.

"You'll give Brezhnev another heart-attack if he glances up and sees you standing there like that," joked Maxim, blinking into wakefulness.

"Doctors have brought him back from death several times already," she replied, neither turning around, nor covering up her naked body now that she had an audience.

"The Belorussian Zubrovka and heavy smoking probably don't help," commented Maxim. "Speaking of which." He lit a cigarette and sat up on his elbows. He looked at Tara's mane of dark hair that cascaded down her back towards the perfectly shaped buttocks at the top of her short legs. Beauty is made by the little imperfections and discrepancies, he thought. With long legs she really would have been untouchable.

"I hope he *can* see me," she said. She was playing with her breasts in full view of anyone who might look up at the window.

When she turned to face Maxim, the plump pouting expression, and eyebrows arched in concentration indicated that she'd been thinking about serious matters. Even naked, she seemed guarded, covered in armour. But his new boss was also horny for both sex and killing, so he fell in love with the soft body, whilst tolerating the hard edges of her character.

Tara padded across the room. She yanked the blankets off Maxim, revealing his naked body and his erection. She was impressed, and he knew it.

Like a jockey mounting its stallion, she swung herself on top of him. She took the cigarette out of his mouth for herself. After a few puffs she left this to burn in the over-full ashtray by Maxim's bed. He reached for her hanging breasts, but she pinned his arms out to the sides as if he were being crucified. She moved her hips, taking him fully inside her.

After a few minutes, as Maxim's expression changed from effort and pleasure to imminent release, she quickly lifted herself up and put her full weight down on his arms.

"Not yet," she whispered in his ear. She watched his face become one of frustration and confusion, even anger.

After a few seconds, Tara repositioned herself and resumed her gyrating. She moved Maxim's arms above his head, clasping his wrists together in as strong a grip as she could manage. Noticing a subtle change in his body movements, she once again lifted herself up and smiled with devilment.

"Breathe," she instructed in another whisper into Maxim's ear.

He struggled against her grip, angry at being denied that which he expected, but also desperate for Tara to resume.

Seconds later she recommenced, repeating the same orgasm control for twenty more minutes until Maxim had been reduced from man to slave.

At each separation she felt stronger, and watched Maxim weaken to her will. She wanted him to overpower her, either to succeed in throwing her off and get dressed, leaving her sexually unsatisfied, or to take control, sweep on top of her, and set the pace regardless of whether she was ready or not, whether she struggled or relaxed. But Maxim did neither.

Tara knew from her childhood years what it felt like to want what you cannot have. But two years before, in bed with the head of one of the KGB's directorates she'd found a way to take control in the same way she now dominated Maxim. The sexual enslavement of Brezhnev's powerful KGB protege back then meant that she was now a senior lieutenant in the State Security Service with forty-five days' annual leave, a good salary, and access to foreign goods.

In her high caste exclusion from normal Soviet life she'd made the system work for her in a society that doesn't usually allow individualisation. She only admired others who had done the same thing. The recent treason of her brother was as unforgiveable a show of weakness as was the meek acceptance of an exploitative system she saw in most others.

Maxim, in his style of dress and rebellion against the special forces career he could have enjoyed, had seemed different. During twenty minutes of sex, he'd shown Tara that he was just like any other weak man.

They both orgasmed, but Tara had been prepared to stop once she'd been satisfied. Maxim was lucky, that time.

"What's the plan, Comrade-Lieutenant?" asked Maxim pulling on his white briefs. His voice now included a tone of subservience that hadn't been there before the sex.

She had no further use for him, sexually.

"For you, checking the sticks-and-bricks where Cooper Bain has been over the last few days." She got dressed into the evening gown from the night before. This wouldn't be the first time she'd walked through the Rossiya lobby in the clothes worn the night before.

Maxim fell back on the bed and groaned at the boredom of his allocated task checking drop sites used by foreign agents and defectors for covert messages. Tara threw the rest of his clothes at him.

"And be thorough," she said. "Remember, people believe what they see. The primary function of that streetlamp may not be lighting, but storage."

"Yes, yes," groaned Maxim. He'd pushed the smart suit to one side and was looking through Bain's luggage for anything with an American brand name on it to wear.

Tara let Maxim leave first, then she searched the rest of the room. She kept the American dollars found, deciding that she'd use them to buy a new pair of Levi jeans at the hard-currency store accessible to KGB officers.

Most of the hotel rooms in the city were bugged, and it didn't take her long to work out where the device was most likely hidden. A small porcelain bust of Lenin, mass-produced across the Soviet Union, had no obvious compartment in which to conceal a listening device, but that didn't mean it was safe, merely that the intended subject of the surveillance was also supposed to think it harmless.

She launched the statue onto the floor of the bathroom.

Amongst the shards of cheap pottery was a small bug. It was a passive device, so called because it had to be activated, or 'illuminated', by radio signal of the correct frequency from an external transmitter. It had no power supply of its own, but the current used to operate the bell of a telephone was of a level sufficient to support such a bug in the room without the need to regularly replace any batteries.

Tara needed to check whether this specific device had been activated, but without alerting the whole of the KGB to any intelligence leads that might lead her to Alexei. She knew where to go to find the answers.

MOST PEOPLE thought The Moscow Watch Factory was just a place to make Slava watches destined for the British company Sekonda. Tara knew differently.

Behind the production lines of women seated at assembly tables compiling the timepieces was a small room. That small office was a listening post, and the place where Tara, in her days working as part of the honey-traps for foreigners, would spend much time corroborating snippets of information she'd been told by the men the Party had asked her to entertain. One of three 'keepers' rotated duty monitoring certain short-wave frequencies on one-way voice links to pick up ciphered messages. They were men Tara could rely on.

A surly, colourless functionary with a mouth of gums rather than teeth checked Tara's identification at the reception counter. He stepped away and consulted his colleagues about her request for admission to the factory.

Admittance was taking some time, as all decisions made by committee usually did. A lifetime spent in Moscow had taught her to tolerate the quintessential Russian character of such gatekeepers. Pressure or threats to hurry up were wasted on such petty officialdom. Losing face would only slow the process down even further, but neither was timid acceptance or, worse, an apology, any more of a guarantee of efficiency.

Even the most obstinate old man or woman who had carried out the same function for decades respected power and authority, when accompanied by a polite smile and the opportunity of a dignified exit from whatever uncomfortable path their inflexible nature had led them down. A détente approach in personal relationships with minor Russian bureaucrats was more effective than either seeking peace or war.

The whole Soviet system worked at the speed of the slowest, as no one feared the lack of his own action. Knowing, and understanding this, kept Tara away from difficulties with such men when other attractive young KGB females had been unable to suppress their haughtiness in such situations, and had been sent away deliberately impeded.

She smiled at the men now considering her admittance. She looked at her watch and paced around the foyer.

There was a poster by the reception kiosk with the pictures of those men and women employed at the factory who had been deemed bad parents by the parent-school soviet. The public shaming for those men who'd chosen to spend their salary on liquor instead of purchasing something of value to their child's education proved effective in some, if not all, of the cases.

Also on the noticeboard were pictures of wives who'd kept the falling grades of their off-spring from the fathers for fear of harsh punishment against the children. The poster reminded parents the committee aspired to establish ties between the educational work of school and family, to ensure parents were fully participating in the realisation of the State's educational goals.

Tara saw the propaganda for what it was. She was glad that such constraints imposed on the masses ensured she kept her privileged access to a life they could never themselves aspire to.

She was no communist.

The mulish gatekeeper approached the glass partition to announce his decision. Before he spoke the factory bell sounded, indicating the time was 11 o'clock. The glass partition was slammed shut before the decision had been communicated to Tara.

Machinery fell silent. Rows of women in matching white coats and headscarves stood and faced the same way. They were then led through a series of repetitive compulsory gymnastic exercises, the instructions for which were broadcast through the union radio, and which they followed with apathy. When fitness, like happiness, was mandatory, everyone became indifferent to it.

Tara smoked a cigarette and glanced at the array of propaganda posters littering the wall of the reception area. There was one of a smiling woman holding a corncob that gradually morphed into pails of milk and cuts of ham, it had the slogan: 'Corn – a source of plenty'. Tara knew that the government had recently asked the USA for more imports of corn while domestic agriculture continued to fail.

Neither the socialist realist artwork, nor the slogans beneath contradicting the reality of life, had any effect on Tara's morale, apart from mild amusement.

'The fate of the factory and the fate of the country are as one!' proclaimed another faded poster. As she stared back into the factory, at the automatons following their radio-broadcast exercise instructions like lack-lustre robots, she hoped this particular poster was not meant literally. She needed the country to continue as it currently did to guarantee her advantages. She opposed anything that threatened that, even her twin brother.

The radio announcements finished. The staff resumed their work, and Tara was granted entry to the factory.

Valentin was the opposite to the grey-faced hollow-cheeked man who had granted her entry to the factory floor. The electronic reconnaissance expert spent most of the year running this small listening station, but he took a break every Christmas.

His large belly and huge white beard made him the perfect choice to play the role of Grandfather Frost. It was also a lucrative source of additional money, going house-to-house in costume for five roubles to cheer up the children and take a glass of vodka from their parents. Valentin could drink, and drink well, but, as the years advanced and his liver weakened, he had been sensible enough to enlist the help of young women dressed as snow maidens to help the progressively inebriated Grandfather Frost get around all the houses on his route. Tara had been one such snow maiden, and would happily be so again, regardless of her advancing position within the KGB.

She found Valentin in the dusty room staring through half-moon glasses perched on the end of his bulbous nose, trying to fix a piece of equipment with a set of children's plastic tools.

"Hard at work, Valentin Ivanovich?" asked Tara.

"There's a shortage of good-quality tools," he grumbled. "I'm forced him to be creative with the contents of my grandson's toy-box."

"Perhaps I can help with that," suggested Tara. "Where everything is forbidden, anything is possible." She tapped the end of her nose and winked conspiratorially. "And I know where the gaps in the fence are."

"If only you could," replied Valentin.

"I have certain connections," whispered Tara, "outside the KGB."

"Alas, my dear Tatiana Ivanovna even the black market can't supply what I need to make this junk work properly." Valentin knew he could be candid with the woman whose tears he'd dried over many years when she'd cried with disgust at the things she'd been made to do in the name of comradeship and duty. Valentin was used to fixing things which were broken, whether human or machine.

"Are you still busy here?" asked Tara, fingering pieces of listening devices that were scattered haphazardly around the small workshop.

"Less so since the Lyalin defection last year," he replied, referring to the betrayal which had led to Department V (Victor) having to replace those Soviet officials in Britain whose identities had been exposed. It was that treachery by Oleg Lyalin which had led Tara to be recruited into Nikolai Borisovich Rodin's 'wet ops' team. New jobs became available on a large scale during the reshuffle of personnel. She was grateful to Lyalin, who'd betrayed his country for the freedom to live in northern England with his secretary.

"A terrible thing," she said insincerely, just in case.

"What brings you back to old Valentin then?" he asked, pleased that someone still valued his expertise. Tara sat down to explain her request.

By the time Tara left the watch factory, Valentin had confirmed the American had not been in touch with his embassy. There was a contact in Moscow, somehow connected to the university, who Cooper Bain had been told would be at that night's final hockey match of the series. But she didn't have any confirmed names or identities from the interceptions Valentin had found.

She paused outside the dilapidated factory while a line of young Pioneers in their blue hats, shorts and red neckerchiefs marched past. She was pleased at seeing indoctrination, especially in the young. They'd all transition into the Komsomol on their fourteenth birthday, and from there become the next generation of volunteer guards in factories like the one she'd just left.

With a certificate, badge and armband, these brain-washed drones would hopefully keep order amongst the masses, preventing anyone from organising dissent and daring to expose the privileges enjoyed by the class to which she now firmly belonged in her own right, not just in the false reflection of her dead father.

In the era after Stalin's terror there had been a vacuum, one which Brezhnev's oligarchy were determined to not let be filled by those who threatened their elite status. For several months, if not longer, Tara had come to fear that her brother was one such dissident because of the sexual deviancy with other men she had suspected.

Alexei's treachery against the Party at the sports stadium had proved beyond question that he was her enemy.

Washington D.C.

26

THE MARINE Corps major had to ask for directions to Henry Kissinger's office. He'd been inside the West Wing only once before.

Entering the room and coming to attention, he knew the tall, grey-haired, straight-backed figure standing in the sunlight of the floor-to-ceiling windows was not the president's national security adviser.

"We're borrowing WOODCUTTER's office for the morning, come in major," said the other man in the room. This man was dressed casually, too casually for the White House, thought the major. "He's with SEARCHLIGHT at CACTUS discussing Vietnam, so you can relax."

The major dropped his shoulders inside his olive-green service uniform. He'd been due to accompany the presidential party to the Camp David retreat for the Vietnam conference, so he was hoping one of the two men in Kissinger's office might explain the reason for his last-minute redeployment.

"My colleague does love to use codenames," said the man standing by the window. He was looking out across the north lawn to where the press camp was situated. "I'm told you're someone to be trusted, major."

"Thank you, sir," replied the marine.

"My name's Alan Rawlings. I work with the president." The man by the window turned around. "One of the testimonies from the Senate subcommittee hearing a few months back has stayed in my mind: how do you ask a soldier to be the last man to die in Vietnam? How do you ask a man to be the last one to die for a mistake?"

"I'm not sure I understand, sir," replied the major.

Alan Rawlings cast his eyes over the marine's smart uniform. He shrugged himself out of whatever melancholic moment had preoccupied him. He was now suddenly more jovial.

"Have you ever been in the Oval Office, major?" he asked, like a child with a new toy he wanted to show off to everyone.

"The colonel usually has that honour, sir," replied the major.

"Then now's the time," said Rawlings. He looked across at the young CIA agent, who gave the smallest nod of approval. "We're in luck, Miss Woods is with the president at Camp David, so there's no irascible gatekeeper to throw us out."

The three men walked through one of the concealed doors into the famous office. King Timahoe, the president's red Irish setter, leapt off one of the plush yellow sofas and hurried towards them. Rawlings brushed the dog aside, irritated by his presence. The marine major crouched down to make a fuss of the excited presidential pet. The major had heard that 'Tim' could shake paws on command.

"Paw," said the marine. He was amused to find out the rumour was true.

"Manolo...Manolo!" shouted Rawlings. He crossed the room to the secretarial office calling for the president's valet, not realising he'd be in Camp David also. "Take the damn dog," he added. A junior secretary called for the dog. Rawlings closed the door once the dog had rushed past him.

"Bloody animal." Rawlings brushed dog hairs off his flared flannel trousers.

The marine found it unreal to be in the room which seemed so familiar from television coverage, and yet so peculiarly unfamiliar in reality. This was the room where Kennedy had played hide-and-seek with his young son; where Eisenhower gave his address about sending federal troops into Little Rock to enforce school desegregation; and where Elvis and Nixon had shaken hands only two years before. It was a room with a sentimental attachment for a proud American such as himself.

He went over to the east doors and looked out to the Rose Garden. He touched the gold drapes, feeling the quality of the fabric, and the door handle; these seemed to him like the only things it would be permissible to touch.

"Impressive, isn't it major?" asked Rawlings. The marine nodded, trying to take in every detail of the room. "You're lucky, when people come in to meet the president, they never get a chance to really absorb the room itself. Most couldn't describe its furnishings once back out in the hallway even if they tried."

Alan Rawlings led the marine over to the huge double-pedestalled glass-topped mahogany desk that dominated the room. In a conspiratorial tone he said, "Take a seat, son."

"I don't think I should, sir," replied the officer. He looked across at the scruffily dressed man standing by the fireplace, whose silence seemed to give him authority. The CIA agent didn't offer any objection to Rawling's suggestion. The marine allowed himself to be eased into the president's black leather swivel-chair.

From the most powerful seat in the world, the marine major looked out across the room of yellow-gold furnishings and royal-blue oval rug in the state colours of California with the presidential seal in the middle. On the desk was a glass star also emblazoned with the presidential seal, a pen stand, and a black phone that he could only imagine had conveyed world-changing instructions. Alan Rawlings sat in one of the striped armchairs flanking the desk.

"I need you to do something for me. In fact, the president needs a favour." He paused to judge the marine's reaction, which seemed receptive. "There are some files in the colonel's office relating to man called Cooper Bain that the president needs to disappear, today." He hoped that the major, sitting behind the president's desk in the Oval Office wouldn't be able to deny him anything at that point.

Before the major had arrived in Kissinger's office, the CIA agent, one of only a few men in Washington who knew about ORCHESTRA, had doubted that Alan Rawlings would succeed. Being able to convince the second-in-command to the Marine Corps colonel serving as the president's military aide to destroy secret files seemed unlikely. They'd become aware these documents were in the colonel's office, to which they had no access without raising questions. Watching the marine officer lean back in the president's chair, his mouth wide open in awe at the unbelievable situation he found himself in, the agent was confident that everything connecting Bain to the White House would soon be wiped clean.

"We need you to bring the files to us at this address." Alan Rawlings scribbled an address down on the same notepad used by the president. He handed the slip of paper to the marine. "Do you think you can organise that today?"

The marine hesitated to take the piece of paper from Rawlings.

"It's very important that you don't tell anyone else," added the CIA agent. For emphasis, he walked over to the desk and slid his CIA identification across the president's desk. "Even if the colonel notices the files have gone. You've aware of the Espionage Act, aren't you?" The marine nodded. "You don't want to be the next Daniel Ellsberg."

"What is it you do, sir?" the marine asked of Rawlings, still not accepting the piece of paper with the delivery address on.

"I work on political intelligence operations for the president's campaign," replied Rawlings. He could tell they were losing the allegiance of the officer, so he changed his approach. "Which is how I know about the calls you've been making to your friend, the staffer on the House Defence Subcommittee." The marine's body visibly tensed.

Rawlings continued, "That's a lot of congressional dollars for your daddy's firm in Iowa that the two of you are arranging. I wonder what Representative Mahon would have to say if he knew about the abuse of his Committee."

The marine officer's head dropped in shame. He took the paper from Alan Rawlings.

"You'd best get on then, major," said Rawlings. He stood aside to let the marine leave. Alan Rawlings was a man whose career had taught him to know when and whether wielding a hatchet or a feather was most suitable.

"Do you think we can trust him?" asked Rawlings on his way back to Kissinger's office with the CIA agent.

"We tend not to rely on trust in the Agency," replied the agent with a cynical smile.

"What does that mean?" asked Rawlings.

"He won't be a problem once the documents have been dropped off later today."

"I don't think I want to know anymore."

"Few do."

"And ORCHESTRA's still safe?" asked Rawlings, his tone now more deferential than when they'd met in the bowling alley a couple of weeks before. "Despite the loss of Bain?"

"If Brezhnev dies, then Nixon can distance himself from the arms treaties he so dislikes just in time for the election campaign. If Brezhnev lives, then the White House can't be implicated in any investigation, once those Cooper Bain files disappear."

"Watergate and the Fielding burglary have made us nervous around here," added Rawlings. He'd been confident of getting the major's cooperation. His earlier melancholic reflections to the marine about honourable men being asked to die for a mistake now seemed more prescient due to the CIA agent's hint about the major's fate.

"That's your mess," replied the agent. "The State Department will remain ignorant of the White House attempt to re-freeze the Cold War, whether CONDUCTOR's mission at Luzhniki is successful or not."

"I wonder if the two enemies realise how similar they are?"

"In what way similar?" asked the CIA agent.

"The serfs were emancipated in Russia at the same time as we had the Civil War here. Our frontier was pushed westwards by cowboys, and theirs eastwards by Cossacks. Both of whom were considered criminals at the time. And here we are dividing the world up between ourselves. It seems like a peculiar series of similarities to me for us to be fighting each other."

"You're worrying me, Alan," said the CIA agent.

"I'm no Commie-sympathiser just in case you're going to scribble this down in some dossier on me," said Rawlings.

241

"Your file's already pretty full," joked the CIA agent. He left Rawlings standing outside Kissinger's office as he strode out through the lobby.

Moscow

27

THE CELL floor was covered in dirty water and human excrement. The holding cell was not designed to keep prisoners overnight, so there was no bed. The raised wooden platform bolted to the wall was the only feature in the eight feet squared room that would usually hold half a dozen inmates awaiting charge, but which had been reserved exclusively for Alexei. The assistant prosecutor and investigator were keeping their prisoner hidden from others. They hadn't even informed the KGB.

At the shift change later in the morning questions would be asked if the KGB had still not been told of his capture. There was only a matter of one or two hours left for the corrupt duo to force a confession from Alexei.

After the third beating, Alexei had still refused to sign the statement which stated he'd been well treated. The paper also had a confession for treason and the murder of Vladimir at the Luzhniki stadium. It seemed both the investigator and assistant prosecutor wanted to solve a few outstanding crimes, and Alexei was a suitable fall guy for several assaults, thefts and vandalism that had been added to the bogus statement.

The clear ups that had nothing to do with Alexei would enable the assistant prosecutor to meet his quarterly quota; actual suspicion or guilt of the accused was a secondary consideration at best. It was this desire for bureaucratic fraud that had kept Alexei's name away from the KGB since his arrest when fleeing from the Kremlin wall the previous night. The fear of redeployment as warden at a penal colony in the forests of the far north was enough to encourage the assistant prosecutor to keep his high-profile prisoner's name away from the KGB for as long as possible to elicit the confession he'd hastily written once Alexei's identity was known to him.

The light switch was outside the cell door, and had not been flicked on, leaving Alexei in a darkness only mitigated by the light creeping in from under the cell door. The toilet was also in the corridor, access to which had to be granted by the guard upon request, something which Alexei refused to ask for as he knew it would be denied.

He felt disappointment more than anything else. Not fear or anger but regret and confusion.

The sister he loved, the twin of himself with whom he shared a closer bond than with any other, was working against him. She'd hidden her true relationship with either the KGB or the CIA, and Alexei had been oblivious, trusting the sister he met, and never suspecting that a different person was concealed behind the facade. He regretted not now being able to ask her why she'd deceived him for so long. Tara had seemed unrecognisable when looking down at him from the Kremlin wall with the gun.

His father, his lover, and now his twin sister had all kept secrets from him.

Vassily's expression at Serbsky had been one of understanding, if not forgiveness. He'd stared at the mirrored glass, knowing Alexei, his betrayer, was seated the other side watching his torture. But Tara's expression had been one of hatred and cruelty. Many an actress playing the role of Lady Macbeth would be envious of the message Tara's eyes conveyed to her brother the previous night at the Kremlin.

Alexei coughed to clear his throat of the fetid fumes of his cell.

Everyone had lied to him. The Party he'd been loyal to since childhood, the father who should have protected his children, the twin sister he'd shared his whole life with, and the lover he'd felt safe next to.

Alexei was alone now.

Everything had been taken away from him over the last few days.

He drew his knees up to his chest. He was overcome with a peculiar sense of emotional liberation. With everything that had mattered to him now lost, it felt as if he'd been cleansed. The loneliness he felt, if that was the correct term, had the opposite effect to that expected; it made him feel peculiarly complete, and free.

There were no guy-ropes keeping him tied to anything or anyone. There was nothing missing in his life, quite the opposite. Everything was as it should always have been. He now saw all those in his life in their most honest form.

He felt strong.

He was unencumbered by guilt, duty, or love.

There was no ventilation in the cell, making the smell from the floor excrement, combined with the years of cigarette smoke embedded in the damp and porous stucco walls, even more potent. The air was so putrid, it felt to Alexei as if his eyes were burning.

His feet had been stripped bare by the guard who'd taken a liking to his relatively new shoes. The faeces squelched between Alexei's toes each time the beatings had forced him off the wooden bench. His clothes had become sodden with sweat within thirty minutes of being put in the cell due to the stifling heat.

The insect-ridden chamber was also visited by the occasional rat that scurried across the floor and disappeared back under the cell door.

The barracks of a barbed-wire labour colony seemed preferable to his current internment conditions. Alexei knew the Soviet Union would never permit him exile to Siberia. Even a life sentence served at the infamous prison called simply '6/12' three hours' drive from Moscow would be too much to hope for.

For him it would either be Serbsky, or a firing squad.

Knowing this to be his fate emboldened Alexei to not let the fire in his belly that had made him leave the kolkhoz and return to Moscow to prove his innocence, dampen, even at this most desperate of times. He was a Guards officer first and foremost, trained to the highest standards of courage. He would use that training to now punish those who had trained him.

Once transferred to either the Lubyanka or Serbsky, there would be no opportunity for a show of defiance, but while he was in the pre-trial police centre in Moscow he could at least try and free himself; to fight back against something and someone.

The beatings had been conducted by both the investigator and duty guard. Alexei couldn't fight off two strong men, but he knew eventually the investigator, more used to paperwork than brawling, would tire and leave the prison guard to continue the brutality for the little time that remained until the KGB had to be informed of his arrest.

When he heard the key turning in the heavy metal door, Alexei didn't have any plan for his attack, but he remembered from his military training that anything can become a weapon if used as such. There was nothing in the cell, apart from the damp clothes he was wearing, and the filth he was standing in.

The first pile of wet shit flung by Alexei hit the guard in the eyes as he stepped into the cell with the wooden club ready to continue the beating. The guard backed up in disgust and hurried to remove the excrement from his face, disregarding the danger this put him in from the prisoner.

Alexei started to beat the guard with the wooden club that had been dropped. The bruises on Alexei's back no longer hurt as they had done moments before. Where his skin had been broken earlier, the pain similarly eased as Alexei unleashed his fury.

The guard, able to see once more, fought back. Alexei pushed the wooden club lengthways under the guard's chin and applied as much pressure to the man's throat as he could manage.

His chance of escape was now more than just a hope.

The guard choked and passed out.

Alexei used the keys to unlock each of the doors in the basement corridor of cells, every one of which was crammed with dozens of desperate filthy men in spaces no larger than the one he'd just freed himself from.

Chaos would be his best chance of escape from the building when the alarm was raised. Once released by Alexei, some prisoners chose freedom and ran to the stairs, while others settled for revenge against the prison guard. The muffled cries as the guard woke to being abused in the most brutal fashion gave Alexei a moment's pause as his conscience debated whether to try and rescue the young man who would now suffer a more unpleasant death even than those at Serbsky.

Alexei carried on up the stairs with those prisoners who'd chosen escape.

Even morally, he now felt a sense of freedom. He didn't care if dangerous criminals were set free against his new enemy of the Soviet state.

The wave of liberated inmates overpowered the guards who tried to quell the surge. At each pinch point, some prisoners were successfully detained, but Alexei remained at the back, letting those in front create a channel to freedom.

After slipping behind a few prisoners who'd decided to raid the commissary for cigarettes, Alexei burst out into the street along with half a dozen others. The sirens of Militsya patrol vehicles could be heard approaching.

Alexei was completely disorientated about where he was.

A vehicle came to a screeching halt next to him, and the passenger door was pushed open.

"Get in!" shouted the driver to Alexei.

Alexei didn't recognise the driver. He paused.

A heavy blow to the back of his head knocked him unconscious.

28

IT WAS light when Alexei opened his eyes.

His head was aching, but the bed was clean, soft and warm. It was tempting to stay cocooned under the sheets and pretend the last few days had been a nightmare he was only now waking up from. But this wasn't his bed, and he had no idea how he had come to be sleeping there, or even where he was.

He reluctantly, and quietly, got up.

The filth had been cleaned off him. He padded barefoot across the polished wooden floor to a mirror. His face was, at first glance, shocking due to the bruising, cuts and swelling from the beatings received in the police cell. Nevertheless, his wounds had clearly been treated, and he could smell the medical lotion on his skin. The smell was something familiar to him from his years as a Guards officer, when witch-hazel had used by medics to reduce swelling, repair broken skin and fight bacteria. He barely recognised his own face, but prodding the injuries only made them hurt more, so he turned away from the grotesque reflection.

The room was sparsely furnished. The items present were clearly of very good quality and looked like antiques. The small square-shaped room had wood panelling and freshly painted ornate cornicing.

A clean set of clothes had been left out for him on a chair. He got dressed quickly.

With his ear to the door to listen for movement on the other side he carefully turned the handle. It was locked. He tried again, with more force. Nothing. He kept his ear to the door panel but couldn't hear anything outside.

There were windows on three sides of the room. The view was of parkland, forest, and a large ruined neo-gothic palace of terracotta stone with white detailing. It was not somewhere he recognised. He tried to open each window, but all had been bolted shut and were locked.

He was a prisoner. Whether this was to keep him in, or others out was yet to be confirmed. Had he been saved or captured, he wondered?

He took the small mirror off the wall, wrapped it in bed linen and smashed it against the side of the table. Unwrapping the broken glass, he selected a suitable shard, tore a strip from the bed sheet to protect his hand from the sharp edges at one end, and made himself a weapon.

The key turned in the lock.

Alexei hurried across the room. He pressed his back to the wall and concealed the makeshift weapon behind his back to maintain the advantage of surprise.

"I didn't expect it to be you, Comrade-General," said Alexei. He instinctively stiffened his body coming to attention. His commanding officer from the Border Guards entered the room and closed the door. Alexei gave a half salute, unsure whether this was someone he could still trust.

"Not every surprise is a bad one, Alexei Ivanovich," replied General Pavel Ivanovich Zyryanov, the sixty-five-year-old military leader. "To ease your nerves, I'll stay over this side of the room, I imagine you're finding it hard to trust people at the moment."

"I am, Comrade-General."

"I think we're way beyond formalities, and I've recently retired anyway." The general stayed by the door as promised. "Please call me Pavel Ivanovich. I'll even let you keep that shard of glass that you're trying to hide, if it makes you feel safer. Although I assure you, I'm here as a friend not an enemy."

Alexei pretended to look confused at the accusation that he had a weapon.

The general smiled at Alexei's bluff and said, "There was a mirror here earlier, which is now missing. I'm assuming the broken remains are in that pile of discarded linen, so don't look so innocent. I'm glad to see your training with us continues to prove useful. You may need it for a while yet."

"Where am I?" asked Alexei. He kept the weapon in his hand but held at his side where it could be seen. He'd been deceived by too many people to trust the assurance of an amiable old soldier.

"As you know, your mother is a close friend of mine —"

"Does she know I'm here?" interrupted Alexei.

"No, she doesn't. She did contact my former office though, which is very brave of her considering recent events. I haven't yet spoken to her. I found out everything I needed to from others." Zyryanov, the son of a Kazak railway worker, was a hero of the Soviet-Japanese war, and a veteran of the Hungarian uprising in nineteen-fifty-six. He had reformed the tactics of frontier forces and was widely regarded by the Council of Ministers and the men who served under him with equal respect, something unusual in the Soviet Union. He was one of the Soviet elite. Alexei had trusted him years before, but not now.

"And you're here to elicit a confession?" asked Alexei with undisguised hostility. He was angry that the KGB had enlisted yet another one of those on the list of people he'd trusted to persecute him.

"I know you're innocent. I did by instinct, but I've been doing some investigating of my own, which proves it, at least to me." He ran a strong hand through his thick salt-and-peppered coloured hair to make sure nothing was out of place.

"So, I'm absolved of blame?" asked Alexei, feeling encouraged.

"Far from it, I'm afraid. I merely said that *I* knew you were innocent. The snippets of evidence to prove that would be easily dismissed by a prosecutor."

"But with your support, a man of -"

"I would simply be tied to the firing squad post next to you. You know how things work here, Alyosha." He called him by the pet name used only by Alexei's family.

"Then it's hopeless," muttered Alexei. "You may as well have left me back at the police station."

"Remember your military training, Captain. The battle's not over yet, and I have a plan." There was a twinkle in the old general's eye. "Shall we go for a walk? I'm an outdoors man."

Alexei followed his former commanding officer through the small house and out into the parkland. He left the shard of mirror on a table by the front door.

"Where are we?" asked Alexei. He glanced across at the palace they walked slowly past. Alexei's limbs were aching and his head thumping, but the general was not a man to be rushed.

"It's called Tsaritsyno; we're a few miles to the south of Moscow."

"I've never been before," said Alexei.

"The main palace was built on Catherine the Great's orders. The Empress visited when it was nearly complete, but she didn't like it. A new architect was brought in to redesign things, but Catherine died before completion, and her son had no interest in it. The unfinished remains have been crumbling here for two hundred years."

"An Imperial folly," interjected Alexei.

"Still the dedicated revolutionary I see," chuckled the general. "I think the place is quite romantic. Some of the buildings have been restored, like the little lodge you were in, but otherwise it is as you see it."

"And not somewhere the other KGB officers are likely to come looking for me?"

"Exactly," said General Zyryanov. "The guards I brought along with me can be trusted, not that I've told them who you are anyway."

"Won't they think this all a little odd? A recently-retired commanding officer from the Border Guards hiding someone out here."

"It's not that peculiar. I'll let you into a little secret. The more military-centred side of the security apparatus uses this place, and others, for our own purposes occasionally. We don't want those in the other directorates to know all our secrets." Zyryanov was KGB, in fact he'd sat on the Council of Ministers as a member of the Board of the KGB, but it was not one homogenous organisation. The rivalries between departments often led to disputes and divisions.

"So what's your plan? For me?" asked Alexei as they meandered through woodland. The foliage was still predominantly green, but some brown leaves were beginning to appear scattered on the ground. "Do you know about ORCHESTRA?"

"I do," replied the general, "but don't worry, I'm not going to ask you any questions about it, this isn't one of those soft interrogations designed to make you feel comfortable until you betray yourself."

"I have nothing to confess."

"Quite so." They walked on a few more steps in silence. "So let me tell you a little something about ORCHESTRA you don't know. They have someone in place to attempt the assassination again at tonight's match."

"Really?" replied Alexei. He was still not willing to trust the general by disclosing he'd met the English assassin, nor that the foreigner had known his parents years before. If the comment had been a test, the general didn't show any signs of Alexei having failed it.

"We'd like you to stop him."

"Who is *we* exactly?" asked Alexei.

"A small group, mostly military, or former military who don't want to see someone like Oleg Grigorevich Zhirov assume the top job."

"So, you're loyal to Comrade Brezhnev?" asked Alexei.

Pavel took a second to think about the question, then replied, "Not especially. We're loyal to détente."

"Why not just ask the Comrade Chairman not to attend the hockey match tonight?" Alexei was trying to problem solve the issue in a way that didn't require him to put his head straight into the lion's mouth.

"He won't be," said Pavel.

Alexei looked confused by the general's comment.

"We're fortunate that Comrade Brezhnev is rather distinctive in his appearance," added the former general. "It wasn't difficult to find some others who could easily assume the same appearance with some theatrical make-up. We have a pool of two hundred and forty million people to source the look-a-likes from."

"Then let the assassin try his luck," suggested Alexei.

"That seems rather harsh on the pensioner from somewhere in south-western Ukraine who thinks he's going to a hockey match tonight instead of his own murder," rebuked the general.

"Sorry," apologised Alexei. His comment had been careless.

"Anyway, it's not the death of Comrade Brezhnev, or the uncertainty of the succession that is chief among the considerations. Any attempt, even if unsuccessful, will destabilise things between us and the Americans. Our Foreign Ministry and their State Department have worked very hard to keep things as they now are. The last thing either wants is a refreeze of relations."

"Even if the assassin is working independently? If that can be proved —"

"Small details like that will be easily lost in the rhetoric of the war mongers on both sides of Churchill's iron curtain," interrupted Zyryanov.

"I'm still not sure why you need me, your troops from here can be deployed to stop the assassin."

"True, but we can't show our hand," said Zyryanov. "There are powerful elements in the KGB. And they want a change of leadership."

"I feel like a sacrifice," said Alexei.

"You're a soldier. And you've met the assassin," said the general. Alexei, realising Zyryanov knew even more that he'd assumed, didn't reply directly.

"What's to stop me from leaving here right now? I could easily outrun you, Comrade-General. Even if I stop the assassination, you've already said you can't help me prove my innocence."

"You don't have to outrun me, Alyosha. I have no intention to chase a man forty years younger than me." The general chuckled to himself with amusement. "I'd suggest you do try to escape, if it will make you feel more like you're nobody's puppet. But if you think you're faster that the two hunting dogs following us, then good luck to you." Alexei had seen the soldier leading two dogs at a discreet distance when they left the vicinity of the ruined palace, so he didn't need to turn around to check whether the general was bluffing. "Shall we sit down for a rest?" asked the general.

They'd arrived at a dilapidated stone pavilion with pillars. There were recesses with seats. The view on one side stretched out dramatically down to a small stream and stone bridge set in the meadow.

"So, I am a prisoner?" asked Alexei.

"Only for as long as it takes an old man like me to finish saying what I had you rescued outside the police station for. Then you're free to do as you choose, and I shall keep the dogs at heel, that I promise you, if you're still giving any weight to promises from friends."

"I'm listening Comrade-General, I mean Pavel Ivanovich."

"As strange as it may seem, Alyosha, you're the only man we can be assured is not part of ORCHESTRA. I've arranged for your exfiltration to a neutral country after the match, regardless of whether you choose to help us or not. It's an unconditional offer for the son of a dear friend of mine. But I hope you're not yet so disenchanted with your country that you'll refuse to carry out this last order from your commanding officer."

"I'm not a traitor, that I can assure you," said Alexei. "But neither am I sure what my feelings towards Russia are anymore."

"That's understandable, but don't confuse the government, or the Party, with the country. I can still appreciate the beauty of this park, even if politically I detest the autocracy that commissioned it two hundred years ago. I can feel great pride in our tactics against Napoleon's invading Grande Armee when listening to Tchaikovsky's overture without having any love for Tsar Alexander the First. And I can proudly wear the uniform of a country, my country, regardless of who occupies the post of Party Chairman for the Soviet Union."

"I'm not sure the two things have ever been, or could be, separate for me."

"Then you will either fail in the mission I've given you today, or not even attempt it. I don't criticise you for that, but I would be disappointed."

"And if I succeed?" asked Alexei, being slowly convinced by his former commanding officer.

"You won't be a Soviet hero. No crematorium spot is reserved for you in the Kremlin wall next to Gagarin."

"Near to yours?" asked Alexei with an attempt at light-heartedness, despite how he felt and the circumstances he was in.

"Hardly." The general patted Alexei's shoulder. "No one will ever know what you'd done. But being an unacknowledged hero is surely better than a dead traitor, albeit if that is a mistaken accusation?"

"I have to ask you about something else," said Alexei.

"Your mother?" asked the general. "I shall make sure she's safe."

"Thank you, but I was going to ask about Tara. I saw something…I don't think I can trust her."

"You can't." Zyryanov lowered his chin. "I wasn't sure you knew."

"Knew what?" asked Alexei. He was hesitant to hear the answer in case it confirmed what he suspected himself after seeing his sister's expression and the gun pointing at him from the Kremlin wall the evening before.

"It seems your sister has got it into her head that she can only save herself by being the one responsible for your capture."

"How can that be, Tara's my sister, my twin?"

"Don't underestimate the power of self-preservation. Surely the biblical story of Cain and Abel is familiar to you?"

"I've never read a bible," replied Alexei.

"Romulus and Remus then, quarrelling over who is most favoured by the gods, and disagreeing over their plans to build the city. Cleopatra and Ptolemy weren't just brother and sister, but husband and wife, that didn't stop her ordering his murder, and those of her other brother and sister."

"That's ancient history. Mythology and fairy tales," said Alexei getting angry. "This is real, and now. She pointed a gun at me!"

"Killing the person closest to you? That's not new," said the general. Alexei thought of Vassily, and the part he'd played in his death. "Constance Kent from England killed her brother with a razor blade because her father showed him more love than she."

"You've made your point," muttered Alexei, feeling uncomfortable at the thought that Tara could be capable of killing him.

"Save her from doing something she'll never forgive herself for, Alyosha. Help us, and then leave Moscow, before Tara finds you. I promise to protect your family once you're gone."

They left the pavilion and continued the walk in silence through the criss-cross of tree-lined pathways.

"You're on your own from here," said the general. They'd reached the gatehouse. "Whatever you decide to do," added the general, "be there at midnight."

He passed Alexei a piece of paper with an address on it. Alexei memorised the address and handed the paper back.

"Thank you," said Alexei.

The general gave him a pistol and a spare ammunition clip.

"Just in case," said the general.

Alexei took the weapon.

"Use your training, Alexei Ivanovich, it will help you."

The two men shook hands.

Alexei tucked the gun under his jacket and walked through the gate towards the main road.

HAVING SENT Alexei back to the city, the general returned to the lodge.

Pimen's aria from the opera *Boris Godunov* was playing on the record player.

"This has always been my favourite opera," said the person listening to the crackling recording, "ever since I saw it performed at the Bolshoi."

The general stood patiently in the doorway, while his guest finished a cigarette.

The person known as CONDUCTOR waited for the aria to finish, then stubbed out their cigarette.

"Will he do it? Go to the stadium?"

"I imagine so," replied the general. He was ashamed that he'd been so successful in convincing the young soldier to do as instructed. But he hadn't told CONDUCTOR everything. He could still help Alexei. For his mother's sake. "Alexei should create enough of a distraction for the police and KGB in the stadium to leave you free to finish the job."

"Good, then I've got a hockey game to get to."

29

BIL YAXLEY had become very cold whilst waiting for Raisa to return to her apartment building.

Raisa walked along the street. She saw him in the distance. He raised his eyebrows in acknowledgement of having seen her also.

She took a detour.

Bill followed cautiously.

They met only briefly in the street. Stopping as two acquaintances might to say a few words of greeting and pass the time. They didn't shake hands, kiss, or have any physical contact, just in case Raisa was being followed.

They walked off together. They turned down a side street. There was just enough time for Bill to slip a piece of paper with directions to the room at the university in Raisa's pocket. This period of only one or two seconds was referred to by spies as 'the gap', being the moment when anyone following them wouldn't be able to see.

A man in a brown suit turned down the street behind them. Bill and Raisa were already a couple of feet apart from each other. If their shadow were a surveillance officer, there would be nothing to suggest an exchange had taken place.

At the end of the street, saying goodbye, Bill and Raisa continued in separate directions.

The hour and place stipulated in the message for Raisa left her with very little time to meet Bill. She needed to go home and get changed first. More sensible shoes than her current ones would be needed.

She was wheezing heavily upon her arrival at the granite bust of the scientist Ivan Pavlov near the main university building. The row of busts lined the pond and fountains. She was regretting never having quit smoking, something she'd been promising herself for nearly five years.

Raisa had foregone the usual flamboyance in her style. She'd tied-up her cascades of raven-black hair under a beige turban-style hat. She was almost unrecognisable in a grey skirt-suit, red blouse, and flat shoes. She waited for Bill.

As with the clandestine meetings many years before in Egypt when Raisa had snuck away from her husband to meet Bill, the exciting young British spy, she had a brooch pinned to the left lapel of her jacket. Bill would remember this as the signal that it was safe to acknowledge each other.

Had the brooch been on the right side, then he would walk on by, knowing Raisa had been followed. Then they would not meet. Bill used to have a pen slipped in his jacket pocket for a similar signal depending on which side of the pocket it was clipped to.

Bill walked past Raisa, but neither acknowledged the other.

The pen was positioned correctly in his pocket and the brooch was pinned on the safe side of Raisa's jacket.

Raisa waited a few minutes then followed the next direction that had been on Bill's instructions. She walked through the university campus to a building undergoing renovation.

"Is it safe?" she asked as soon as Bill entered the lobby behind her.

"I've been gas-baggin' with one of the gardeners while you walked here. No one followed you," replied Bill. He checked once more before closing the door.

"Is Alexei here, is he all right?" Raisa hoped that Bill would have found her son, their son.

"No, I'm sorry."

"Oh God, Bill. Where is he?" Raisa embraced Bill and kissed his neck, trying not to cry.

The familiar perfume worn and hint of tobacco that she'd always smoked brought back memories of passion to Bill that he'd not allowed himself to think about for many years.

"What do we do?" she whispered in Bill's ear. She released him from her grip and placed a foot on the first step of the dusty stairwell. She cast her eyes up to where she'd hoped her son might be waiting, the son she now knew was still lost.

"Hold up a minute," replied Bill, taking Raisa by the hand to stop her.

"Is he dead, Bill? I've prepared myself."

"I think he's still alive."

"How? Why?" she asked impatiently, pulling against his strong grip.

"A contact of mine called CONDUCTOR thinks Alexei will be at the game today. I can get him out of Russia tonight."

"But?" she asked. She stepped away from the stairs.

"I need you to convince him to leave. I need you there tonight. Even after everything that's happened, he'll think there's a way to clear his name, and he won't trust me."

"Can he?" she asked, "trust you, I mean?"

"How can you ask that?"

"I'm sorry, Bill," she said. "Ignore me."

"To the State he's either a fool or a traitor, and they treat both the same way."

"But you can help him?" she asked.

"There's a truck that has an engine tank modified with a compartment that he can fit in. It leaves Moscow from the Novodevichy convent in five hours. I hope he's not claustrophobic."

"The Americans?" asked Raisa.

"I wouldn't trust them anymore than I would the Russians," replied Bill. "It's an exfiltration route used by the crime gang known as the 'brotherhood'. I've done the odd favour for 'em. But my credit doesn't extend to an open invitation. This is a one-time offer."

"If we can find Alexei tonight, I'll convince him," promised Raisa.

"There's something else," said Bill.

"What is it, Bill?" She looked fearful.

"It's Tara." Bill shook his head, not sure how to tell her what he knew. Raisa covered her mouth to stifle a potential scream. Bill stepped back and lit a cigarette which he passed to Raisa. He lit another for himself. "I think she's with the KGB."

"That's not a surprise to me. Our daughter's very secretive, Bill. And ambitious." Raisa was relieved the news wasn't worse.

"But she's trying to find Alexei."

"Good."

"You've got it all wrong. I think she means to kill him."

"Never." Raisa's hand was shaking as she took the cigarette out of her mouth, her eyes frowning in disbelief. She wasn't trembling with surprise, but with fear that the daughter she'd never been able to love enough might betray her own brother, her own family. There was something about what Bill suggested that didn't seem implausible; that was frightening.

"I don't like the idea of it any more than you do," said Bill.

"You're wrong, Bill," replied Raisa.

"Let's hope so," he said.

"Will you stay, Bill, after tonight. In Moscow. Whatever happens? I can't stay here on my own."

"You know I can't, Raisa."

"I'm used to you leaving," she replied, her tone heavy with resentment. "Because of Margaret."

"I love you both. But I owe her more, for all those years she's stayed with me while I was…well, they didn't nickname me 'Wild Bill' for no reason now, did they?"

"While I raised our children, alone. That earns me nothing I suppose?" Raisa's comment was followed by a silence from them both, acknowledging something.

"She doesn't deserve the pedestal you've put her on, you know?" Raisa immediately regretted what she'd said.

"What do you mean?" asked Bill.

"Ignore me; it's just spite."

"Look at me," ordered Bill, turning Raisa to face him. "I've interrogated enough people to know when someone's lying. What did you mean, about the pedestal?"

"Nothing." Raisa tried to free her arms, but Bill's grip just tightened. "I'm just upset, I was saying any old thing. Ignore me, Bill, darling please!"

"Tell me again that it's nothing," insisted Bill. "Let me see your eyes as you deny it a third time."

"Please stop asking me, Bill." Raisa didn't trust herself not to reveal the secret she knew to the man she loved, something which she had always known would hurt him. But, with her children in danger, she was not herself.

"Margaret doesn't deserve your malicious lies."

"All right Bill, I'm just a hateful jealous woman!" screamed Raisa, shaking herself free from his grasp.

Once out of his grip, she had nowhere to go.

They both stood, eyes cast downwards to the dusty floor.

"You ain't none of them things, Raisa, which is why I know there's something about Margaret you're not telling me. I want to know what it is. We don't have time for you to play silly games. Alexei needs us."

"Then let's go, forget about this. I shouldn't have said anything. I'm sorry." She tried to take Bill's hand to lead him towards the exit. He pulled away from her, walking back up a few steps of the stairwell, indicating he was not leaving. Raisa turned to face him, trying to decide if he was bluffing. She couldn't gamble with her son's life.

"All right, Bill." She let go of the door handle and walked across to the stairs, looking up at him standing a few steps higher than her. "It was Margaret that betrayed Ivan, back in Egypt."

"She couldn't have done. Betrayed him, how? Why?"

"Jealousy. Perhaps she wanted to hurt me, or maybe she knew it was a way of ensuring the children and I returned to Russia, where you couldn't get to us. I don't know why, Bill, all I know is that she confirmed what Alexei had told the Rezidentura in Cairo about Ivan and the Americans. She provided enough corroboration for them to believe Alexei. That's why they killed Ivan."

"It's not true," said Bill, sitting down on the stairs, steadying himself against the wrought-iron banister. "How would you know this anyway?"

"I've seen Ivan's file."

"Why didn't you tell me?"

"I haven't always known. Once I was back here, after a few years a gentleman friend of mine in the Border Guards showed me the file before destroying it. I needed to make sure Alexei couldn't have any stain as he started his career."

"You should have told me," said Bill.

"There seemed no reason to. I couldn't have you, so she might as well. Saying something wouldn't have helped you."

"I don't believe it. The files could be wrong. I need to get back to ask her."

"And you will, Bill. But we need to save Alexei; you and me."

Bill stared ahead blankly. The information about his wife seemed so inconceivable and yet part of him believed it.

"Come upstairs for a minute, Bill," suggested Raisa. "Do you have a bottle of something up there? We've got some time for a quick drink before the match, haven't we?" She needed to get him out of his shocked state quickly. She needed Bill to help her son.

Bill struggled to stand up as Raisa pulled his arm from under the shoulder. He had to sit back down to rub his knees, which had seized up.

"We've got time," he replied, knowing he needed a drink.

"Neither of us is so wild anymore, hey, Bill?" joked Raisa. She wiped away a tear that had formed in the corner of her eye. She once again helped Bill to stand up.

"YOU DON'T look much like KGB," said the gardener.

"Who said I was?" asked Maxim. He was dressed in flared jeans and a turtleneck jumper.

"That's who I called," replied the gardener, "and here you are."

"How long have you been working here, comrade?" asked Maxim.

"About four months."

"And what made you suspicious about this man you saw?" asked Maxim.

"Well, the building over there was being upgraded, but the workmen got moved to another project about four weeks ago." The gardener pointed across at the dormitory building. "I saw the old man coming and going over the last few days and that seemed odd."

"Perhaps he's working there," suggested Maxim. He was irritated that the gardener's call had got through to Tara, and that she'd sent Maxim down here to ask more questions. The final hockey match of the series started soon. After a day spent pointlessly checking drop sites around the city, he was eager for the match.

It was only the memory of Tara in the bed that morning that made him acknowledge the instruction to meet her. She'd cast some sort of sexual spell over him by bringing him to the edge of orgasm and then repeatedly denying him that pleasure.

Fortunately, the university campus was only a short distance from the Luzhniki stadium where the hockey match was taking place. He could still make the game, assuming whatever enquiry Tara needed him for proved to be a dead-end.

"This man's too smartly dressed to be a builder," said the gardener.

"But what prompted you to call us, today?"

"He asked me for a light for his cigarette," said the gardener.

"So?" asked Maxim, growing impatient.

"When I asked for a cigarette in exchange, a box of matches fell out of his pocket as he reached for the cigarettes."

"Being absent-minded isn't a crime, comrade."

"His accent sounded foreign," said the gardener. He was excited to have discovered what he thought was useful information for which he might be rewarded.

"What accent?" asked Maxim. He checked his watch.

"I don't know. When the woman arrived, they both went inside the building."

"A woman?"

"Yes. Middle-aged," said the gardener. "She's not a builder either," he added mockingly.

"Watch it," warned Maxim.

266

Maxim saw Tara striding towards him across the lawn. Whatever annoyance he'd felt about being summoned here dissipated. She was the untouchable woman he'd now touched, more than touched in fact.

When he saw that she was without any other agents, Maxim also knew that Tara had decided their close partnership should continue. He felt trusted and intimate. The hockey match was now of no importance.

TARA HAD reluctantly summoned Maxim to assist her. He'd given over his power to her too easily in the hotel room that morning. He'd shown her just how easily he could be controlled.

However, finding her brother was a priority. Being the one to deal with him would protect her against any residual suspicion that might be cast against her. Maxim was someone she now knew could be easily controlled and would be unlikely to report being summoned to the university to anyone else. Other agents all had line managers and secondary managers to report to who were monitoring the activities of the first manager, such was the pervasive sense of mistrust in the KGB at that time. Maxim's rebelliousness and lack of institutional loyalty made him useful to her, for now.

"Has anyone come out since you've been here?" she asked of Maxim. She didn't acknowledge the gardener.

Maxim expected some sign of intimacy between them. Tara gave none.

"No one," replied Maxim. He felt the rejection.

"And you haven't told anyone about meeting me here?"

"Why?" he asked.

"It doesn't matter," she said. "Let's go inside."

"There's a woman with the old man," said Maxim.

The stairwell was covered with residue dust from the renovations. Tara tracked the footprints in the dust up to the third floor, where they stopped. She drew her gun. Her finger twitched over the trigger.

Maxim left his gun in the pocket of his jacket. The intelligence report from the gardener confirmed an old man with a foreign-sounding Russian accent had been making use of the building, and that a middle-aged woman had recently met him there. To Maxim, the report indicated an illicit sexual affair. But Tara clearly had an instinct that the people were connected to her traitor brother.

Tara pushed open the door to one of the sets of student rooms where the footprints in the dust led her.

The corridor smelt of paraffin.

Tara walked forwards silently on her toes. She took deep enough breaths to wrest control over her nerves.

Maxim waited disinterestedly by the door.

She walked towards the room where the smell of recently extinguished paraffin was strongest. The creaking sound of Tara's knee-length leather coat seemed to echo down the empty corridor. She tried to keep her arms still so as not to disturb the leather more than necessary.

She paused for no more than two seconds to exhale a deep breath.

Tara stepped into the room.

Her gun was raised.

30

RAISA WATCHED from a window on the second floor of the dormitory as Tara and a young man walked out of the building, having left the floor above. Her instinct was to rush outside and ask her daughter to explain why she was there; to plead with Tara to help her find Alexei.

"That confirms she's KGB," whispered Bill. "I saw the gun."

Raisa considered whether to argue against Bill's statement, then said, "They've gone."

She glanced down at the length of metal pipe Bill had armed himself with. He'd picked it up after pushing Raisa into the second-floor room when someone entered the stairwell as they were leaving the dormitory building.

"You don't need that," said Raisa. It was a rebuke. She was horrified that he'd even considered hitting his own daughter with the weapon. Bill put the pole down, understanding Raisa's tone, and feeling ashamed of himself.

Raisa looked back out of the window as her daughter strode across the lawn. Tara looked different, so much so that Raisa even questioned if the confident, serious woman really was her high-spirited, girlish daughter.

"I've got to speak to her." Raisa pushed past Bill.

"Why?" asked Bill. He grasped Raisa's wrist to stop her.

"We can look for Alexei together. She obviously has connections with the KGB we didn't know about."

"If she was trying to help him, she'd have told you about those connections before now, wouldn't she?"

"Of course she's trying to help him. He's her brother, her twin brother; they're two halves of the same thing, Bill." Raisa was irritated. She tried to unlock Bill's fingers from her arm. "Something you and I created," she added, hoping this reminder would weaken his grip.

"I hope you're right," replied Bill. He didn't defend himself against the clawing, but neither did he release his grip. "But it's clear she ain't got any more of an idea where Alexei is than we have. She came here looking for him."

"I need to go to her, Bill."

Her scratching had begun to draw droplets of blood on Bill's loose-skinned and aged hand. Her shoes were slipping on the rubble-strewn floor she fought against him.

"I know," he replied.

His grip remained in place, but he'd begun to question his own assumption that Tara, his daughter, was looking to betray her twin brother. Only Tara herself could contradict that unconscionable theory.

"Let me go," pleaded Raisa. "Please, Bill."

"I won't," he replied. He decided to trust his instinct, even if the information about Margaret had made him begin to question everything. "You can't help her." He pulled Raisa into his arms.

"Then who can?" she asked. She pulled herself away from him and straightened her back.

"Perhaps I can," he replied.

Despite the warnings, Bill knew Alexei would have gone to the hockey match. Alexei knew CONDUCTOR had commissioned Brezhnev's assassination, and Bill's earlier failed attempt was unlikely to be the end of it. Bill's most recent contact with CONDUCTOR had not been reciprocated so there was a chance that someone else had been asked to carry out the assassination. If Alexei had gone to the stadium, then so must he.

"Rescuing Alexei will save Tara from herself," said Bill.

"Save them both, Bill," Raisa instructed softly, hopefully. "I'll do whatever you say."

She stepped aside. Bill released his grip. He kissed her on the cheek; it was a kiss promising something he knew would be difficult to deliver.

Raisa felt a hollowness in her gut at the thought of Alexei not coming back to her. It was a greater anticipated grief than for Tara. She crossed her arms against her stomach. The conscious realisation of something she'd always known about her feelings for Tara made her feel undeserving of motherhood. There was no survival without Alexei.

"Stay here until I've left, then head to the stadium. I'll find you there," instructed Bill. "We can't be seen arriving together."

Raisa was too upset to reply, she just nodded her agreement.

The evening had started to draw in and she flicked the light switch on once Bill had left. She was surprised that the bulb worked.

She moved around the room. She lightly touched the few items left by the builders. She untied her hair, shook it out, and sat on the only chair in the room. She held the sheet from the bed to her face as she cried, muffling the sounds in case Bill returned.

Despite the years of high living as one of the Moscow elite, she now felt poor at the prospect of being without her son, the most miserable person in Moscow. She felt worse, realising the lack of a similar feeling she had for her daughter.

Her life had been one of regrets, and she had never minded that her son seemed to have such little affection or even friendship for her. She had been happy to worship him from a distance. But the prospect she now had to consider, if Bill failed, seemed unbearable.

HAD MAXIM not asked Tara whether he could now go to the match, she wouldn't have turned around when getting into her car. Had she not looked back, then Tara wouldn't have seen the light being switched on in the supposedly empty building they'd just left.

They crept slowly back up the stairs, knowing they would now find someone in the dormitory. It was someone who'd deliberately hidden from them.

Maxim now also drew a gun from his pocket.

Tara left her leather jacket at the bottom of the stairs.

The palm wrapped around her pistol was damp with sweat as Tara adjusted her mind, getting ready to shoot her brother and those harbouring him; there would be no hesitation as there had been after the opera at the Kremlin when the American died. She had no father, and a mother who was more interested in entertaining powerful men than in raising children. That had been Alexei's fault.

Finding out about Alexei's complicity in the ORCHESTRA plot, and his fugitive status, had come as a surprising relief to her. She was ready to pull the trigger of the gun that her finger now tightened itself against.

The light from the room drew Tara and Maxim towards it. They both stepped through the door frame with their weapons drawn.

Tara recognised her mother. She lowered her gun.

Raisa, relieved to see her daughter, stood quickly. She dropped the bed sheet.

Maxim fired. Two quick shots. As he was trained to do.

He'd misjudged how tall the target was as she'd stood up. The second shot missed her head.

Raisa fell.

Her body bounced off the chair onto the floor. A fast-moving stream of spreading blood mixed with the dust and rubble.

"I thought she had a weapon under the sheet," he explained.

Tara didn't react.

"Fuck!" exclaimed Maxim.

"It's all right," said Tara in a whisper. She grabbed Maxim's arm as he rushed forwards to her mother's body.

"Who is she?" asked Maxim. He kept his gun raised in case anyone else came into the room.

"I don't know," lied Tara.

"I'll get help," said Maxim. "She's still breathing."

"No," said Tara. She quickly wiped a tear away from her eye. "Leave her. There's nothing we can do now."

She led Maxim to the hallway.

"Let's both go and enjoy the match," she suggested. "Neither of us wants to explain what happened here."

She kissed him.

"I'll follow you," she said.

Maxim was pleased of the permission to leave.

Tara turned back to the room. She concentrated on the trail of her mother's blood as it formed a channel through the dirt on the floor. She could hear her mother's gurgling breaths.

A feeling of relief surprised her.

Tara walked down the stairs to meet Maxim.

31

THE LUZHNIKI sports complex was full of spectators awaiting the start of the eighth, and final game of the hockey series. The score was level. This match was the decider.

The blue jeans of the three thousand Canadian fans contrasted with the grey burlap trousers of the Soviets. The crowd of sports fans was almost outnumbered by the uniformed security presence that had been brought in for the game.

Inside the Sports Palace the Canadian fans on the six-hundred-dollar package trip had created a party atmosphere. They waved flags, and cheered, "da da Canada, nyet nyet Soviet." A trumpet was being blown and passed amongst the foreign fans as the Soviet police tried to find the culprit of the disruptive noise.

From outside the stadium Alexei could hear the noise. He needed to use his training in the art of warfare to plan a way into the heavily guarded building. He might get lucky and pass through the security checkpoints without being identified as the KGB traitor. But the cuts and bruises to his face would set him immediately apart from the other spectators and raise the interest of all the uniformed personnel in the stadium.

He'd been trained to turn a weakness into a strength.

He stole a tracksuit from the merchandise stands with ease. In a nearby public toilet cubicle he looped his feet into the elastic stirrups of the bottoms and zipped up the shiny fabric of the track jacket emblazoned with the letters CCCP on the back plate.

Alexei hurried to the side entrance of the stadium. He kept hidden for a few minutes. The remaining staff of the Soviet hockey squad arrived, and Alexei joined the huddle of men and women wearing the same tracksuit as he now was. The bruises on his face made him a plausible member of the Soviet hockey squad. His entry into the sports stadium went unchallenged.

ACCESS TO the stadium would be difficult for Bill.

He arrived after most of the Canadian fans had already entered. His description from the department store chase a few days before would have been circulated to all security staff on duty at the match. Everyone would be looking for him and his supposed accomplice, Alexei Dimichenko.

At the first attempt on Brezhnev's assassination, CONDUCTOR had duped the KGB, specifically Alexei, into ensuring Bill's access to the stadium and the target was almost completely unhindered. Bill had no such assistance this time. He would have to adopt a more creative method of infiltration. This meant identifying weak points of the enemy and either bypassing the strongpoints or isolating them using deception and attack.

Having been inside the Sports Palace before, Bill had the advantage of knowing the layout. He was likely to get caught, so he prepared for that eventuality. Remaining calm was the priority, not letting panicked thought processes lead to bad choices. If caught, stealth would become useless, and force would be needed.

The principles of successful infiltration he'd been trained in during the war highlighted the need for clothing that was suitable to the environment, and a means of knowing the whereabouts of the enemy at all times to judge when to move and when to remain. Using his training, Bill kept a safe distance from the area until he'd carried out enough reconnaissance to determine the weakest entry point.

The outer boundary had mobile patrols, static guards, and dogs.

Bill bought a meat patty from one of the food stands. Into this he squashed a tranquiliser tablet, what other assassins called a hush puppy pill. He threw the meat across for a guard dog which was tied to a long rope; this dog was the only one without a handler.

The dog ate the meat. He paced around, stumbled, then laid down on the tarmac. The animal was unconscious.

Bill administered a syrette filled with adrenalin to reawaken the dog once he was safely past. An unconscious dog would raise suspicion that the perimeter had been breached. Bill was always thorough.

He approached the stadium at the point where a solitary guard was out of the sightlines of the colleagues either side of him around the perimeter of the Sports Palace.

Bill smiled and waved at the guard – this was the last thing a suspicious person would do. This made the guard hesitate. He slowly raised his 9mm submachine gun. He didn't even shout 'stop'. That uncertainty was all that Bill needed. He sprinted the last few metres and, in one fluid movement, was behind the hesitant young man. Bill pressed a trench knife against the guard's throat, ensuring immediate compliance.

"Move!" ordered Bill. He marched the guard into the building. "I *will* kill you if you speak," Bill added. He held the guard's submachine gun in his opposite hand to that with the knife, ready to open fire if he found himself walking into a hotspot.

They were in an empty section of the maintenance corridor. He'd been lucky so far, thought Bill.

"Give me your uniform," said Bill.

"No, I –" The guard stopped speaking when the tip of the knife pushed harder against his neck. Bill stopped just short of puncturing the skin.

It was only a couple of minutes before the guard was dressed in just his underwear and socks.

"Turn around and put your hands behind you," ordered Bill. The young guard turned his back and put his hands behind him. His pressed his wrists together ready to be tied.

The blade of the trench knife sliced open the guard's throat. Bill cut cleanly from one ear to the other, severing the guard's windpipe and veins. The young man tried to call out for help but was rendered mute by the surging gurgle of blood his hands tried to stop in the last seconds of consciousness.

It was a quick death. It was a necessary death.

Bill had no intention of leaving a witness alive to raise an alarm and describe him to others. He'd only let the guard live long enough to strip so that no blood would stain the uniform Bill would now wear. This was war, and the survival of his children depended on its success.

Once the blood had stopped pumping out of the dead guard, Bill wrapped the neck wound in his old clothes to prevent a trail being left. He dragged the dead body out of sight.

He set fire to some old newspapers left in the corridor and covered the pool of blood with these. A sprinkling of sand from the fire bucket helped to disguise the origin of the mess, should any patrol come by.

Bill cracked his knuckles, flexed his knees, and stretched his back to remove all tension in his joints.

He tuned into the security service channel using the guard's radio. He had now infiltrated the building and had both the clothes suitable for the environment and means of tracking the enemy.

THE USSR tracksuit that had allowed Alexei to enter the stadium so easily would have become too distinct once he was inside. He found a staff locker room and changed into maintenance overalls. The door he walked through brought him unexpectedly rink-side.

In front of Alexei, Parise for Canada slammed his stick down on the ice in frustration, causing it to splinter. He swung the broken hockey stick at the referee.

Uniformed police pushed past Alexei.

From the Canadian team bench Harry Sinden threw a metal chair onto the ice in protest at his team's treatment.

As the police and military surged forwards, Alexei hurried backwards to the corridor behind the seats.

He looked at a building map on the wall to check where he was.

The smell of his sister's perfume reached Alexei a second before he felt the gun pushed against the back of his head. There was no need to turn around.

Neither sibling spoke for a few seconds. Alexei was waiting, either for his sister to alert others on the radio to their position, or for the shot.

Tara said nothing.

Alexei could feel the gun barrel shaking against his head.

"Not as easy as you thought?" he asked.

After a pause Tara said, "Don't be so sure." Her voice was unusually timid.

"Why, Tara?"

"Be quiet," she ordered. "Please." She put both hands on the gun to try and steady the weapon.

"You'll never forgive yourself, trust me, I know." Alexei wondered if his sister was alone. He still had his back to her.

"Vassily?" she asked. Alexei didn't need to reply. "That was a mercy killing after what you done to him."

"And you have no clemency for your twin brother?" he asked.

"I hate you." She jabbed the gun forward against the back of her brother's head. "You've ruined everything."

"You'll kill me for access to blue jeans and Wrigley's gum?"

"No. But I could kill you for our father."

"It's a bit late for that, Tara."

She lowered the gun and took a couple of steps backwards. Alexei kept his back towards his sister, waiting for permission to turn around, and to know that it was safe.

Tara had lost track of time. The end of the period caught her by surprise. A surge of spectators burst through the doors to stretch their legs, use the toilet, or get refreshments ahead of the next twenty minutes of the hockey game. The crowd engulfed Alexei.

When he turned around, Alexei's eyes met Tara's.

The spectators had pushed her back, creating a distance between the siblings, something she hadn't resisted.

She was crying and her shoulders were slumped forwards.

278

Oleg and several uniformed KGB officers surrounded her. Maxim, on Oleg's instruction, took the gun from Tara's hand. She could have alerted them to her brother and saved herself. She didn't. She hated Alexei, but hate wasn't enough to kill someone she'd loved so deeply, only love could do that.

Alexei ran towards his sister. He used his elbows to push people out of the way. He was shouting, trying to make himself known and to give Tara a chance to escape. But the noise of the crowd was too loud for him to be heard.

"Alexei Ivanovich! It's so good to see you!" exclaimed Yuri, Alexei's neighbour from the Gorky Street apartment.

Yuri took hold of Alexei's arm. Maria, Yuri's wife, blocked Alexei's path to his sister.

"I'm glad we've found you," said Yuri. "Maria and I wanted to thank you again for the tickets."

Alexei tried to keep Tara in sight, but she was soon lost amongst the mass of spectators.

32

BILL HAD searched the stadium thoroughly during the first two periods of play. He hadn't found Raisa, Alexei, or Tara. The locations most suitable for an assassin to take a shot at Brezhnev were also unoccupied.

He positioned himself as others in the same uniform as himself had done at a security checkpoint while he continued to listen on the radio for information which would either lead him to Alexei, or to whoever CONDUCTOR had arranged as the new assassin to complete the ORCHESTRA mission.

As the crowd spilled out from their seats at the end of the second period Bill was trying to think of a new plan. There was only twenty minutes of the match left. Alexei's exfiltration with the crime gang from Novodevichy was a one-time opportunity, and the clock was ticking.

He plotted and replotted ideas, thinking about tactics to identify Alexei in the stadium. He followed each idea through to the same conclusion: dead ends.

There was only one scenario which achieved the necessary outcome.

To save Alexei, Bill realised he would have to kill Brezhnev and let himself get captured.

Bill considered whether that had always been CONDUCTOR's plan. Maybe there was no other assassin. However, after contact between them had ceased, there was no way CONDUCTOR could guarantee Bill would attend the hockey match, much less that he'd realise he had to be the one to complete the assassination.

The only reason Bill was back at Luzhniki was to save Alexei. Bill was sure CONDUCTOR couldn't know Alexei was his son. The only person who knew that was…

…Raisa.

The moment of revelation was as if someone had just given Bill the final piece to a jigsaw which only now made any sense. Bill wondered if he, the veteran assassin, the man who'd outwitted some of the world's most accomplished criminal minds, could have been duped by the woman he fell in love with nearly thirty years before in the aftermath of the war: Raisa Dimichenko?

Bill questioned the last thirty years. Had Raisa, realising her husband was working for the Americans in Cairo, been the one, not Margaret, who'd betrayed him and secured a life of luxury for herself back in Moscow? Had she been the mysterious Soviet contact known as CONDUCTOR for all these years, supplying Bill with lucrative contracts?

It seemed so unpalatable, and yet completely conceivable to him now, that the rebellious gypsy-like woman he loved could be the most loyal of Soviet agents. Was she someone who had meticulously plotted the events of this last month's hockey series to guarantee that Oleg became the next Soviet leader? Had Raisa hoped to sit as the true power behind the Politburo throne?

Bill felt sick with the taste of betrayal. Everything fit together too easily. There was also a slither of respect for a fellow operative, one who had bested him for decades. Raisa Dimichenko should have played against Bobby Fischer at the recent chess championship, instead of Spassky, thought Bill; she had been several moves ahead of them all for years.

He couldn't believe it.

The crowd started to dissipate as people returned to their seats for the final period of the match.

Amongst the remaining spectators Bill saw the face of the middle-aged woman who was so familiar to him. She hadn't seen him. She looked pale.

Bill questioned himself to make sure he wasn't seeing things. It was definitely her. He was in disbelief that she was there.

He followed a few metres behind her, undetected in his disguise. The uniform also eased his path through the spectators who instinctively moved away from anyone in uniform, especially those walking with such purpose.

Bill made sure he chose the right moment. As the woman approached an access door to the maintenance corridor, Bill paced forwards quickly. He grabbed her by the elbow and thrust her through the door.

Those spectators who'd seen it just shrugged at the brutish behaviour of the uniformed officer. They were glad on this occasion it was not them being apprehended for the office supplies they'd deliberately double ordered, or the petrol stolen from the company vehicles to be sold on the black market. Every Soviet citizen expected a leather-gloved hand to suddenly land on their shoulder.

"Evening, Bill," said Margaret. She smiled. She reached into her coat pocket for the gun.

"Looking for this?" asked her husband, holding up the compact pistol he'd found in the pocket of her long denim coat.

"That was quick of you. But of course the arthritis is in your knees, your hands are still as sharp as ever."

"Tell me it's not true, Margaret. Tell me you're here by accident, here to help me." The whirr of the refrigerators for the stadium rink meant that Bill had to step closer to be heard.

"And you'll give me the gun back, so we can head out there like Butch and Sundance? This isn't a romantic reunion of husband and wife, Bill. But I would like the gun back; it's a prototype for the Soviet high command that will be missed."

"What are you doing here?" asked Bill. "Did the British send you?"

"No, Bill."

"Then who? Why?" he asked.

"Haven't you guessed, darling?"

Bill didn't reply.

"I'm with the Soviets," she said.

"You're working…" He couldn't believe it. "For them?"

Margaret nodded.

"How? No, I mean why? Since when?" His words couldn't keep pace with his thoughts.

"All along." She smiled; it was almost an apology, but not quite.

"For our whole marriage?"

"I'm afraid so, Bill. Even longer than that in fact."

"Does your sister know?" Bill realised it was a pointless question as soon as he'd asked it.

"There is no sister, Bill, in France or anywhere else. All those trips were back here. Do you mind if I smoke?"

It seemed strange to Bill for his wife of thirty years to be asking permission to have a cigarette. He nodded his agreement and didn't even tighten his trigger finger when she reached into her coat.

Margaret lit two cigarettes in her mouth and held one out for her husband, as she had done hundreds of times before at their semi-detached house in Buckinghamshire. When Bill didn't move forward to accept it, she cast the second cigarette off to the side with a shrug of her shoulders.

She seemed unrecognisable to Bill. Margaret had never been a shrew-like woman, but neither had she ever seemed quite so self-confident, to the point of arrogance.

"You seem pleased with yourself," said Bill. It was an accusation.

"I'm not going to apologise and there's no need for me to give you a confession, Bill."

He was distracted by a faulty fluorescent strip-light flickering above Margaret. He shot the bulb, covering his wife in shards of glass. It pleased him to see the flash of fear on her face. She brushed the fragments off her shoulders and shook more out of her honey-ginger hair.

"You know it all, just connect the dots, Bill. I often thought you'd realised, when you'd slump into a bad state, that deep melancholy of yours."

"I thought it was me that was throwing things off kilter in our marriage, that's why I got like that."

"I won't say it was all there for you to see, I credit myself with more skill than that, but no one can keep up the act for three decades without the odd slip."

"An act." From his tone it wasn't clear whether he was asking this as a question or making a statement.

"I do love you, Bill, or I grew to. I enjoyed being your wife." She took a deep drag on her cigarette. "For Christ's sake Bill, I am your wife. They didn't warn me about that. There's a truth to some of it."

"Truth?" he asked.

"Bad choice of words." She took more long drags on her cigarette. The nicotine was helping to steady her inner nerves which were masked by an exterior calm.

"Who recruited you?" He was trying to review the pieces of his life, as she suggested, seeing everything in a different light.

"Kim Philby. I'm not so much the fourth man, as the token female." She could see the pain on her husband's face, a man she'd spent her whole adult life with. "It's like someone having an affair, Bill. There are lies of course, but enjoying a dinner together in a restaurant, laughing at a comedy show on the television, these things were real."

"And in bed?"

"Yes, that to, I suppose."

The roar of the crowd reached them in the maintenance corridor. Bill looked up towards the noise.

"NONE OF this makes any sense," said Alexei.

Yuri and Maria had taken him to the large loading bay of the Sports Palace, where they had a car parked.

"You weren't placed in our apartment by accident," explained Maria. For months she had, as the apartment steward, been nothing but hostile towards Alexei.

Maria now fussed over him like a devoted aunt. She checked that his facial wounds. Then she rummaged through a bundle of her husband's clothes to find something suitable for Alexei to get changed into.

"Placed?" asked Alexei, accepting the flask of vodka offered to him by Yuri.

"The old accordion player who'd lived there before isn't really in a Siberian work camp," explained Maria. She held up a sweater to see whether it might fit Alexei. "I concocted a show trial to free-up a room for you. The accordionist is living happily in a very nice apartment in Leningrad. His new neighbours might not be so pleased. I really don't miss that infernal noise."

"But who? Why?" asked Alexei. Everything was moving too fast for him. He was also worried about his sister.

"We have a mutual friend in General Zyryanov," explained Yuri. Maria turned her back for Alexei to get changed out of the tracksuit. "He's your guardian angel."

"More specifically, your mother is the guardian angel," added Maria, "but the general can pull the levers for her." She also took a swig from the flask of vodka.

"He made sure we were here tonight, a pair of faces you'd recognise to help get you away from here if needs be," said Yuri. He stuffed the discarded overalls into a nearby bin. "At the end of the match, when all the official cars leave, we're to join the motorcade and drive you to the exfiltration point arranged by the general."

"I can't leave," insisted Alexei.

"Don't be foolish," rebuked Maria. She turned back around. "That was a narrow escape back there. The young woman with the gun was about to shoot you."

Alexei hesitated then said, "She's my sister."

FROM BELOW the stadium in the maintenance corridor Bill heard the roar of the crowd. It was followed by a rousing rendition of, 'Oh Canada, we're number one!'

"Well, I guess the plan's failed," said Margaret. "Brezhnev will be ushered away fairly speedily, if indeed it is Brezhnev sitting up there."

"You'd really have let me kill him? And get caught?" asked Bill.

"If you hadn't, I would have. But that's what you do, Bill. You wouldn't have enjoyed retirement in the Home Counties playing bridge with people like Sir Hilary Redfern. This was to be your blaze of glory to go out on."

"I'd prefer bridge to torture, or to breaking rocks in Siberia."

"Don't be so dramatic, Bill. I'd left instructions with Oleg for you to be dealt with –"

"Humanely?" he asked, interrupting.

"Quickly, and painlessly."

"You're all fucking heart, Maggie." Bill was still recovering from the shock, but his grief and surprise was turning to anger.

"So, are we going to stand like this all night?"

"I know people who would like to talk to you, maybe even to make the mysterious CONDUCTOR a decent proposal. I'm assuming a second honeymoon in say, West Berlin's out of the question?"

"It is, Bill. No one ever leaves the KGB."

"What made you so sure I'd come here tonight and kill Brezhnev?" he asked.

"Alexei."

"You know about him then?"

"Of course. I've always known. He wasn't supposed to be part of this, but when he accidentally stepped into ORCHESTRA, I realised he'd be useful."

"Callous bitch."

"Guilty," she replied with a smile. "I'm a killer, Bill. Just like you."

"There have been others?" he asked. He still couldn't believe it.

"My first kill was back in forty-seven. I rammed a thin knife into the skull of an Austrian diplomat during the final notes of *Boris Godunov* here in Moscow at the Bolshoi. It was easier getting you to do the dirty work all these years, but make no mistake, Bill, I can still ram a knife into a man's brain if I have to."

"I'm beginning to believe it," he replied. "Is he dead, my son?"

"I gave instructions for him and his sister to be arrested but not killed. With your death and Oleg, essentially their stepfather, as the new Soviet leader, that should have exonerated them. But you've messed my plans up rather."

"And Raisa? She was gonna meet me here."

"I'll tell you what I know, Bill." She took a few steps towards her husband. Bill stiffened his grip of the gun. "But on one condition."

"Go on," said Bill. He didn't step backwards.

"You give me the gun." She held out her hand.

Bill didn't hesitate.

He released the clip, freed the chamber, and handed the pistol to Margaret. He threw the loaded clip off to the side.

"Both guns, Bill," said Margaret. She held out the other hand. "If you really want to know where Raisa is."

"You want full disarmament?" he asked. Margaret nodded.

He similarly dismantled the Makarov that had belonged to the owner of the uniform he was wearing. He threw the clip away, out of both their reaches. He also tossed the Makarov itself down the corridor away from Margaret.

"That's détente, comrade," said Bill. Neither of them was now armed.

Margaret shrugged her acceptance of his compromise.

"Police were called to investigate a report of shots being fired at a disused dormitory building behind the university before the match started," said Margaret. "I assume that location means something to you," she added.

She walked up to her husband. She stood on her toes to kiss his cheek, as she had done during many years of marriage. Bill's body didn't respond. Her lips were icy cold.

Margaret whispered into his ear, "Goodbye, Bill."

He watched her slowly walk across the corridor and out through the door. He then hurriedly reclaimed the Makarov and clip.

By the time he was back in the main area of the stadium with a loaded gun Margaret was nowhere to be seen. He had other priorities now anyway.

"YOU CAN'T come with me," said Alexei. He held out his hand for the car keys. The roar of victory from inside the stadium made its way down to them in the loading bay.

"Our instructions from the general are quite clear," said Maria. She didn't give Alexei the keys.

"Well, I'm giving you new instructions," said Alexei. "Too many people have been hurt already. I won't let you put yourselves in danger; you've got children."

"Maria, give him the keys," said Yuri. He lifted his wife's hand that held the car keys. "He's right."

"Get out of Moscow, Alexei," instructed Maria. "Go to the address the general gave you." Maria pressed the car keys into Alexei's hand, but wouldn't let him go. "You can't help Tara now, leave that to the rest of us once you're safe." She clasped her other hand over his. "Promise me that this hasn't all been for nothing. You must get out."

"I promise," replied Alexei. As he kissed Maria on the cheek, she released her grip of the keys.

Alexei shook Yuri's hand, and hurried to the car.

Yuri and Maria walked back to the stadium to join the spectators leaving the building through the regular exit points. Alexei inserted the ignition key and let the car's engine turn over. His friends had secured a Volga sedan, a vehicle reserved for doctors, lawyers and government officials, so he would easily blend in with the other official vehicles leaving the stadium.

As he selected a gear, Maria dashed back towards the car. Yuri was in the doorway shouting for her to return inside. Alexei opened the car door just as Maria reached him. Without saying anything she thrust something into his hand and ran back to her husband. Alexei looked down at the picture of Vassily he kept hidden in his room at the Gorky Street apartment. He wiped tears away from his face and waved back to Maria. She blew him a kiss, then the door closed behind her, and his friends were gone.

Alexei slowly edged the vehicle out of the loading bay.

One of the other sedans flashed their headlights to let Alexei merge in the queue of official vehicles slowly creeping out of the stadium complex.

He checked the time on the vehicle's dashboard clock. He only had fifteen minutes to get to the meeting point specified by the general. It was a twenty-minute drive away.

The motorcade came to a halt. Up ahead Alexei saw a flurry of security officers exit the side entrance to the stadium. Behind them walked Brezhnev, or at least someone who was playing the part of Party leader that night.

Another minute ticked by on the car's clock as the Soviet leader slowly made his way into the waiting limousine.

Alexei wondered what had happened to the Englishman, who'd apparently failed to kill the Soviet leader for a second time.

The vehicles started to move again as Brezhnev's car drove off.

Seconds later everything came to a stop once again. Emerging from the same exit as Brezhnev, Alexei recognised two or three senior Party officials, amongst them was Oleg.

A rage coursed through Alexei's blood as he watched Oleg laughing, shaking hands, and patting the other dignitaries on the shoulder as he supervised them each getting into their own vehicles. He was acting like the supreme leader he'd hoped to have been by now, had ORCHESTRA worked.

Alexei was sure that someone like Oleg, a man who had survived two revolutions, the purges, and four Soviet leaders, there would be another opportunity to achieve his ambition, regardless of the victims sacrificed such as Vassily, or Tara.

Alexei gripped the steering wheel. He pumped the accelerator and swung the vehicle out of formation. He had no concern for the rendezvous or his own safety.

It might have been wishful thinking, but in that second of impact between Alexei's car and Oleg's body, Alexei was sure Oleg recognised him. The vehicle smashed into the old man without stopping. The expression of terror mixed with recognition that he saw flash across Oleg's face made Alexei smile. He changed gear, pushed down on the horn to warn others out of the way, and forced the vehicle through the exit under the railway bridge.

Alexei drove at speed onto Bolshaya Pirogovskaya Street.

He had ten minutes to get to the rendezvous.

Wednesday 8th November

Moscow

EPILOGUE

MARGARET STOOD by the record player. Her arms gesticulated wildly as she pretended to conduct an imaginary orchestra to the sound of the final scene from *Boris Godunov*.

The Moscow apartment had been obtained for her by Kim Philby. She was now in retirement.

It had been nearly six weeks since the final hockey match of the Summit Series. She hadn't been debriefed by the KGB, nor had she been updated on the whereabouts of Bill. In fact, Philby had been her only visitor.

The music finished. The needle-arm returned itself to the cradle. She turned the volume up on the television set to hear the coverage of Nixon's re-election from the day before.

The Soviet newsreader announced that the Kremlin had conveyed Comrade Brezhnev's good wishes to President Nixon via Ambassador Beam at the American Embassy. Margaret raised an eyebrow and took a deep sigh of disappointment that ORCHESTRA had been unable to facilitate the refreeze in East-West relations, which she still favoured. Nixon's re-election was the largest in American election history. He'd won forty-nine of the fifty states with sixty-one percent of the vote.

The Cold War was over, thought Margaret. And the Soviets had lost, even though they didn't realise it yet.

News footage from the night before at the Shoreham Hotel in New York showed President Nixon taking to the stage.

He'd been heralded by the anthem 'hail to the chief'. In his speech, Nixon gave thanks to the wives of the candidates. This prompted Margaret to raise her glass of vodka to an imaginary Bill, someone she had surprised herself by missing over the last few weeks.

When Nixon started talking about building a world of peace with honour, Margaret turned the volume back down and flicked through the other records Kim Philby had lent her.

Had Margaret continued to watch the previous day's footage from New York, she'd have seen the man she was raising a glass to moments before.

Mingling with the crowd of campaign staff and other supporters at the Shoreham Hotel 'Wild Bill' Yaxley and Alexei Dimichenko, both wearing celebratory plastic boaters and waving small American flags edged their way closer to the area where the senior campaign staff had gathered to listen to Nixon's victory speech. Amongst these men in suits was Alan Rawlings, the man Bill and his son had infiltrated the event to meet. Bill and Alexei were there to ensure Rawlings wouldn't make it to the intimate dinner Nixon was hosting after the speech.

The bell rang, and Margaret dashed barefoot over to the padded leather door. Flinging it open, she expected to see Kim Philby with a bundle of British newspapers giving her the news from the place she still referred to as home.

One of the two KGB agents aimed the barrel of his Makarov pistol at her.

RAISA DIMICHENKO was in a hospital outside of Moscow for her own safety.

Her friend, Pavel Zyryanov, had used whatever influence he still had, despite his recent retirement, to get her the best treatment available. She'd spent the last six weeks in hospital insisting that she was well enough to leave. Maxim's bullets had collapsed a lung and shattered her shoulder.

Only now, and against the doctor's advice, was Raisa remotely well enough to be discharged.

"Have you found her?" she asked. The vehicle sped into the city.

Yuri and Maria had been enlisted by Pavel to once again help the Dimichenko family. They'd borrowed an ambulance from a contact of Yuri's.

"Yes," said Yuri. "But it's not good news." He hesitated. "She's at Serbsky."

"Is she…" Raisa couldn't finish her question. Serbsky, and the treatment on offer there, was well known to her. It conjured up images too horrific for a mother, even one who was only now rediscovering the feelings for her daughter, to imagine. Alexei was safe with Bill, so Raisa needed to devote herself to the remaining twin. Tara was in danger.

"We don't know," replied Maria. She was driving so her husband, a doctor, could monitor Raisa. "But she's been there since the hockey match apparently. But we've got a plan to try and get her out today."

Raisa coughed violently; her lungs were struggling to withstand the jolts of the car.

"I think we should go back," suggested Yuri, seeing how difficult Raisa was finding the journey.

Raisa dabbed the spots of blood away from her lips with the back of her hand, the one not in a sling. She then pushed Yuri away from her.

"No!" demanded Raisa. "Just get me to Serbsky, please." She leant back. It was a struggle for her to get air into her weakened chest.

Maria made eye contact with her husband in the rear-view mirror, signalling that she would continue to Serbsky. They both knew there might never be another opportunity to get Alexei's sister, and they'd made a promise to Alexei.

Maria had also made a promise to her father, a victim of Stalin's show trials years before, that she would devote herself to bringing down the system which had destroyed him. Maria was certainly no foreign agent, she was a nationalist revolutionary, even if it meant becoming a leading figure in her local Party Soviet to fight the beast from within.

The plan which Pavel had designed was dependent less on them escaping from Serbsky with Tara, although that would not be easy, but more on gaining access to the facility with Raisa posed as a prisoner being brought back from surgery. The ambulance, the medical outfits, and the KGB identification arranged for Yuri and Maria were all to enable them to break into the institution that every citizen feared, the name of which, if ever spoken, was only done so in whispered tones.

Maria slowed the vehicle down as she turned into the street which looked in most respects like every other residential avenue in central Moscow. What made Kropotkinskiy Street different was the grey steel gate set into the stone wall surmounted by rolls of barbed wire.

The engine of the ambulance stuttered, as if the vehicle itself was nervous.

Maria pulled up outside Serbsky. She handed the identification papers over to the guard. Those in the borrowed ambulance all knew that they would be arrested once inside if the plan had failed, and the papers provided by Pavel hadn't passed the authenticity test.

Maria was waved forwards.

The gate closed behind them and the papers were returned to Maria.

Yuri reached down to help Raisa out of the vehicle. Raisa pushed his hand away and glared at him. He realised his mistake and stood back up to watch as Raisa struggled unaided to get out of the ambulance. Raisa knew that a KGB agent wouldn't help a prisoner.

The uniformed guards hadn't noticed Yuri's mistake.

When the guards did glance over, they saw two KGB medical staff watching as their middle-aged female prisoner, dressed in hospital robes and with skin so pale it was almost translucent, struggled to get herself out of the back seat of the ambulance.

The soldiers returned to their guard house.

In the reception area, Maria handed the papers over once again for inspection. Yuri clasped his hands behind his back to stop himself from helping Raisa. The patient carefully climbed the steps into the building; she was fighting against her failing lungs.

Raisa's appearance was so sickly, genuinely so, that the reception staff gave the admittance papers only a cursory glance. The guard by the door stood aside to let them through to the wards.

They were inside.

"Walk slowly," whispered Maria to Raisa. The older woman reduced her steps down to a shuffle.

Maria and Yuri quickly scanned the lists of names posted outside each of the wards as they passed. At the third ward Yuri stopped. Both he and Maria double-checked the list. A collection of traumatised faces appeared at the small window staring out at them blankly.

"Excuse me," said Yuri to a passing female nurse. "We need this door unlocked." He tried to give his voice as much authority as needed.

"We need to return our patient," added Maria.

The nurse looked across at Raisa.

She unclipped the ward key from the chain attached to her belt and said with irritation, "Return it to the duty officer when you're done. I haven't got time to wait around."

Inside the long white ward Yuri and Maria distracted the clamouring patients. Raisa scanned the faces crowding around her. Tara wasn't amongst those clawing at them.

Raisa hurried as quickly as she could along the rows of those who were bed-bound.

A third of the way down the room something made Raisa return her gaze to the small shaven-headed body lying in the bed she'd just passed. Backing up, Raisa couldn't believe it was her daughter. But it was Tara.

"Can you walk?" asked Yuri, carrying out as quick a medical examination of Tara as he could.

Maria helped regulate Raisa's breathing. Her lungs couldn't cope with the shock at seeing her daughter in such a state of decrepitude.

The figure in the bed looked twice the age that the twenty-seven-year-old Tara was. Aside from her mane of thick black hair having been removed down to the pale scalp, her cheeks were wrinkled, her eyes had sunk back into their sockets, and her scrawny neck indicated the emaciated state that the rest of the body covered by a shapeless grey tracksuit was likely to be in. Tara was unresponsive, but her body didn't resist as Yuri eased her out of the bed to test her mobility. Tara could walk, albeit not unaided.

"Tara, what have they done to you?" pleaded Raisa. Her own bony hand squeezed the skeleton-like hand of her daughter.

Tara showed no sign of recognising her mother.

"We can't help either of you walk," said Maria to Raisa. The older woman nodded her understanding.

The fragile Raisa forced a loud cough to clear her throat. She then supported the frail body of her daughter. They walked back along the corridor to the entrance.

A group of male nurses hurried out of a medical room inside of which was a metal bed frame and an unusual bathtub.

The floor inside was soaking wet.

At the next corridor, they were only a few metres away from the reception area and the exit to the waiting ambulance.

Yuri walked on ahead to hand over the paperwork and speed the process up.

The reception officials examined the fake identity documents declaring Yuri and Maria to be medical staff with the KGB, and the temporary release authorisation for medical treatment that Pavel Zyryanov had organised for Tara.

Maria, Raisa and Tara joined Yuri as the papers were being stamped.

"The release is for one prisoner, comrade-doctor," said the guard.

"No, comrade, both prisoners need surgery at the hospital. The papers are there." Yuri passed the bundle of paperwork back across the desk. "We don't want the prisoners to die before all the necessary intelligence has been extracted, comrade?" Yuri tried to disguise the nervousness in his voice. "The papers are there, I'm sure of it."

The reception staff went through each of the documents in the envelope.

Maria and Yuri checked their watches.

Raisa resisted the urge to show too much affection to Tara.

"Comrade-doctor. The papers are for Tatiana Ivanovna Dimichenko. No mention of this other prisoner."

"Let me check," replied Yuri. He snatched back the documents. His search showed the guard to be correct. There were only documents for Tara's release.

"I'll call Comrade-Doctor Luntz," said the reception guard. "He'll be able to check and sign a new authorisation so you can take both. What's the other one's name?"

Yuri and Maria looked at each other. Dr. Luntz would confirm that no prisoners were to be released for treatment elsewhere.

The guard looked up at Yuri, confused by the delay in answering his question.

Maria looked across at Raisa. Her expression conveyed an apology.

Raisa understood what needed to happen.

"We haven't time for this, comrade!" exclaimed Maria, stepping forward. "Here's the key for ward three, you'll have to take the older one back. It's not our mistake. We'll take the other one and someone else can sort this mess out later."

Maria pushed Raisa away from her daughter. She took a firm grip of Tara's elbow to keep her upright.

"We need to leave, comrade!" said Maria. She walked with Tara towards the door.

The guard pressed the button to release the lock.

Yuri, Maria and Tara walked through. They didn't look back.

The door closed and automatically locked behind them.

One of the guards picked up the key and said to Raisa, "Come on then." He walked back to the ward, glancing behind to make sure Raisa was following, which she was.

He took a short-cut to the ward through the room the medical staff had left earlier.

Raisa was struggling to keep up with the pace of the guard as she moved around the metal bed frame and peculiar bathtub. Her shoes slipped on the wet floor and she fell. She grasped onto the side of the bath to steady herself.

Raisa looked at the body strapped down inside the bathtub.

She saw the dead, wet face of Margaret Yaxley, and thought to herself, no one ever leaves the KGB.